TREY

The K9 Files

Dale Mayer

TREY: THE K9 FILES, BOOK 28
Beverly Dale Mayer
Valley Publishing Ltd.

Copyright © 2025

ISBN-13: 978-1-778866-51-7
Print Edition

Books in This Series:

Ethan, Book 1

Pierce, Book 2

Zane, Book 3

Blaze, Book 4

Lucas, Book 5

Parker, Book 6

Carter, Book 7

Weston, Book 8

Greyson, Book 9

Rowan, Book 10

Caleb, Book 11

Kurt, Book 12

Tucker, Book 13

Harley, Book 14

Kyron, Book 15

Jenner, Book 16

Rhys, Book 17

Landon, Book 18

Harper, Book 19

Kascius, Book 20

Declan, Book 21

Bauer, Book 22

Delta, Book 23

Conall, Book 24

Baron, Book 25

Walton, Book 26

Cage, Book 27

Trey, Book 28

Austin, Book 29

Boxed Sets and Bundles

https://geni.us/Bundlepage

About This Book

Welcome to the all new K9 Files series reconnecting readers with the unforgettable men from SEALs of Steel in a new series of action packed, page turning romantic suspense that fans have come to expect from USA TODAY Bestselling author Dale Mayer. Pssst... you'll meet other favorite characters from SEALs of Honor and Heroes for Hire too!

A trip home was always in the back of Trey's mind, just with no date set, until he was asked to find a War Dog in his former neck of the woods. He was all about saving the dogs that kept him safe while on tour, so finding out Missy and her father and the War Dog were all missing adds a sense of urgency to the situation.

Missy had gone fishing with her father, as she had done many times before. Not that she was as fishing crazy as he was but just that she loved spending time with her father. What she didn't expect was to end up in a dire situation that had only bad news written all over it.

When Trey found the missing trio, he was overjoyed. Missy was the same as always—still beautiful even years later. Silas, her father, was in a bad way. Schooner, the War Dog, was the hero of the rescue. Only after getting everyone safely home did Trey realize that this event had been no accident. This was sabotage. And only a few people had access to the equipment, which meant they couldn't trust anyone any longer ...

Sign up to be notified of all Dale's releases here!
https://geni.us/DaleNews

PROLOGUE

"WE'LL HAVE TO go visit them," Kat announced to Badger, as she finally put down her phone, still stunned at the turn of events for Cage and Risa. Kat beamed with satisfaction, proud of having guessed it or for prodding this one into being.

Badger chuckled, shaking his head. "I can't believe that the whole lot of them are together, and even the old man is moving down to join them."

"And yet, why not?" she asked, with a giddy smile. "Being alone is a terrible position to be in."

He caught her head between his hands, kissing her, then whispered, "Which is why I am so grateful that you came into my life."

She smiled up at him. "You know I'll never let you forget that, right?"

He burst out laughing. "Yep, I know that, and I think we've done pretty darn well together."

"We have, indeed," she declared. "Now if only I could find some help and some good news for Trey."

"Trey?" Badger asked, staring at her in confusion.

"Yeah, Trey, one of your guys … and now my guy."

He blinked at that and then nodded. "He's relatively new here, so why all of a sudden is he at the top of your concern list?"

"It's not that he's at the top," she clarified, "but he's definitely somebody I want to see happier. I feel as if he's had an awful lot of trauma in his life, so he's due for some good stuff for a change."

"Sure," Badger agreed cautiously, "but we're also talking about finding lost War Dogs, not starting human relationships. Despite the mounting evidence to the contrary, you aren't a matchmaker." When she just smirked at him, he relented. "Okay, so you *are* a matchmaker, but we're really supposed to be doing this for dogs."

She smiled. "If it works out for both, why not? That's perfectly fine with me."

"Sure," he conceded, with an eye roll, "but I don't know how it's happened. I recognize that it has, but we can't expect a love match to happen every time. And, for that matter, I would think you would be all about Timber getting a partner."

"Oh, I think Timber's partner is coming," she said, with a chuckle. "I just don't think he'll recognize it when it happens. How is he doing right now?" she asked, looking over at Badger.

"As far as I know, he's doing just fine. We plan to head out there this weekend and take a look, remember?"

"Yep, I know," she said, "but I still keep thinking about Trey. I was wondering about him for the next job."

"I thought we didn't have any next job," Badger noted.

"Just a couple," she said. "I know you keep thinking that we're done, but they are still trickling in."

"Right. And how much of that trickling in is due to the fact that you keep finding all the dogs and each of the men involved in finding them? And what of Timber? We should be helping him."

"Hey, I'm not the one who's involved to that extent," she pointed out. "That's all you and your guys. I don't know if we have money to send people anywhere, unless I check with you. Besides, we are already helping Timber, and Trey's still on my mind right now."

"Where is this next dog?" Badger asked cautiously. "You know we always try to find the money for expenses on these War Dog jobs. Sometimes it's just easier than others."

"No doubt about that," she agreed, "and this one's in Maine."

"Maine, *huh*? That entails a flight or a drive, maybe of a decent distance. What's in Maine?"

"It's more a case of *who*'s in Maine."

"Meaning?"

"This case is one where, chances are, … it's not good news. That's why I'm hesitating about sending Trey out there. I don't want him to feel as if this is a loss, and it could be our first situation where the War Dog is gone for real."

"Explain, please," Badger stated in a sharper tone. "I don't think I've heard about this one."

"Maybe not," she noted. "So, the K9 dog went to its handler, and they were in Maine. He's a fisherman and goes out all the time. Anyway, he got caught in a big storm, and there's been no sign of him."

"Oh, *great*," Badger muttered. "Don't tell me the dog was with him."

"The dog *was* with him, and, of course, as far as the military is concerned, both were lost at sea because nobody has seen any sign of them."

"How long has it been?"

"It hasn't been as long as you might think," she said, looking down at the paperwork. "Three weeks."

"That's long enough. If he's caught out somewhere, three weeks is a long time to try to survive."

"Yes, except the K9 handler was also a survival specialist."

"So, he would have a better chance than most, but—"

"I know," she replied, "and that's why I was a little worried about asking Trey."

Just then somebody poked his head in and greeted them. "Are you talking about me?"

She smiled at him. "Yes, we are. I asked you to come by, didn't I?" She gave Badger a look and continued. "I do have an open opportunity. You know the K9 dogs we've been dealing with?"

Trey nodded. "Yeah, I sure do, and I was wondering if you had one of those jobs that I could do. It's not that I'm *not* happy to help out around here, as I have been. It's just that a War Dog job would make me feel a little more useful."

"What? Roofing doesn't make you feel useful?" Badger teased, with a smile.

"Hey, I'm happy to do any grunt work you have, but tracking down one of these dogs would be something that would always warm my heart."

"And we've had great luck up until now, but the thing is, this case isn't the same as the others."

When she explained it to him, Trey frowned. "If he's lost at sea, there's really nothing I can do."

"I understand," Kat said, "and that's why I was surprised when the War Department asked us, except that both the veteran, who is Silas, and the dog, Schooner, are both survival specialists."

"Ah." Trey nodded, his interest evident from his facial expression. "So, am I looking for the dog or am I looking for the handler … or both?"

"In a case like this, your official job is to look for the dog, but obviously, if you found either or both, we would be ecstatic."

"Christ," Trey muttered. "This seems to be a foregone conclusion and could be a very depressing job."

"I know it," she admitted, "which is why I was a bit hesitant to send you."

He nodded slowly. "But"—he stopped for a moment, then nodded—"still better to know, one way or the other, right?"

"It absolutely is better to have that closure, but, if it'll drag you down, it may not be worth it to send you. We don't need you to suffer from any more depression."

He glared, his jaw tightening at her words.

She nodded. "I get it. That's not something you want to hear or to talk about, but I don't want to send you to a job that could trigger you into a downward spiral."

"I already know what I'm diving into," he pointed out, "and obviously I would do my best to find everybody involved."

"You're a good fit for it," Kat declared, with a smile. "You are definitely uniquely qualified."

He stared at her and smiled. "Don't suppose you saw my file by any chance, did you?"

She gave him a fat smile. "You would be surprised at the things I can find out if I apply myself."

"Right. So, I probably have just as much survival training as they do. Plus, I'm a Marine, and I was raised in fishing communities not that far from that region. Do I know the guy?"

"I don't know." Kat pulled out the file. "You tell me.

His name is Silas Ragner, and it's his daughter—"

"Missy, … oh my God." He stared at Kat. "It's Missy, Missy Ragner?"

She looked through the file and then nodded. "Yeah, Missy Ragner. Does that make a difference?"

"Just tell me how I'm getting there, and I'll be on my way. Missy Ragner was …" He stopped and smiled. "She's a few years younger than I am, but she was that bright kid on the block, who would go pick flowers and deliver them when you were sick, even though that was the last thing you wanted anybody else to know. She was the girl who just couldn't stop herself from helping people. She was really one of the brightest lights in town."

"Did you know her on a personal level?"

"Outside of being in the same town, no, not really," he said. "I did go to school with her, but she was years behind me, but she was always, you know, pretty special." He shrugged. "It would be a huge loss if the community lost her too."

"It sounds like you need to go find out," Kat noted.

"I would be happy to, and, if I'd known, I would have gone already."

"Exactly. So, in this case, it's the dog and two people."

"What about search and rescue?"

"They gave up," she shared.

He winced. "That bad, *huh*?"

"Rough terrain," she shared, "and I don't have all the details, but you can contact search and rescue as soon as you get there, and they'll have more for you."

"Of course." Trey glanced around, as if already looking to grab his go bag.

"So, if this is a yes on your part, we'll arrange a flight

and a rental vehicle."

"A flight would be good," he said. "I already have a vehicle available to me. My brother lives there, and I haven't been back in a bit. It's well past time for a visit, but somehow going there was just one more thing on my list that I didn't get around to."

"Now you'll have a chance to take care of that too. Is there any reason not to?"

"No, not at all, and, as a matter of fact, they'll be delighted."

"Good. How about Missy?"

"Missy," he repeated, clearly looking back in time and picturing her for a moment. "If she's still alive and out there struggling to survive, she'll be mad as a hatter. She had good outdoor skills because her dad made sure of it, but that's a long time to be out there."

"They are together hopefully, and the weather's been good," Kat pointed out. "So, if they've managed to get grounded somewhere, you and I both know they have a chance."

"Yeah." Trey turned and headed to the door. "Fly me out tonight, will you?"

"It might have to be tomorrow."

He shook his head. "They don't have time for it to be tomorrow. Get me out tonight." And, with that, he was gone.

CHAPTER 1

TREY DORCHESTER HOPPED out of the taxi, waved to the cabbie, and, with his bag over his shoulder, strode up the driveway. His gait was a little awkward, and he was still a bit sore, but he was mobile and doing a hell of a lot better than he had any right to be, considering all he'd been through.

He'd barely reached the door when it opened, and his sister-in-law threw herself into his arms. With a big shout of laughter, he picked her up and gave her a big hug before dropping her back down again. That's when he realized a rather rounded belly was between them.

He looked at her with one eyebrow raised, and she smiled. "Jackson wanted to wait to tell you when you got home."

"Nobody needs to tell me anything," he muttered, with an eye roll. "It's pretty hard to hide that." She flushed and nodded. "On the other hand, I am thrilled for both of you." He gave her a much gentler hug this time.

"I'm not breakable," she protested.

"Maybe, but you've waited a long time for this," he noted, "and I certainly won't cause any distress."

She smiled. "I don't think you could, even if you tried. Come on in. Jackson is waiting for you." Spying his brother behind her, patiently waiting his turn, Trey stepped around his sister-in-law and opened his arms. The two men hugged.

"It's been too long, damn it," Jackson muttered, as he stepped back and looked at his brother with a critical eye.

"You did come see me when I was in hospital," Trey reminded him, with a smirk, "and, believe me, that was appreciated."

"You could have come home. I wish you would have come back for your recuperation," Jackson pointed out again. "I would have loved to have you here."

Trey smiled at him and nodded. "I know it, and it was a difficult decision, but, in the end, this was really tough mentally. So I needed some time to come to terms with everything."

"And I get that," Jackson agreed, "and that's the only reason I left you alone for as long as I did." The two of them chuckled, and then his brother added, "But now that you're coming home, I am happy, but it's a godawful reason."

"You heard about Missy Ragner?"

"I heard about Missy and Silas," Jackson confirmed. "And you know search and rescue's been called off."

"I know," Trey stated, "and they had a K9 dog with them. The dog was also in the military service."

"Sure, he was always around. Silas has been darn proud of that dog. He's been showing him off everywhere in town."

His sister-in-law, Elizabeth, nodded. "It's a lovely dog."

"Was," Jackson corrected her.

She winced at that and nodded. "That's the problem, isn't it?" she asked, looking at Trey. "You're here about the dog."

"I'm here about Missy, Silas, *and* the dog," he corrected. "Yet you're right in a way. It's because of the War Dog that I got sent here initially," he explained. "I didn't realize all three of them were missing until then."

"If anybody could still be out there," Jackson declared, "it would be them."

"It would certainly be Silas, and I know that Missy has a lot of skills too, but it's a wilderness, and we don't know if anybody is injured. The injuries are always the worst because one will often stay with the injured partner and not leave them. Then they all end up dying due to exposure," he shared. Turning to his brother, he asked, "Do we have any marine maps, anything that shows where they went that day?"

Jackson nodded. "Yes, and the trouble is, everyone's been to all the expected places," he muttered, shaking his head. "Just because search and rescue was called off doesn't mean that the rest of us have given up on them just yet. I was out there last weekend, but I saw no sign of anything," he shared. "The trouble is, it's miles and miles of ocean, with small craggy coves and tiny islands everywhere. You know what the place is like. You could go up and down the coast for a lifetime and not find them."

"Oh, I hope it won't take a lifetime," Trey muttered soberly. "Missy is such a great person."

"You always had a great relationship with her, didn't you?"

"It's not that I knew her all that well, but, what I did know, she was great," he replied. "She was always good to us."

"And you were always good to her," Jackson pointed out. "If she's out there and keeping her hopes up by thinking of who might be out there looking for her, would she think of you?"

"No, of course not," he said. "I haven't had anything to

do with her in what, ten years? That's how long since I enlisted."

"Has it really been that long? Good God," Jackson said, staring at him. "That is not what I expected."

"It's true, for better or for worse, right?" He smiled at Jackson. "Besides, I'm here now."

"Yes," Elizabeth added, eyeing him intently, "but it sounds as if you're heading out to look for this group, and I suspect you are going alone."

"It's not as if anybody else can come with me," he pointed out. "You're not in any shape to be boating, and I wouldn't want to take my brother away from you at this point in your pregnancy. Plus, I don't know of too many other people around who would be willing to go. I really need someone with survival training."

"And, if there was someone, would you take anyone?"

"Maybe," he conceded, looking at Jackson. "Why? Are you looking to come?"

"No, you're right. I can't go. … I guess I'm just a little worried about your mental state."

Trey nodded. "Understandable, but I'm fine. I'm here to see if I can do anything about the sticky situation with the War Dog. It's not as if my construction gig will be impacted if I spend a couple days or even a week or two out there, trolling for them. You and I both know the Ragners have great outdoor skills. So, if there's a chance that one more search will make a difference," Trey added, "then I'm all for it."

Jackson grinned boyishly. "I'm really glad to hear that because I've been feeling damn guilty. Yet it's pretty hard to keep going out. I've got a job to go to, and Elizabeth's pregnancy hasn't been easy on us. She's having a lot of health issues, and she's more or less been ordered to bed rest."

Trey turned to face her, and she immediately shrugged. "I don't think it's that bad, but the doctors are being pretty insistent about it."

"Considering what you went through to get pregnant, I would highly suggest that you strictly follow those doctor's orders," Trey suggested.

"As if your brother would allow me to do anything else," she said, with a smile. "But Missy, if she's out there and waiting for a rescue, … that's got to be hard."

"It's more than hard," Trey clarified. "It's horrific." He watched the two of them exchange glances at his tone, and he brushed off the solemn moment. "So, I sent you a list. How did you do with collecting that stuff?"

"I've got it all," Jackson confirmed, "and most of it we already had, so you should be good to go."

"And the gun?"

He nodded. "Yes, I have that covered too. I was thinking you could take Dad's old hunting rifle."

Trey pondered that and then nodded. "It was a really decent one. As long as the sight and the barrel are still good, that should be fine."

"It's good," Jackson stated. "I was using it myself, and I took it out when I was looking for them."

Trey nodded. "Good enough. I'm hoping for a good night's sleep." Then he turned to Jackson. "As long as I can have the boat."

"Of course you can have the boat," Jackson stated in that tone from years past. "It's hardly had any use. That always was your favorite damn thing. I don't know why you wouldn't accept it from Dad, when he wanted to give it to you before."

"Because he gave it to me to keep me in town," he explained, with a shrug. "You know that as well as I do, and I just couldn't accept it. It felt like I was taking a bribe and then walking away with the prize, and I just wasn't comfortable with that."

"Got it." Jackson nodded in understanding.

"Speaking of which"—Trey cast a glance at his brother—"how is Dad?"

Jackson shrugged. "Considering the fact that he doesn't really know who we are, I would say he's probably doing fine." Jackson grimaced. "It is tough to see somebody give you a blank look when you stop in to say hi."

"Right," Trey muttered. "I'll stop in at some point, though I'm not sure I'll make time for it before I leave. He won't know the difference either way."

"No, he probably won't, and yet sometimes I wonder if he's there still."

"You mean, inside?" Trey asked.

"Yeah, and just not capable of coming back out again."

"I hope not," Elizabeth said with a shudder. "That would be one of the worst nightmares for anybody. To be locked in their own mind, not able to let anybody know that they're still there, yet everybody else treating you as if you've completely lost it."

"I don't think *completely lost it* is quite the term," Jackson corrected, with half a smile in her direction.

Trey shrugged. "But dementia is not nothing either. As long as he's happy in his current state, I don't want to rock the boat. Seeing him could set him off, and I don't want to do that either and then leave it for you to deal with."

Jackson frowned at that but then nodded reluctantly. "You could be right, though he does ask for you a lot, but ..."

"Right, it's the *but* part. You know how he reacted to my leaving."

"I know," Jackson replied, "and yet you felt you needed to do what you needed to do."

Trey stared at Jackson. "You don't feel as if I needed to do it?"

"I don't know what you needed to do," Jackson admitted, staring at him, "but it doesn't matter now. You did it, and this is where we're at."

Something was off in his brother's tone, but Trey wasn't exactly sure what. Glancing over to Elizabeth, her gaze tried to tell him something that he didn't catch the meaning of. He figured that wasn't today's issue. He just nodded at Jackson and let it be. "So, the boat and everything is ready?"

He nodded. "I filled up the fuel, and you've got a couple extra tanks. We've got it stocked with food supplies, but you'll need to take fresh groceries with you."

"I'll go shopping in the morning," he noted.

"No need. I've already got some stuff here for you," Elizabeth shared. When he looked over at her, she shrugged. "We knew what you would do when you got here, so there wasn't any point in not preparing for it."

"Right." He nodded his thanks. "I appreciate that."

"Find them, and we'll all appreciate that you came home to find the family," she said.

"No guarantees," he murmured.

"My bet's on you," she declared, with a smile. When her husband looked at her, she shrugged. "You forget that, growing up, Trey was the one who found everything—lost keys, that ring of yours, or whatever was misplaced, it didn't seem to matter. Trey had this weird ability to find lost things."

Jackson looked at her and then laughed. "You're right. I completely forgot about that." He turned and stared at Trey, then shook his head. "Damn, maybe you are exactly who we've needed after all."

"I don't know about that," Trey replied. "I'm just trying to help out."

"And it's a good thing you're here," she said firmly. "Come on. Let's get you settled into your room before dinner, so you can get some sleep tonight. If I know you, you'll be up and out of here early."

"I will," he agreed. "I even wondered about sleeping on the boat. I don't want to disturb you guys."

She frowned at him. "In what way would you be disturbing us?"

Trey rolled his eyes. "I just didn't want to cause any trouble."

"There is no trouble," she declared. "You are family, and we've wanted you to come home for a very long time."

"Fine," he said, staring at her, "but it would be okay if I slept on the boat, you know?"

"You'll spend enough nights on the boat," she stated, "so you might as well get some sleep tonight upstairs. Getting some quality rest will only prepare you a little bit better."

He laughed at that. "Fine. You always were stubborn."

"*I'm* stubborn?" she repeated, rolling her eyes as she moved toward the kitchen. "I'm easy to get along with in comparison," she protested.

Jackson laughed at that. "God, you even said that with a straight face. I don't know how you managed that."

Smiling, she just waved him off with her fingers. "Get your brother settled in his room and then come down for coffee," she ordered. "Dinner will be ready in about forty minutes."

"You heard the boss," Jackson said, as he waved his brother upstairs. "You still know which room is yours?"

"Of course I do, assuming my room is still my room."

At that, Jackson stopped and asked, "Are you pissed off that we got the house?"

Trey shook his head. "No, if anybody needs it right now, it's you."

"Yeah, well, it's your house too, you know? We're living here, and I guess we're living here rent-free," he noted, as the two men climbed the stairs. "However, you weren't here at the time, so it didn't seem to really be an issue."

"And it isn't an issue now either," Trey stated, keeping his tone steady as they headed toward the room he'd spent his childhood and teenage years in. "Being here just brings back a lot of memories."

"And they don't have to be bad memories," Jackson pointed out. "You and I don't have any problems."

"As long as you're okay with my going into the military," he said, turning to look at his brother, "but I sense there are still some reservations there."

"Not reservations," he clarified, "but you were missed. I know that Dad has been calling for you a lot, until he went silent this last time." Jackson grimaced. "That was really hard because I couldn't give you to him."

"I was stationed overseas."

"Or," Jackson added, "you were recovering from your accident. Either way, I feel as if I failed him because I couldn't give him a chance to say goodbye to you."

Those words alone were enough to break Trey's heart. "That's a rough way to put it."

"But it's the reality of what we had to deal with," Jackson explained. "Now that he fully doesn't recognize any of us, it's easier in a way. It's hard to see him brought to this point, but it's also easier in the sense that we aren't watching him always fighting for memories just out of his grasp. Now he doesn't even seem to remember that he had memories."

"*Great,*" Trey muttered. "That'll be a tough visit."

"It will be, and you need to prepare yourself for it."

"Okay, well thanks for that at least." He didn't know what to say and was wondering if he should have come home more often. He didn't have a particular reason why he didn't. He was just always busy living his life, which had resulted in his more or less forgetting about everyone else's. "It's not that I was thinking of *not* coming home. I was busy at work, and, even on my time off, I was traveling the world." He shook his head. "It was an obsession."

"I know," Jackson replied. "You used to send us some of the pictures of the crazy things that you would see and do. Elizabeth was quite jealous for a long time."

"And yet you never really wanted to travel, did you?"

Jackson shook his head. "No, I'm a homebody through and through. I never really could see hassling with airplanes and all those crazy flight schedules and the stress of people going in and out all the time," he shared. "I'm just as happy to be right here."

There wasn't a whole lot to argue about there, since flying in general had only gotten crazier since COVID. "Dad was never affected by COVID, was he?"

"That was another odd thing, as we thought maybe COVID had something to do with his declining health. He did get the symptoms and all, but he seemed to recover fairly well from it."

"I don't know if there's any research into that yet," Trey

murmured, as he dropped his bag on the bed, then looked around the room he had spent all of his childhood and his teenage years growing up in. Shaking his head, he shared, "It's hard to see this room in a way because it brings back so many memories."

"But are they bad memories?" his brother persisted.

"No, of course not."

"Yet you never came home."

He winced at that. "I feel as if you're looking for a reason why I didn't come home very often."

"Very often?"

"I did come home three times," Trey pointed out, "but, for a homebody like you, three times just wasn't enough."

Jackson went silent at that. "Maybe that's part of it, but the other part of it is, … I just missed you. And knowing that Dad was missing you just made it that much harder."

"Right, but I can't go back and change it now," Trey stated, "and I don't remember ever hearing from you how bad his condition was."

"No, and that was Elizabeth's doing," he said, as they moved downstairs to join her. "She didn't feel it needed to be emphasized. If you came home, you would know, and, if you didn't, what would be the point of pushing it? You were obviously very busy doing what you wanted, and she wanted you to have a life doing what you wanted."

Trey looked over at him. "And, for you, that's a hard thing to understand?"

"I don't know if it was a hard thing to understand, but it was a hard thing to accept," he shared, with a nod. "But she convinced me, and here we are."

As they walked down the stairs, he stared at Jackson carefully. "Was she wrong?"

"I don't know whether she was wrong or not," he said.

"I'm sure seeing Dad will be very difficult because I didn't have the interim months of seeing him decline. I've gone from having a bright and mentally alert father who was always busy and off doing things on his own, to somebody you say is mentally not there anymore."

"Oh, he's mentally not there all right," Jackson noted, "with zero recognition. I was honestly hoping if he saw you that he might remember you."

"Maybe he will," Trey suggested, "but I won't go in that direction yet. Not until I've had a chance to see if I can find Missy."

Jackson nodded at that. "Honestly, considering how long they've been gone, you know as well as I do that you're the best chance she has."

"I wouldn't say that."

"You really came because of a dog?"

He stopped and faced his brother. "Look. I didn't know about Missy. I didn't know about Silas. I didn't know anything about any of it, until about four hours before my flight took off. However, I'm here now," he pointed out, "and the reason doesn't matter. I'll do what I can. If I can find them in any condition that I can bring them home, you know I will."

"I know that," Jackson said, with a wave of his hand. "We just ... We feel defeated because we tried and got nowhere."

"That's the other thing. I'll need a map of where you guys have been, what areas you have looked through."

"I've got that for you," Jackson replied, as they entered the kitchen area.

"But for the moment," Elizabeth said, "you'll eat. Then

we'll sort out the details, so you can go have a good sleep. Then, after a good breakfast in the morning, we'll say goodbye."

He looked over at her and smiled. "I can see how you've been keeping Jackson in line these last few years."

She rolled her eyes. "You're not the first person to mention that," she muttered. "I just like to keep things organized and on track."

"I'm not against organization," Trey noted.

"It makes life a whole lot easier."

"Tell your brother that," she said, with a laugh. "He's against anything that slows or changes his plans."

"He's always been independent, hating to be held back," Trey pointed out.

"I know," she admitted, "and I keep trying to come back to the fact that I knew what he was like before we got married, but I'm telling you, dealing with that on a long-term basis is a very different story."

Trey smirked at her. "You wouldn't have it any other way."

She grinned. "Maybe every once in a while," she suggested, "but you're right. Most of the time I wouldn't have it any other way."

And, with that, dinner carried on into a lovely evening. They spent some quality time, exchanging stories and remembering their days together. Then, after making sure he was all set for an early start, they finally called it a night and headed for bed, each of them thoroughly exhausted.

WHEN TREY GOT up bright and early the next morning and

came downstairs, ready to go, he found Elizabeth in the kitchen, cooking sausage and eggs for him.

She pointed to a big bag on the kitchen counter. "Here are your food supplies. It should be more than enough for a week, even with four mouths to feed, but, if not, you'll have to improvise."

"I've also got extra food storage, if I need it," he added.

She nodded. "I sure hope you find them."

"I do too, and I need to find them in a location where I can rescue them from. I need to get them out of where they are holed up, and, depending on what trouble they've gotten into, it could be bad."

"I know," she muttered. "I've spent all my life here. So believe me that I know."

"Do you know Missy?"

"Sure," she replied in an offhand way, "but I didn't really have any dealings with her. Still, she's one of us, and that's all that matters when it comes to these things."

And that was so very true. As soon as Trey had his brother's vehicle loaded, Jackson waved him into his truck and drove Trey to the closest grocery store.

"How did you know I would want even more supplies?" Trey asked.

"Because Elizabeth understands, but she doesn't understand," Jackson explained. "She's never been out here. You have a boat. You have storage and space, and you may end up having to pick up a few extra people," he noted. "You'll need all the supplies you can carry. You could be out there for a while."

After gathering more fresh groceries, as an afterthought, he picked up a big bag of dog food and put it in the cart. His brother eyed it, shook his head, and muttered, "You're obviously very positive."

"It's not that I'm positive," Trey clarified, "but a dog is out there somewhere. If he's had any way to survive, he'll be doing just fine. If he didn't have a way to survive, there's nothing I can do for him—or for them for that matter. But this War Dog? … He could be the reason they're all still alive."

"You think so?" Jackson asked, staring at him.

He nodded. "Yeah, I do. I've worked with these dogs, and honestly there is nothing quite like them. They saved our bacon many times. Plus, this one was survival trained."

"I'm glad to hear that," Jackson stated, "because, honest to God, I know Elizabeth doesn't say a whole lot, but she's pretty freaked out at the idea of locals, who have been here all their lives, yet ended up in enough trouble that they might not come home again. I suspect that, if Silas and Missy are not found safe and alive, I'll have a hell of a time ever going fishing again." Looking over at Trey, Jackson added, "I think the baby may have something to do with that as well."

"I'm sure it has a lot to do with your life from now on," Trey stated, with a nod at his brother. "Think about everything she's already gone through and about the family she's already lost. In this case, I don't think she's prepared to lose anymore, and that includes you."

"I know," he conceded, "but it still feels as if I need to be out there helping everyone else."

"Is anybody else looking?"

Jackson sighed. "No, not anymore. There was hell of a ruckus over it, but all the searches have been called off."

"Now you know one more is ongoing," Trey declared. "The radios are all working?"

"Radios are in fine shape," Jackson stated. "The only thing *not* in fine shape"—Jackson turned to glare at his brother—"is you."

"I'm in as good a shape as I can be right now," he declared calmly, completely ignoring what his brother meant. Jackson was not sure Trey could handle this rescue with his disabilities. "This is just one more in a long line of challenges." Shaking his head, he continued, "But, if it's something I can do, something I have the time for, … you can damn well believe I'll do it."

MISSY SAT BEHIND the big rocks, protected from the wind and the little bit of rain that was starting up. Her arms were wrapped tightly around her knees. Beside her, her father lay ever still in the same unconscious state that he'd been in for the last couple days. She no longer had any hopes of his making it through this, but she was damned if she would die too because she would never give up, would never let whoever had sabotaged their boat get away with it. She hadn't even considered sabotage, but her father had made it very clear in the early days of this *adventure* that he had serviced this boat and knew his boat had been tampered with.

Schooner was tucked up against her father, the warmth of his large furry body wrapped around his side, attempting to transfer some warmth to the injured man. Her father had been awake until two days ago, and then he'd slowly slipped into unconsciousness. For her, that was a death knell, and she knew what was coming. It was hard knowing that she could do absolutely nothing to stop it.

It was heartbreaking to watch anybody die, but, in these circumstances, it was beyond painful. She glared at the radio at her side, wondering if she should try it yet again.

Would it make a difference?

Would anything make a difference at this point?

A million thoughts ran through her mind. It was one thing to watch her father go down, and it was another thing to let her and Schooner die too. Without Schooner, God knows she would not have survived this long.

Shifting her position ever-so-slightly broke that warm cocoon she'd built around herself, and she winced as she tried to relax her sore muscles. If it had been summertime, she wouldn't be anywhere near as worried, but it was fall and settling into cold, muddy, cloudy weather, enough to make anybody anxious. In her case, she cast another worried glance at her father, knowing these conditions could have fatal implications for him.

She shifted far enough over that she could pick up the radio yet again. It wasn't her thing at all. It was her father's little hobby, one she had never really intended to get involved in. Now though, she wished she knew a whole lot more, just for these situations. She understood the battery life could be extended, but she didn't know how to do that, which drove her even more crazy.

She'd lost innumerable hours trying to sort it out and, even now, still didn't quite understand this radio. She kept it off most of the time in order to preserve what little battery power was left, and she'd taken it from the boat as it was. Silas Ragner was nothing if not meticulous and prepared. He'd bought this backup radio that he attached to the boat, but it could be taken on land as needed. Taking this radio was one of the first things he'd told her to do after they crashed into this cove. That was a good thing because, as she cast a glance back over at her father's boat, it was hidden in the rocks, with the wind knocking it about over and over.

Their boat had been beached several days ago, with a big hole in the hull. Ever since then, Mother Nature had taken several more swings at it. Thus, the boat was in much rougher shape. In the beginning, she'd tried to keep every-body close to the boat because it provided some shelter, but she couldn't control where it was going or how it was drifting once they'd lost power and the rudders. So now, tossed up against the rocks, she had zero control over the boat.

If she could have somehow secured the boat, she might have at least been able to keep her father sheltered better. Yet no point in worrying about what could have been. The fact was, this was their current situation, and whatever would happen would happen out here. Her dad would put up a good fight, but no one in his condition and in this circum-stance had ever won that fight for long. She just didn't want it to happen on her watch, but she had very little in the way of control.

She'd just finished her veterinarian exams, and her father wanted to go out for a boat trip to celebrate, before she started working with him at his clinic. It had always been her intention to work with him, and veterinary school was a part of the plan from a very young age. She'd always been fascinated with animals and helping them, and now here she was, fully licensed and stuck out in the middle of nowhere, slowly watching her father die, something she just couldn't stomach.

As she glared down at the radio in her hand, she turned it on once again and started playing with the dials to try to find the right frequency, where she might get through to anybody out there. She hadn't had it on for more than thirty seconds when she heard a cackle and a man's voice coming through, calling out for Silas and Missy.

She leaped into action as she screamed into the radio, "I'm here. I'm here." More crackles came, amid more strange noises, but she couldn't tell if anybody heard her or not.

"I'm here. I'm here," she repeated, panicking like crazy. Then came a moment of clarity and a man's voice came through.

"Missy?"

"Yes," she screamed, "yes, I'm here." Then she held her breath, and his voice came through again, calm and calculated.

"Thank God for that. Where are you?"

She stared out at the ocean and whispered, "I have no idea. We headed toward Boulders' Gates and then came around the side of the island. … From there on, I don't know. We got caught in a storm," she explained.

As soon as she got all that out, the man called out, "Missy, are you there? Missy, Missy." He kept repeating her name, and she realized that, once again, nobody had heard her. She groaned after trying several more times, but then the static died, and she was left with a dead radio. Beside her, Schooner woofed, and she placed her hand on his neck.

"The good news is, somebody heard me. That means they know I'm alive. That in itself should trigger more of a search. Let's hope the rain stops, so I can start a fire."

She couldn't believe that they hadn't been found already. When this nightmare started, she thought they would be stuck out here one day, maybe two. But instead of days, it had been weeks now, weeks where they'd gone through all their supplies. If not for Schooner, she didn't know what she would have done to survive on this rock.

Schooner kept appearing with dead animals. As much as she hated to see them all mangled and gory, she refused to die. So she found a way to deal with whatever dead animal was delivered to her in the mouth of a dog. She realized more than once that she owed her life, and her father's life, to a rescue dog that they had taken in, a dog that her father had fallen immediately in love with and wouldn't part with under any circumstances, which was why Schooner was in the boat with them in the first place.

She didn't think Schooner particularly liked being out in the water, but he was always right wherever her father was. As she glanced down at him again, she gave him a hug. "I don't know what I would do without you, buddy."

He woofed again several times and nudged her closer.

"I know. He's not doing very well, is he?"

She'd done everything for her father that she could in these conditions, but he needed X-rays and medicine. She was pretty damn sure that when he'd been tossed from the boat and then slammed up against the hull, he had sustained some internal injuries, but he was holding on. All they needed was a rescue, any damn rescue to get them out of here, so he could be airlifted to safety, where he would have a good chance of surviving.

But if nobody knew they were alive, she didn't have much hope. She stared down at the radio, again realizing that somebody now did know she was alive. It may not have been much communication, but it was enough. It had to be enough because, without it, then both she and her father would die.

All she had was hope that a rescue would come and would be in time.

CHAPTER 2

M ISSY SLEPT FITFULLY, waking up several times when she heard her father groan. Each time she told him to stay calm, to stay quiet, then explained over and over again what had happened. She knew whenever someone was unconscious that they thought everything was dead and gone. Yet really your mind just didn't know how to make sense of the new circumstances you found yourself in. So she explained the situation to him each time he woke up, just to keep him calm. He needed all his energy to heal, not to be freaking out and thrashing about. She had to get him through to the point where somebody could come and help them.

She had tried twice to turn on the radio, but nothing worked now. Still, she had to hang on to the hope that somebody was out there looking for her. Hopefully they had heard her voice and would be looking even harder. She sat back, frustrated, and yet, for the first time in days, she was hopeful. Somebody was out there looking for her. She just had to trust him, maybe not for her sake but for her father's.

He was a well-loved member of the community. She hoped that she was at least considered a part of that community too. As with most communities, they helped each other, and she couldn't imagine anybody letting them stay out here like this. Still, she also knew that search and rescue would call it quits at some point, if only for the bad weather. She had seen plenty of that. She also realized that any searchers would have a hard time keeping up with the boat and its erratic trajectory. When the boat had gone ashore on this island, she'd been hard-pressed to get them off in one piece.

When the weather had calmed a bit, she went back to the boat and grabbed a few supplies. Ever since then, she watched the boat being slowly destroyed, as the waves tossed it against the rocks. It would break her father's heart to see it right now, yet he would also understand that a boat really didn't matter. When the going got rough, what really mattered were the people, and he was a firm believer in people and families and animals.

He'd helped out so many families in town who, for one reason or another, found themselves in difficult circumstances with their animals. He would do surgeries at half price or sometimes for free, just to help them, which was why, when Missy thought about working anywhere else, it had been an immediate no. Her heart and soul were a part of this community. She just needed the chance to give back to it.

It had always been her dream to be at her father's side, and yet here she was at his side, and he didn't even know it, which was just another part of the heartbreak she felt right now. They'd lost her mom years ago to breast cancer, and the thought of watching her father die slowly at her side was enough to make Missy tear up immediately. She had to be strong, hanging on as much as she could for her father's sake. Now Missy couldn't rouse him again, and it just broke her heart a little bit more.

She stared down at the dead radio, wondering if she should try it again, but she didn't have the location information to give. All she knew was that she was out here. She'd given the last location she knew, and then the storm had tossed them about, so who the hell knows where that would have taken them? Still, she believed that somebody who knew the area well would find them—or if not one somebody, several.

With a last check on her father, she sat back to eat the last of the rabbit stew that she had made, making sure to share as much as she could with Schooner. He might have been fully capable of looking after himself out here, but she wasn't about to treat him any differently than he had treated her. He'd been there for her this whole time, and, damn it, she would ensure he survived this nightmare. That poor dog had been to war several times, and even now he wasn't in the best shape, which is why she was so surprised at his ability to hunt. That had been the saving grace for them, and, with that, she sat back, closed her eyes, and tried to rest again.

TREY WAS BLOWN away when he heard that panicked, fearful, *please somebody be out there* voice, but it was definitely a woman, and she'd called herself Missy, so he knew he was on the right track. The panic was evident in the full sentence he heard. *Yes, I'm here.* He quickly relayed that information to Jackson. Trey was a good 120 miles away from Jackson's home at this point in time, motoring steadily in the direction she had shared.

The fact that they had been blown off course could mean a lot of things. She could literally be hundreds of miles away, but his instincts always told him to go back to the source, to the last-known location, and take a look at the tides, take a look at just where the ocean could have taken them.

It had been Missy's voice on the radio, not Silas's, so that didn't bode well for her father if she was the one handling the radio. Silas was a radio buff, and everybody knew it. He had short-wave radios all around, definitely connecting to some friends who were almost as crazy about them as he was. But nobody had heard from him since they'd gone out that fateful day. Now at least Trey knew that somebody was still alive out there.

Jackson sent him a text message, which Trey received, which was pretty awesome, considering where he was. Of course Jackson doubted what Trey had reported. Shaking his head, he immediately sent his brother another text. **I know what I heard. They're alive.**

With that, he turned off his phone because no point in wasting his battery charge by arguing. That was always one thing Trey could count on about his brother. Jackson never really believed until he had actual proof, but the only proof this time would be finding them, and Trey was more than determined to do that. As it was, trying to find them out in this vast ocean was a needle-in-a-haystack operation for sure. Of anybody in this area, Silas would know that it would be almost impossible to find them unless they had some SOS system, something that somebody could somehow see from far away.

Planes flying overhead were often a great way to do that, but that didn't mean Missy had any means or was physically capable of garnering attention from above. Just because she answered the radio call or had been on the end of that radio transmission didn't mean that she was physically capable of doing anything about her situation. Trey had to keep that in mind. He also couldn't confirm anything about Schooner. Was the War Dog alive? He had no idea. If he could find them, that would be a godsend, and he would have answers then, but right now it was all just guesswork, and he hated that.

Still, he'd been lucky enough to have a natural affinity for this search and rescue business—or at least good luck. He was quite happy to be out here, alone, doing something to help somebody else. The fact that three lives were at stake made it that much more important. Plus, knowing the people involved was something else altogether.

Remembering the radio transmission about their location before the storm, Trey checked his maps and realized he was pretty close to their original location, at least their original *intended* location. Of course, that was always the challenge. It was impossible to know if they changed locations and had gone somewhere else. With Silas being a crazy fisherman, it was hard to say where and what decision Silas Ragner would have made, but, if the fishing was no good, he may very well have headed someplace else. At that thought, Trey quickly turned on his phone to send a text to Jackson, asking for Silas's favorite fishing haunts.

It took a moment for his brother to answer, but he gave him a list of three others. Trey studied those on his map and then nodded. That brought back memories of some of Silas's personal fishing spots that he shared with only his inner circle. Trey ticked off all six and found them not too far from his current location.

As it was, one was relatively close to here and would make sense that Silas detoured over there, especially if the fishing at their intended destination was no good. Silas might very well have made an executive decision to try another spot. Trey did a slow search around this point, checking all the rocks, nooks, and crannies, shutting down the motor and calling out over the building wind, using a boat horn to try and raise as much noise as he could.

Even after that, he wasn't sure most of it could be heard over the gathering wind. They may have heard it, but that didn't mean anybody was capable of coming to shore. If they were there, this would be one of the things that would bring them into sight. Everybody, if they had the ability, would stay somewhere close where they could be seen, but he saw absolutely nothing as he moved around the rocky corners, checking out the nooks and crannies, looking high up onto the rocks in the back. He found no sign of the boat, no sign of people, no sign of them anywhere.

Frowning, and yet knowing that this was just the start of what could be potentially a very long day, he checked his maps and then carried on toward the next rock. With no luck there, he headed out to the next island, which also wasn't very far away. As he came closer, he realized that dusk was already settling in, and he would have to make a decision about a safe place to spend the night. He checked the bays, and one in particular up ahead looked decent. It appeared to be out of the wind. Plus, if any storm should come up in the night, his anchor should hold.

There was no point in continuing to run around like crazy if he couldn't see what he was looking for. He pulled into the next small inlet, chugging along slowly and checking out the area around him. He hit the old fog horn again, letting that deep, low sound blast out into the air, hopefully causing somebody somewhere to wake up and to move. Just as he was about to row past one of the rocky crags, a dog's head appeared above the rock, and he started to bark like crazy.

"Well damn," Trey muttered, as he immediately

changed course, found a place to pull into a spot close enough that he could drop anchor, yet not close enough that he could hop his way over to the rocks without pulling out the dingy. Knowing he might need the dingy anyway, he quickly got it into the water, then, battling against the growing wind, moved the short distance toward shore. As he got there, the dog met him, his tail wagging like crazy.

Trey immediately spent a minute greeting the dog, physically checking him out and realizing that this most likely was Schooner. "Hey, Schooner. How're you doing, boy?"

Hearing his name, the dog went ballistic and started to jump up and around, trying to knock him down to the ground, so Schooner could shower Trey with love. He gave the dog a couple good cuddles. "Okay, now take me back to Silas and Missy."

With that, the dog bolted forward into the area just up ahead. Trey followed quickly, his medical bag on his back. As he got around the corner, he couldn't see anything, and his heart dropped. The dog was sitting off to the side. He called him over, and the dog came immediately, willing to do anything to keep the man here. Just as Trey wandered around, his flashlight out, trying to find something in the dark, Trey heard someone.

"Hello?"

He immediately raced toward the sound, and, sure enough, there was a young woman, all bundled up under blankets, wrapped around what looked to be another human form. "Missy?" he asked.

"Oh my God," she said, bolting up and staring at him. "Oh my God, oh my God." Without warning, she threw herself into his arms.

He held her close and whispered, "It's okay. It's okay.

You're found."

"Oh my God, thank God, thank God," she whispered. "My father, he's hurt. He's hurt bad."

"Right," Trey noted, peeling himself off her. "Let me have a look." As she shifted out of the way, he handed her his flashlight and said, "Hold this for me. What happened to him?"

"He was trying to secure the boom when he got thrown overboard. He went into rough seas. I think the boat hit him alongside the head," she explained. "Then, when I tried to get him back on board again, he took a heavy beating from the boom."

"Right." Any head injury wasn't fun, but out here it was almost a death sentence. Trey looked over at her, studying her closely. "What about you? Are you okay?"

"I'm fine," she muttered, "a little dehydrated, a little exhausted, and terrified of my father's condition."

"Right, okay." He took a look around and stated, "We'll have to spend the night here."

"No, no, no," she cried out hysterically. "We can't. We can't stay here. He hasn't got another night." Trey eyed her sharply, and she shook her head. "He's been like this for days."

He nodded. "In that case, hang on. Let me try my phone." When he had trouble with that, he spoke to her calmly. "I'll be back in a minute. I'll head to my boat and see if I can raise some help on the radio."

She asked, "You have a boat?"

He nodded. "I do, and, yes, I can get you on it, where it's warm and dry, but I do want to ensure that we can get somebody in here to help your dad. For that, we'll need search and rescue, depending on the weather."

She shivered. "Seems as if it's always the weather," she muttered.

He nodded. "Out in locations such as this, it absolutely is." He looked down at the injured man, frowned, then looked back at the dog. "What do you think, Schooner?" Schooner barked several times, and he nodded. "Right, got it."

"What do you mean, *got it*?" she asked, looking at him funny.

He smiled. "I asked for Schooner's opinion, and he gave it to me."

She laughed. "He's kept us alive out here, so anything he says goes, as far as I'm concerned."

"He's a damn good dog," Trey declared. "As a War Dog, he's been well trained."

He headed back to the boat and tried to raise somebody on the radio, but the wind had picked up, and all he got was static. He sent out an SOS and sent several text messages to Jackson, hoping that something would get through. The fact that he'd found the three of them was huge, but he still had to get them back to the boat, back to safety. Those presented some issues he wouldn't solve all at once. So, getting them onto the boat would have to do for now, and then he would find a safer place to lodge for the night.

With that plan in mind, he made several trips in the little dingy. With a great deal of effort, Trey got Silas up into the boat. Trey had bumped Silas a couple times on the way, but there was no help for it. In these situations, you did what you had to. With Missy coming up behind, he soon had all three of them on board, including Schooner, who'd had a little trouble jumping from the dingy up onto the boat. No way he would be left behind.

Once Trey had his new guests ensconced below the deck, he put on the kettle and made her a hot cup of tea. Then laid out food for her and a bowl for Schooner. He made some sandwiches for them all. She fed Schooner her meal before sitting back and huddling over her tea. Schooner emptied his bowl and asked for more.

"I need to brace for the current, and we should move to a better location, with the heavy winds coming."

She looked at him and nodded. "I would really love to get home tonight."

"You might love it," he replied, with a bit of warning, "but I can't change the course of the weather conditions out here. We can only do so much."

"Of course," she muttered, huddling deeper, but casting a worried glance at her father.

"I've hailed the Coast Guard on the radio," he shared, "and I've got an SOS out. My brother knows that I found you three."

"You're sure they know?"

"My brother knows that I'd made radio contact, and I sent texts that I'd found you after that," he explained. "Now it's a matter of making sure we can get some place where they can get to us."

"Right," she said.

He could tell that the fatigue and the cold had taken its toll on Missy, as well as all the days out here without much in the way of provisions. "We'll do the best we can."

And, with that, he headed topside, checking on the weather. It was definitely rising, but if he could get a little bit farther south, he might make it back tonight. With Silas and Missy safely below, and the dog sitting beside Trey, he pulled anchor and immediately turned on the motors, heading toward home. He knew of a couple nice little bays where he might rest, waiting for the worst of the storms to pass, or he could possibly make it straight home again. The fact remained that he couldn't count on that entirely. All he could do was the best that he had to offer, and sometimes Mother Nature just wouldn't cooperate.

CHAPTER 3

MISSY WOKE, FEELING surprisingly warm. She shifted uneasily, trying to figure out what was wrong and realized that she was on something moving. Then awareness hit her. She'd been rescued, picked up off the damn rock, and now hopefully heading home. They were motoring, so they were going somewhere.

She leaned over to check on her father. He was warm for a change and curled up on his side. Maybe it was her imagination, but his breathing was a little bit easier too. Feeling incredibly grateful to the stranger who had picked her up, she grabbed one of the blankets, wrapped it around her shoulders, and made her way topside. When she came up to the deck, she shivered immediately.

The man heard her movements and turned, smiling at her. "Hey, how are you feeling?"

"Now that I've had some sleep, I would like to say I'm warm, but I'm not anymore." She clutched the blanket to her chest as she studied her rescuer. "I'm feeling a lot better, though still hungry." She looked around. "Where are we? I'm Missy, by the way."

"About two hours from home, if we can get there before that squall. It's picking up off to the east." He pointed to the incoming weather. "And I'm Trey... Jackson's brother."

She stared out in dismay, missing Trey's response to her

introduction. "Can you beat it?"

"I don't know," he admitted, "and I also have to ensure that we have enough fuel to get home. I do have extra, but I don't want to end up in a worse situation than we're already in."

"Damn," she muttered.

"I have heard from the Coast Guard, and they're on the way."

"Really?" She looked at him in delight.

He nodded. "Because of your father's condition and the potential for the weather to keep us from getting back, they're on their way to us."

"That's something at least," she said, looking around. She searched the skies, but all she saw was the incoming cloud cover. "Of course these clouds won't make that easy either."

"No, and the only reason the Coast Guard are even trying to reach us is because they were already close enough to make the trip," he added. "Otherwise we would be home before they could get to us."

"Right," she muttered, as she released a deep sigh and took in a deep breath of the salty air. Looking over at him intently, she smiled. "I wanted to say thank you."

He looked at her and nodded. "You're welcome," he murmured. Schooner, who she hadn't realized had been happily ensconced on the passenger seat beside him, barked.

"Yes, Schooner," she said, "I owe you thanks as well." She gave him a big cuddle. She'd always loved the dog, but he had been very bonded to her father. Schooner was obviously a man's dog, which she never thought would upset her, but she longed to have that same connection with something in life. Somehow the strays and the rescues always gravitated more to her father than to her.

"Grab the wheel and I'll go get the thermos of coffee and sandwiches I have with me," Trey announced, racing below. He returned almost instantly, handing her an oversized thermos full of coffee and several thick meaty sandwiches and quickly retook his spot.

"Did you check over my father?" she asked greedily biting into the first chunk of sandwich.

"I did," he stated but said nothing more.

"*Right.*"

"Nothing we can do except get him some help as soon as we can, and I'm doing everything to make that happen."

"I'm sorry. I don't mean to sound ungrateful." She stared down at the sandwich he'd provided. She really wasn't at her best.

Surprised, he immediately shook his head. "You're not. You're worried sick about him. It's been weeks, hasn't it?"

"It's not been weeks since he went unconscious, but it has been weeks since we got lost in the first place and when he first got hurt," she stated, shaking her head. "He's been injured for, … gosh, I don't know how long." She frowned. "I've lost count of the time."

"That's okay. The fact that he's unconscious and that we can't rouse him is the main part. If he's just happy to have a good old snooze, that's one thing."

"That's not him. He would revel in this weather," she murmured. "He was always happy to go out when Mother Nature would kick up her heels. I'm the one who was much less content with that." He smiled at her. She frowned and admitted, "You look familiar, but I'm sorry. I don't know who you are."

"Sorry, I should have introduced myself," he replied,

with a chuckle. "You may know my brother, Jackson."

"Oh my gosh, you're Trey."

He nodded at her. "You were a couple years or so behind me in high school," he noted, giving her a searching look.

"Yes, I think so. Whatever brought you back here? You're not someone I would have expected to run into out here."

"The search and rescue crew was terminated," he shared. "They can only give so many days to these searches. When the possibility and the timing looks even worse for a recovery mission, they just can't continue."

"Right, I know," she said. "My father and I did talk about it beforehand, what I should do, but … what you should do with your father's help versus what you do when your father is dying beside you is different. That's been the horrific part."

"Let's hope he's not dying."

"He's been out cold for a very long time."

"I understand, but did you rouse him at all?"

"Once or twice," she confirmed, "but then he just crashed back under again."

"You're a veterinarian, so you must have some idea of what he's dealing with."

"Sure." She nodded. "A concussion gone bad. He's most likely comatose now, and there are all kinds of related scenarios that I don't even want to contemplate."

"We don't have to right now," he stated, "because, first off, we're looking for a way to get home. Barring that, a place to pull over and to get out of the worst of the weather for a time. We could try fighting our way down, but I don't think either one of us really wants to battle Mother Nature when she's in a bad mood, like this."

"God no, not again. I just want to get Dad home, safe and sound."

"We're working on it, and we're only a couple hours away. Still, that's a long time, considering. Unless the winds change, Mother Nature will try and hit us sideways, and that won't be a good scenario."

"Jeez," she muttered, as she stared out at the blackness, feeling her heart sink. "I was so hoping that, now that we were found and rescued, we would be safe."

"It's not that you're *not* safe," he corrected. "We're just out on a regular fishing trip, and bad weather has come up."

"Sure, and that's exactly the scenario we had when I left with my father. And now he needs a whole lot more than that right now."

"I agree, and we'll get as far as we can, but, if you have any pull with Mother Nature, tell her to back off on that storm," he suggested, pointing off to the approaching storm. "Now would be a really good time to test out those powers."

She snorted. "As if."

He looked over at her and asked, "So, this was all just bad luck?"

She looked at him sideways and shook her head. "I'm not so sure about that." His glance when it came her way was curious. She shrugged. "I got the impression that this was deliberate. My father did too."

"What was deliberate?"

"That our radio onboard didn't work, that our fuel tank that had supposedly been replenished wasn't, and that the emergency medical kit we always keep on board was missing. He mentioned something else about repairs that were supposedly done but didn't appear to be done."

"So, you're thinking that either somebody was sloppy

and that got you into so much trouble, or you think the boat was vandalized in such a way that it would only become an issue if you had bad weather?"

"When you say it like that, it sounds foolish."

"Not necessarily. People do all kinds of stuff if there's a reason to get rid of you or to make your life a whole lot more difficult. Is there anybody in particular who would do this?"

She shook her head. "No. ... I don't know of anyone. I know that my father was rambling on about sabotage, but I didn't have any reason to feel that way, and Dad didn't mention any names. It's not as if he was making sense, you know?"

"Right," Trey muttered. "So even if somebody had done a lot of repairs, the storm itself could have caused a mess on its own."

"It's possible," she conceded. It was hard to understand how mixed up her feelings were over the entire topic. "I get it," she murmured. "From your perspective, the thought of anybody sabotaging the boat is probably foolish."

"Not at all," he clarified. "The work that I've been doing for a lot of years involves people being absolute shits to each other, ... and I've seen plenty examples of bad behavior. But, if somebody has done something to sabotage your boat, the wrecked boat will be completely messed up now. I won't have the time or the inclination to search the wreckage. I'm not sure what the local authorities would do about the boat either."

"It would be hard to prove anything at this point, given all that the boat has been through," she agreed. "That's the evidence you want to see *before* the rocks get a chance to hide any evidence of tampering."

He smiled at her. "On the other hand, if somebody

wants you guys to never return, we'll find out pretty quickly, once we get you home."

"Not necessarily," she countered. "If somebody didn't want us to come back, they could just play it cool for a time, and we would never know."

"Something to keep in mind at least." He didn't say much more.

She looked at him and declared, "I'm not making it up."

Surprised, he shook his head. "What makes you say that? I am not assuming that you made up anything. … It would be nice to get your father's take on it too."

"It sure would," she muttered, as she stared where Silas Ragner was tucked safely inside the boat.

"How are you doing?" he asked. "Do you want to go below and get warmed up?" When she shivered, he nudged her toward the galley. "Go ahead. Go downstairs, stay warm, grab another coffee. Eat more. I'll do the best I can to keep us going toward home," he murmured. "You just stand strong. You've survived the worst of it, and now we just have to get through this last bit."

She smiled up at him. "Thank you. I think I'll curl up downstairs with my father." And, with that, she turned and headed back down. If this trip was the last she got to spend with him, she wanted to make the most of it. Though it's not the way she would have chosen to say goodbye, at least if this was goodbye, she'd had the chance to spend these last few days with him.

TREY STAYED UP top, guiding the boat safely back toward home, knowing that time was of the essence. He really had no business looking to find a place to hide from the storm when they had someone injured on board. At the same time, he also knew it was foolish to continue to risk all their lives if it came to that. Just as he was wondering how bad it would get, the winds cleared away the clouds, and, weighing his options, he looked up and off to the side, then spotted a Coast Guard cutter racing toward him. He smiled, signaled that he saw them, and immediately stepped below to tell Missy that the Coast Guard was on their way.

She looked up at him in disbelief and then bolted up top. "Oh my God." She saw the boat racing toward them. "It's really them, isn't it?"

"It's really them," he confirmed, with a smile.

It took another twenty minutes before they were alongside and got her father transferred to the larger ship. She went with him, but then she stopped and looked back at Trey. "You can't come with us, can you?"

He smiled and shook his head. "No, I'll take my boat back, but it's clear weather, and you're safe now, so that's all that matters."

She threw her arms around him and gave him a huge hug. "I'll call you as soon as you get back again." And, with that, she was gone.

Trey had to admit, finding and rescuing all three of them gave him a huge sense of relief. After his accident, a part of him always wondered whether he would be of any value to anybody anymore, or if he was just so injured, so broken, and so mentally racked over everything he'd gone through that his old confidence and tendency for success wasn't anything he could count on anymore.

It sounded terrible, even pathetic in a way, and he certainly didn't want to experience that, so he felt a huge relief to have found her and her father and the War Dog. It gave Trey a mental boost that he really needed.

Why had nobody found them yet? Still that was neither here nor there. As he made his way in the boat to the dock, he saw Jackson standing there, waiting for him. Trey pulled in alongside, tossing the rope to his brother, who immediately tied them off and swung him into a big hug when he arrived.

"Look at that. The mighty hero has returned home and what? In two days you found people who have been missing for over three weeks."

Trey shook his head. "I'm just glad that they're found."

"You and everybody else," Jackson stated, with an amazed expression. "How is it that you even found their location?"

He laughed. "I used to go fishing in and around this place, remember? I knew of a couple fishing holes that I could always count on when it was a shitty fishing day and the fish weren't biting. Silas, being a regular, was always determined to change the location, but, in this case, that location is one that he likely turned to after trying out his favorite spot."

"And of course everybody went looking through all those known locations," Jackson said, "but nobody seems to have had that particular spot locked down in their mind, and the fact that you did is huge."

"I don't even know that it's anything I had locked down, so in a way I hit the jackpot," he shared, with a laugh, as he picked up his bag, took another look around the boat, right as his brother told him to just leave it.

"We'll come back here tomorrow and take care of that. You need some sleep and some food."

Trey shook his head. "I've had sleep and food, and I'm feeling pretty decent, I'll have to admit. It's enough knowing that she's fine and"—he gave a sharp whistle, watching as Schooner hopped up on his side at the edge of the boat—"and I found the War Dog."

"Good Christ," Jackson muttered, staring at the dog in fascination. "You really found him, didn't you?"

"I really did, but we didn't want to send Schooner with the Coast Guard, so I just kept him myself. I know the Ragner family will really want Schooner back."

"I haven't heard any update on Silas, have you?" Jackson asked.

"No, I haven't, but we haven't been back very long. I'm sure they've got him airlifted to a hospital by now."

As it was, they had just barely made it back to the house when Trey's phone rang. He didn't recognize the number but answered anyway.

"Hi," came the quiet voice. "It's Missy."

"Missy, how are you doing? How is your father?"

"We're at the local hospital. He's in the ER, and they're doing all sorts of tests of course. I don't know what the prognosis is yet," she muttered, her misery clear in her tone, "but I wanted to let you know that we made it this far. Did you make it home?" she asked anxiously.

"I did. I just now stepped in the front door of my brother's house."

"Oh good," she said. "When we left you, the bad weather was still around, and I was afraid that something might have happened."

"Nope, nothing happened to me," he stated, with quiet reassurance.

"I never thought it would ever happen to me either," she

stated, her voice choking. "But the one thing you can never do is imagine that you know more than Mother Nature," she whispered. "I just wanted to thank you again."

"I'm fine," he replied. "Go spend time with your father, and, when things have calmed down, give me a call. We'll go out for coffee or something, and we can talk about it."

"Thank you," she whispered, "that would be lovely."

He ended the call, and Jackson raised his eyebrows, watching him intently. "And now you're getting a date with Missy?"

"Just checking in with Missy and her father."

Jackson added, "I'm pretty sure she realizes you saved their lives."

"That's true," Elizabeth confirmed, coming up behind them.

Trey smiled as he turned, opened his arms, and she gave him a big hug.

"I can't believe you came home, headed out, and immediately found them," Elizabeth exclaimed.

"Not sure I would put it quite that way. It wasn't a case of immediately finding them, but I did have some idea of which fishing holes to check. I'm surprised that nobody else knew about Silas's favorite spots."

"I don't know that *nobody* else knew," she corrected, "but Gerald, who was running the search and rescue efforts, certainly didn't know about them, and he's been best friends with Silas since forever."

Trey nodded at that. "That could just be because, as we know, fishermen tend to be very competitive about their special spots and keep them secret."

"Oh man"—she nodded—"are they ever competitive. Hard to believe that they would argue over fishing locations, their *super secrets*," she muttered, followed by a chuckle. "Come on in. I've got a meal ready to sit down to."

Trey shook his head. "I never really understood how you could always do that."

"Always do what?" she asked.

"Always have a meal ready. It's like, at any point in time, somebody turns up, and you always seem to have a meal ready."

She shrugged. "Been cooking a long time, and you learn what you can do quickly, without a whole lot of effort," she replied with a smile. "So, you don't worry about it. The more cooking I do, the better off you are."

"Ha." Trey smiled. "I won't call you a liar, but …"

"Ah," she quipped, "but you'll call me a liar." Laughing out loud, she stopped when she took one look at Schooner, her eyes glued to him. "Wow."

Schooner immediately barked and nudged her hand.

Trey nodded. "I hoped you might have a little bit of spare food for him. I did pick up a big bag of dog food, and I've got it, but I'm sure he's looking for a treat. According to Missy, he kept them alive, which I wouldn't doubt for a moment," Trey declared.

"I'm not even sure I want to hear all the details," Elizabeth admitted, "but the fact that they're even alive is huge. Everybody gave up." At that, she gave Trey a curious look. "And yet you never really had that thought, did you?"

He shrugged. "I didn't know for sure. I just knew that Silas and his daughter had a certain amount of survival training that gives them an edge, and an edge is all that is needed. Also they had found a place that was safe and out of the wind, and they were all tucked up, with all the blankets."

"Would they have lasted much longer?"

"Probably not a whole lot longer, but they did survive, and that's what's important," Trey said.

Elizabeth nodded. "A returning hero—animal or human—deserves a treat, so come on in."

CHAPTER 4

MISSY SHIFTED, AWAKE yet again in her uncomfortable spot on the hospital cot beside her father. The hospital staff had brought the cot in for her, after she'd begged to not leave him. They'd wanted her to get some quality rest at home and to ensure that she wasn't suffering any further ill effects from her ordeal, but, as long as her father was on death's door, she wouldn't do anything for herself. There was just too much trauma involved in watching somebody you loved suffer, like he had suffered.

When the doctor came in, he raised an eyebrow when he saw her awake and asked, "Did you get any sleep at all?"

She shrugged. "Maybe a little."

"In other words, no," he declared, with a nod.

She smiled. "Did anybody really expect me to leave him?"

"No, I sure didn't," he stated, with a smile. "If it had been my father, I would be here too."

"Exactly," she murmured. "So, how is he?"

"He's holding his own. He did have surgery to open up the pressure on his skull from that bleed on his brain. Over time it had built up and had definitely become an issue. We got that cleaned out, and the pressure on his brain released, so we're hoping that he will pull through, but honestly you need to be prepared for anything. There's no way to know yet."

She just nodded as the doctor made a few more notations and then turned to face her.

"What about you?" he asked Missy.

"I'm fine," she replied, "obviously tired and stressed, but I'm okay."

"Good," he said, "and being okay is a large part of it, but you also need to ensure that you aren't hurting yourself further by staying here and looking after him."

She smiled. "Even if you ordered me to leave, I wouldn't," she declared. "He's all I have in this world, and I spent far too long watching him sink every day, without being able to do anything to help him."

"I get it," he noted, "but my concern still stands that you don't do anything that will put yourself into further trauma."

"You mean, outside of watching my father die?"

"Yes," he confirmed, "outside of watching your father fight for his life. Don't shoot him down too early. He's always been a fighter, and I can't imagine he would be anything less at this stage either."

She smiled. "I gather you know him?"

"Yeah, I sure do. I was jealous as hell at every one of those fishing derbies. He had a *supersecret* fishing spot, and he would head out early in the morning alone, never tell anybody, always coming back with some of the biggest fish ever."

"Of course." Missy had to laugh. "He held those derbies as the biggest events of his year. Everything else could go by the wayside, but, as long as he got to do his derbies, he was good."

"And you know, as a crazy fisherman myself, I totally understand."

She nodded. "I gather you've never been to any of his special spots?"

"Nope, I sure haven't. He's not one to share," he pointed out, with a chuckle.

She smiled and didn't say anything. Interesting that Trey knew where to look, but nobody else did. She hadn't realized just how competitive her father had gotten over his fishing spots. It didn't mean that the spot they had gone to was one of the ones that he had kept secret for the derbies, but it could have been, in which case it would make sense why nobody found them. He may have paid the ultimate price for that secrecy.

She sighed as she settled back. A few minutes later a trolley came around, and she was given a tray of food for breakfast. She smiled her thanks and stared down at the very unappetizing food in dismay. Funny, it wasn't very long ago that she would have been absolutely screaming for joy to have this, but the minute you recover the tiniest bit, you sure look for the better things in life, and hospital food just wouldn't cover it.

While she sat here, staring at it, trying to figure out what to do, somebody cleared their throat at the door. She looked up to see Trey standing there, holding two cups of coffee and a small bag. Her face lit up, and she carefully put the hospital tray off to the side and headed toward him. "Oh, I could give you a big hug right now," she said, as she eyed what he carried. "Please tell me some of that is for me."

"Absolutely," he stated, with a chuckle. "In my experience, hospital food was never great."

"I was just thinking how spoiled and terrible I am because it wasn't very long ago that I would have been thrilled to have anything on that tray, but now? It just seems awful."

Trey nodded in understanding. "I've been there and done that too. I spent way too much time in hospitals myself," he shared, with a smile. He held out one of the cups of coffee for her. "I did have to guess how you like it, so it's black, but in the bag are a couple creamers and some sugar too, just in case."

"I don't need the sugar." She sniffed the lid and groaned with relief. "Thank you, thank you, thank you," she muttered. As he held out the bag, she peeked inside and smiled. "Breakfast sandwiches too?"

"I didn't even think I was coming to the hospital, but then I woke up this morning, and I just couldn't stay in bed. I have Schooner out in the parking lot, if you want to come say hi."

"I absolutely want to come say hi."

Together they walked outside, and, as soon as Schooner saw her, he went berserk trying to get out of the vehicle. She waited until Trey quickly opened up the door to let him out, then handed him her coffee and let the dog have a few minutes of running around, doing zoomies.

When Schooner finally calmed down, she laughed and cuddled him. "See? We didn't desert you, buddy."

"I think he knows it," Trey added comfortably, "but the hospital wasn't exactly the place to keep him."

"No," she murmured, "it's not." She looked over at him and smiled. "So, now you're a lifesaver again."

He frowned at her, and she pointed at the coffee. He chuckled. "I don't want to say anything bad about the hospital, but it is hospital food, and I figured that you were still here, though I did call to confirm it."

"Of course you did," she said, with a smile, "but there is no other place I'll be, not until I know how he's doing."

"And can you tell me how he is?"

"I just spoke to the doctor. They did surgery to relieve pressure on his brain last night," she shared, with a shrug. "It sounds as if he can potentially recover, but the doc emphasized that, with all my dad's been through, something could easily go wrong, and we could lose him. I know I should have listened more closely and asked more questions, but honestly I'm just so grateful that somebody else is here to make whatever decisions need to be made. I feel as if decision fatigue hit while we were stranded out there in a big way, and, for now, I just want to know that he's being taken care of by the professionals."

"He is," he assured her.

"I do know what they're doing," she stated, with a smile, "and it's not as if I'm trying to hand over my responsibilities. … I'm just so grateful that they're doing something for him."

"Of course," Trey agreed. "So now maybe you can ease up on yourself and quit feeling so guilty for not being able to get you guys rescued."

She looked up at him, and the tears immediately came to her eyes. She wiped them on her sleeve and grumbled, "How did you know?"

"Because you just finished your education as a vet, didn't you?"

"Yeah," she confirmed, "and that's the trouble. I've just completed my exams, but I still have a year of residency, and I was supposed to do that with Dad. Now, I wonder, could I have opened up his head and done something for him on that rock? Believe me, I went through that possibility time and time again, and, if I had really thought I could do something, I might have considered it. Yet I also knew that I could kill him. Plus, I didn't have any equipment, and I didn't have any medicine to fight infection or any anesthesia. I didn't have any way to test exactly what was even wrong with him, so, from my perspective, everything I looked at as an option seemed more harmful than good. But, man, being out there alone like that, not able to help? … I don't ever want to go through that again."

"So, it's a good thing then that you're a vet and can spend a lifetime helping guys like this one." At that, Trey pointed to Schooner, who was basically sitting on her feet, so she couldn't leave without him.

She laughed, then bent down and gave him a big hug. "I would absolutely love to do that," she confirmed, "though it would be doubly hard if my father wasn't with me going forward. Not to mention he signed for me to do the residency with him, so I can't even complete my training without him. I would have to leave and do that somewhere else, before I could even come back and take over his practice."

"So, in that case," Trey noted, "we won't even contemplate that possibility, and we'll just assume that he'll make it and that you'll be working together in no time."

She looked up at Trey and smiled. "And again that voice of cheerful confidence," she murmured. She studied him for a moment. "Didn't you go through an accident or something?"

"If that's what you call it," he said, with a hard look. "Let's just say I got injured while in the military, and I'm no longer in the service because of medical reasons."

She looked him over carefully, without trying to make it seem she was checking him out, but he seemed healthy enough. "I don't really know what happened," she confessed, "but you seem fine."

"I may look fine, but I do have a prosthetic." Surprised, she looked him over another time, and he smiled. "That's just life."

She nodded. "I would think a prosthetic might be the least of the issues."

"It absolutely is," he agreed, with a gentle smile. "Military service can be tough, and, when you go through everything we went through, a prosthetic is not the worst thing."

"Isn't it amazing," she stated fervently, "how a traumatic event completely changes your perspective? I've barely had a chance to even realize I survived, but I know—without a doubt—that I'll look at the world differently from here on out. And, with my father's life still hanging in the balance, life seems incredibly fragile."

"As it should," Trey stated. "We can get pretty flippant sometimes, thinking that everything is good. Then, all of a sudden, something like this happens, and you realize that you didn't have any real respect for what you had, and you didn't appreciate it all, and you didn't have any gratitude for the things that really counted. Now that you've seen how easy it is to lose everything, it helps you rediscover the things that really matter."

She smiled. "I can't argue with that." She looked at Schooner beside him and bent down to give the War Dog a big hug. "My God, he was so great to have out there, and just … knowing I wasn't alone was a help, you know? And then all I could think about was how he would do so much better if he wasn't sitting there with us."

"Did he take off on you?"

"Yes," she said, with a laugh. "He left a couple times, but he always came back, and, as disgusting as this may sound, he even brought me a rabbit or two."

Trey smiled. "Schooner was trained in survival tactics. So some of the War Dogs have more training in that area than others."

"It blew me away," she admitted, "and I ended up making a rabbit stew that lasted for days. I gave him the bones because I needed him to have food too."

"That's good." Trey nodded. "With that level of bonding, he would have done his best to keep you in food as well." He reached down, gave Schooner a very big hug and a good scrub. "You did good, buddy, really good."

Schooner barked and jumped back and forth, running around as if looking for a tug-of-war toy or something to play with.

"He's always been so full of energy," she said. "I never really understood what happened to him that he would be moved out of the military."

"I haven't looked at his record that deeply," Trey shared, "but I can probably find out. It could easily just have been his age or the situations he'd been in."

She looked down at the dog, then scrubbed the back of Schooner's head. "He'll be on Easy Street from now on."

"And that's because he did something that a lot of animals would have done, and that was to look after you, but he did it at a much higher level," Trey explained. "With the training and experience these War Dogs get, they end up with a heightened instinct for survival, not just for themselves but for others too."

"It never occurred to me that a dog would have been such a help."

"Didn't you grow up with pets?"

"I grew up with rescues," she clarified, with a smile.

"When your father's a vet, you get used to having strays all over the house. And I was terrible, forever asking him to bring home animals, spending every day I could with him in the clinic. It was a given that I would end up being a vet too," she said, nodding. "In a way that saved me a lot of turmoil that my friends went through, trying to figure out what classes and programs they should focus on as they determined what they might want to do in life. That never happened to me because, from a very young age, I planned on being a vet. And, more than that, I've always thought I would be a vet with Dad and would eventually take on his business."

"You still might," Trey pointed out. "Don't give up on him yet. Your dad's a tough cookie."

She nodded. "So, hang on a second. I did want to ask you one thing." She looked up at him. "I was talking to the doc here, and he mentioned that my father was well known for having some really excellent but very secret fishing holes, which is how they think he does so well in the fishing derbies."

Trey laughed. "Are you thinking that the area I found you at was one of the spots he was protecting? It's possible. I did go fishing with your dad some when I was in Boy Scouts."

"Oh my goodness. I wondered what you were talking about when you told me that you'd been fishing with him. I couldn't remember that at any point in time, but he did do several programs with the Boy Scouts, didn't he?"

Trey nodded. "He did, and I did take to fishing quite nicely, so your dad and I did go out quite a bit for a while there. That may be one of the reasons I thought you guys might still be alive, since he was always so well prepared for almost anything."

She pondered that and nodded. "I don't recall much about that, but I do remember something about your being a very able fisherman. He was hoping that one day, when you grew up, you could end up going out together. Did he show you that place? Where you found us?"

He nodded. "That place and a couple others too. He may have forgotten and might not like it if I enter a derby and end up beating him," Trey teased.

"I think, in a way, he would like it. I think he would absolutely love it. He always wanted a son, never had one, since my mom got sick and died when I was young," she explained. "I think he was just full up with the business and meetings and the challenges of single parenting, so he never married again."

"Maybe he was happy because he had everything he needed," Trey suggested. "He had you, the memory of your mom, and the love of the work that he did."

"Oh wow," Missy muttered, turning to look in the general direction of her father's hospital room. "I hadn't thought of it like that."

"I think a lot of people forget that having children is a choice. So, when you already have a child you absolutely adore, and life shifts such as his did, maybe you don't need to go through that process again. Maybe what you have is absolutely the very next best thing to what you had and all you could ever ask for. Thus, all you need to do is go through life and enjoy it."

She stared at him and said, "You do say the darndest things."

He chuckled. "I don't know if I told you, but almost dying—"

"Right," she agreed, "absolutely right, just like I did."

He nodded. "You might find that, from now on, your mind-set will be focused on other things."

"Maybe," she murmured, "it does still feel very much as if I don't really know what I'm doing and where I'm going right now, and everything is on hold for my father."

"It's on hold to a certain extent, but you can't just sit here and put your whole life on hold. You don't know how long your father will need to recover."

"I appreciate the fact that you didn't say *if he recovers*."

"No, I won't say that," he stated. "I have seen medical miracles happen so often that I won't write off your father. He has a strong will to live."

"I hope so," she whispered, turning to stare back at the hospital. "I feel as if I should go back up."

"Go ahead. I just wanted to stop in and say hi."

She looked up at him. "And bring coffee and breakfast sandwiches."

"Which you haven't eaten yet."

"No, but I will," she promised, as she turned toward the hospital.

"I also wanted to ask you something." She turned and looked at him curiously. "Remember what you told me about potentially some deliberate vandalism to the boat?"

She nodded. "I know what I said, and I know what I heard my father say, but I just don't know how to get to who it could have been or why—or if it was literally his pain talking or just something in the subconscious of his mind," she replied. "I don't have any reason to suspect anybody, and I have nothing outside of a terrible accident to even consider it, except an unexplained inkling that somebody might have done it. So, I'm not saying, *ignore my words*. I'm just saying that maybe there wasn't anything there to begin with."

"Got it," he noted.

"But you won't let it go, will you?" she asked, eyeing him closely.

Trey laughed. "I will think on it."

"You do that," she said. "I spent a lot of days thinking about it, and I didn't get anywhere, but maybe you can figure it out. For the life of me, I don't have a clue."

"Just one other thing. Do *you* have any enemies?"

"Me?" she asked, staring at him in shock.

He shrugged. "Two of you were on that boat, weren't there?"

"*Hmm.* I hadn't even considered that." She wrapped her arms tightly around herself at the thought. "That's …" Just like that, she was bereft over the question, unable to say anything else.

He nodded. "It's terrible to even think of, I know, and I'm not trying to scare you. I'm just asking."

"I suppose I do have enemies. I suppose everybody does. I just don't know who that would be. This was my hometown for many years, although I haven't even been in town all that long this time. I've just come back after my last term of schooling. I've always been heavily involved in the clinic. Yet I get along with everybody who works there, and I don't know who would consider me an enemy."

"Okay." Trey nodded. "I just needed to ask."

"I'm glad you asked," she added slowly, "but it's a very disconcerting thought."

"It is," he agreed. "It's also one of the reasons why I wanted to bring it up. So, while you're in there with your father, maybe you can think about it."

"I don't want to," she stated immediately.

His smile was gentle. "I know, but, from now on, it'll be something you'll struggle to *not* think about."

She winced. "Yeah, thanks for that."

He grinned. "You're welcome. Now head on up to your dad. I'll take Schooner back to my brother's place, and I'll touch base with you later."

She bent down and gave Schooner another big hug, watched until the two of them got into the truck, and then headed back to the hospital and her father.

Did she have any enemies?

What a question. She really didn't even know, did she? She hadn't had an answer for if her father had any enemies, and who was to say that now Trey was really asking a better question? Was somebody out there who might have sabotaged their boat because she was on it? Surely not, but it was a thought that disturbed her throughout the rest of the day and the night, as she waited for her father to show signs of improvement.

TREY WALKED TOWARD the house, Schooner by his side. They had been down on the beach enjoying a walk, just the two of them out in the fresh air, away from all the looks, the phone calls, and the queries. *How did I find them? Why had I gone in that direction? How had I known?* Things like that. The deputy had come, and he'd given a statement, albeit brief, but a statement nonetheless. Then it had been relatively quiet in the house, outside of Elizabeth and Jackson fielding phone calls, mostly from well-wishers with congratulations and the regular gossipy shenanigans.

It still felt weird to Trey. Search and rescue had been a

job he had done many times over in his military career, going in to help, in various places, for various people, of various nationalities, even completely different countries. He'd been involved in picking up immigrants at one point in time, who had been dumped into the Mediterranean Sea when trying to cross to get to peaceful lands, free lands.

Yet there was no such thing as a free land anymore, and Trey doubted that any of those people had a much freer life, even after all that effort. Rescue work was something he had done a lot of, and it still felt strange and uncomfortable to be thanked for it. If someone could do something to help another, then one should do it. It was as simple as that, and it was that creed which Trey lived by.

Back at his brother's house, as he approached, Elizabeth looked up from the deck where she sat and waved. "I just put on a fresh pot of coffee."

"I swear to God I could smell it down there."

"I'm not surprised."

As soon as he poured himself a cup of coffee, he rejoined her out on the deck, where she was busy peeling potatoes. He looked at her and asked, "You need a hand with those?"

"Nope, I'm fine. It's one of the things that I like to do when I'm tired but not so tired that I want to go lie down. It's a nothing job. I don't have to think about it, but, if I don't need the potatoes today, I'll need them tomorrow."

"Smart," Trey noted. "If you know that you'll need it anyway, why not?"

"Idle hands and all that, as my mother used to say," Elizabeth shared, with a bright smile.

"That was my mother too," he agreed, "not that I remember a whole lot about her."

"Jackson doesn't talk about her at all."

Trey nodded. "It's still a painful subject in many ways. When you lose somebody you care for, it's hard, and there's no other thing for it. It's just plain hard."

"I get that," she said, "and I think, in some ways, being pregnant has triggered some of that for him."

"It's sure to have triggered some nostalgia over it all. She would have been a grandma soon, and that's something that I'm sure she would have appreciated."

"Of course," Elizabeth agreed.

"What about your family?"

"I only have a few left, but they are in town," she replied, "and they hover constantly, but this is their sixth grandchild. It just happens to be my first, so they're not exactly leaving me much space."

"Of course not," he muttered, with a big smile.

They sat in companionable silence for a little longer, and then she asked, "Have you got any plans?"

He looked at her, not exactly sure what was going on, and asked, "You mean, like for the next five minutes, up to three or four hours from now?"

"For the next few weeks to the rest of your life," she stated bluntly.

"Are you trying to get rid of me already?" he teased.

"God no." She stared at him. "No, … not at all."

"So, where's the question coming from?"

"I guess I'm wondering if you'll stay around or not. I know Jackson really wants you to stay."

Trey frowned at her. "I haven't really thought about it, you know?" he admitted. "I came here—"

"For the dog, I know," she interrupted, rolling her eyes.

He shrugged, then shook his head. "And Missy and Silas."

She immediately nodded, her tone turning contrite. "Sorry, that wasn't fair. You saved Missy and Silas, which is huge."

"We don't even know that Silas will survive," Trey clarified, "but even being able to get back to that work again gives me more sense of value, a sense of still having something to offer." He hadn't really meant to bring that up, but, when he looked over and saw the surprise and then the understanding on her face, he smiled. "I've had a lot of things to work out since my accident."

"You'll always have a place here," she stated firmly.

He laughed. "That's fine for short-term, but it isn't exactly anything I need to do long-term."

"Are you okay financially? … Since you're not working?"

"I'm okay for a while," he shared, "but I do need to sort out what I'll be doing, and that's partly what I was working on in New Mexico."

"These people that you were with, you were doing a bit of everything that has to do with construction?"

"Kind of," he replied. "It was more a hands-on therapy, in the sense of, … if your life has gone all to hell, and you don't know what you can do anymore, then come over and help us help others. They were building houses for vets and people in need, and we all just pitched in."

"As in free labor?" she asked.

"Yes, but not. We got free room and board. Yet it wasn't so much about that as much as it was a chance to see other people who were doing better than you, people who had the same type of injuries and life experiences, yet who had come out on the other end and were not just surviving, but thriving," he explained. "I'll never think of that time as being without payment because, to a certain extent, we really did get paid. And in a way with something much more valuable than money."

"So, they sold the houses you built or what?"

"The houses weren't for sale in the usual sense. They were for vets who couldn't afford housing, who didn't have a place to go, or those who needed adjustments made to their houses to adapt to their new physical circumstances. In those cases we often just helped because that's what you do. They were all in the same boat as I am, and anything I could do to make their life a little easier made me feel as if others were out there to make my life a little easier too."

"And yet you don't appear to be physically handicapped or needing any of those kinds of modifications."

"Right now, for the most part, no," he agreed, looking over at her. "But what happens in the future?"

She frowned, then went back to her potato peeling.

In truth, she had never stopped. She was so comfortable with the task that she was doing it blindly, while her mind worked on other issues.

"But that goes for anybody," she said finally. "Any of us could have an accident. Just because I'm pregnant, that doesn't mean that the baby will be born without any issues. But, when life gives you lemons … I think it's a lesson we all have to learn. You do your best to make lemonade."

"I agree," he stated, with a smile, "and finding Missy and her father and the War Dog went a long way to that end." At the sound of Missy's name, Schooner, who was stretched out beside him, lifted his head and gave a rough chirp, almost half a bark.

Trey laughed at the dog. "What was that about, buddy? I mentioned just her name, *huh*? Are you pretty close to her? How about Silas?"

At that, Schooner immediately woofed again. Trey was about to say something, when his brother walked outside to the porch.

Jackson looked at him and smiled. "See? Look at that. You're home two days, and you're already a hero."

Trey laughed. "Hardly."

"You went straight to a location nobody else knew about, and I think some of us were out in that general area."

"I was wondering about going back out there, trying to secure the boat, until we could go back again," he shared. "Do we have any floats we could fill to keep it safe and raise it up, then drag it back to the harbor?"

Jackson frowned in thought, then said, "I guess it would be a good thing to do, instead of leaving all that debris out there."

Trey hesitated, looked over at Elizabeth, and added, "Silas also mentioned something to Missy while he was delirious, about how he seemed to think that it was no accident, that the boat had been deliberately sabotaged."

At that, Jackson's eyebrows shot up, and Elizabeth gave a shocked gasp. "Well, hell," Jackson muttered, as he stared off toward the ocean. "What are the chances there would be any evidence of that, especially after it was bashed around as much as it has been?"

"That's what I don't know," Trey admitted, "and another reason I was thinking about bringing it back."

His brother eyed him sideways. "Are you doing this for yourself or for Missy?"

Trey shrugged. "How about for the truth? How about for Silas, who may or may not ever open his eyes again? How about for all his practice and all the patients that he's worked with and done so much for over the years? ... When you think about it, an awful lot of good will is felt toward Silas. He's done a lot of good things for the community, and, if there is any evidence of somebody deliberately sabotaging his boat, that puts them on the wrong side of the law. So, if we can prove it and get them brought to justice, I think we need to do just that."

"That could have been in fun, not deliberate sabotage, you know," Jackson pointed out.

Trey frowned at him. "How do you sabotage a boat in fun and it not be deliberate?" he asked curiously.

"I don't know. I'm just saying that if giving him the wrong maps or telling him to go somewhere because the fishing was good, things like that, … that's not sabotage, is it?" he asked, shaking his head.

Trey got up and looked at the two of them. "I'll go talk to Old Rob."

"Rob?" Jackson asked.

"Yeah, he's the pro at bringing derelicts back, right?"

"This is hardly a derelict," Jackson noted, "if she's floating at all."

"I don't know that she was floating so much, as she was up on the rocks," he pointed out. "She was floating but taking on water. Yet she was at the shore, so we could patch her, pump out the inside, and potentially bring her home again."

Jackson nodded thoughtfully. He looked over at Elizabeth and asked, "How long until dinner?"

"Probably about forty minutes. Why?" When Jackson hesitated, she just nodded. She knew him all too well, and it showed. "Go talk to Rob," she declared dismissively. "You'll be useless if you don't."

Jackson laughed. "Only because Trey put that idea into

my head," he countered, turning to look at Trey, who was already heading to the street. "At least we'll see what the possibility is of bringing her back."

"You know how much having that boat back would mean to Silas, if he survives," Trey added, with a shrug.

"Yeah, most guys would want their boats back," Jackson agreed, as he fell into step behind him.

"It was his dad's, you know."

"Was it?" Jackson stared off in the distance and then nodded. "I think you're right. I'm pretty sure his dad did give it to him. Or maybe he inherited it, but that's an old memory. I remember his dad was pretty obsessed over it, but he had a heart attack a little on the young side, so Silas ended up getting it."

"What did he do with his other boat though?"

"I think he sold it to somebody," Jackson said, with a shrug. "I don't really know. If he lives, you can ask him."

"Right," Trey muttered, the gloom landing suddenly on his shoulders. "It'll be awfully tough on Missy if he goes."

"True," Jackson noted, "but losing a parent is never easy on any of us."

"No, but she had to sit there and watch him all that time, trying everything she could to get signals out, to put up flares, to build fires, anything that was available to her, and yet there was still no help."

"It never even occurred to me that he would be that far out," Jackson noted, as they walked toward the marina.

"I don't know that he was that far out on purpose. I just think the storm blew in, and they ended up out in the middle of nowhere, where they didn't have much in the way of options."

"True, but that was quite a ways out," Jackson said, "and

it's not exactly the easiest thing for people to find when they go that far."

"And yet the Coast Guard was out looking."

"Sure, everybody was looking. We all had quadrants that we were searching, but it's a pretty deserted coastline, and depending on exactly where they were, where the boat was, … they may not even have been visible from the ocean," Jackson explained.

"You came around each of the shores and slowly moved around each island, didn't you?"

"Yeah, of course I did."

"And that's what I was doing, but I was in a different location," he pointed out.

"So, you just ended up"—Jackson winced—"and I know this sounds terrible, but you ended up being lucky."

Trey snorted. "Yes, if you want to go that direction. … Yeah, I was lucky."

"I didn't mean it in a bad way," Jackson explained, "but, honest to God, a lot of us were out there, spending many hours each day. Then you go out on day one, and suddenly there she is."

"She?" he asked, raising an eyebrow.

"Missy," he said, with a shrug. "And her dad and Schooner," he added, looking at the dog always attached to Trey now. "He seems to have really taken to you."

"I think that probably has a lot to do with the fact that I got him off that island and brought his owners to a hospital, where they could get some care," he murmured. "So hardly a surprise."

With that, Jackson laughed.

CHAPTER 5

MISSY SAT BESIDE her father, one hand holding her father's hand. She stared down at him, feeling the tears threatening to slide down her face once again. Her sleep had been fitful since returning, as she kept seeing her father unconscious and helpless beside her on that rock of an island, unable to do anything for him.

For all her medical training, there was still only so much that was available to her when she was out in the middle of nowhere, without any access to equipment or supplies.

The hospital doctor walked in just then, took one look at her, and offered, "He's doing better, you know?"

She looked at him hopefully. "Seriously?" she asked, not able to believe him. "Or are you just telling me that?"

"I'm not in the habit of just telling people stuff," he replied, with a smile, "but he's doing a bit better, and he's definitely resting more comfortably. As I told you, the tests revealed a brain bleed, which we've implemented a fix for, and that's all been safely drained away. You know better than anyone what a horrible assault his body went through, but we're hoping that, given enough time, he'll heal and come back to us."

"But there's no way to know if he will, and there's no way to know a time frame, is there?"

He shook his head. "Modern medicine is wonderful, but

it has its limitations. Sometimes we just can't get them back," he shared. "One of the biggest things you can do is just be here for him, remind him that you're here, remind him that you're safe, remind him that the ordeal is over now and how you need him back in your life."

She smiled. "That's easy enough to do. I've already told him all that," she murmured. "We've always been very close."

He nodded. "That's what I understand, so keep that up. Meanwhile we'll give him a chance to do what he needs to do—heal. We can't rush this, and, if his brain and his body need a little longer, we'll give it to him."

"You won't just pull the plug or anything, will you?"

His eyebrows shot up, and he shook his head. "No, that's not something we do. He's not even close to that point where we would even consider that," he noted. "So rest assured that your father has a really good chance of making a full recovery, now that he's getting care." Then he frowned at her and asked, "How are you doing? I don't want to forget that you were also out there, as part of that nightmare."

"The worst part," she confessed, "is that I can't sleep. I keep seeing my father in this condition out on that island, but I'm unable to help. I keep waking up, reaching for him."

"Got it." The doc nodded, with full understanding. "I could offer you something to help you sleep."

She immediately shook her head. "No, I would rather just work my way through this. I don't want any pills."

"How about talking to somebody?" he suggested, studying her carefully. "We don't always have to do everything ourselves."

She smiled. "Is that personality trait so obvious?"

He grinned. "It is something that we see often," he noted. "If you have friends you can talk to about it, anybody who's there for you, give them a call. Spend time remembering that you're safe, that you're back, that you survived. As your father recovers, these nightmares, although they may not go away for quite a while, they'll become easier to handle." And, with that, the doctor was gone.

She sat back down beside her father, having moved away from the hospital bed while the doc was checking out her father's vitals. Then she smiled at the relaxed expression on his face. "Did you hear that, Dad? The doctor says there's a good chance you'll come out of this and be okay. That is way more than I could have hoped for, so start listening and pull yourself out of this. Do you hear me?"

A chuckle came from the doorway, and she looked over to see Jackson. Behind him was Trey. She lit up when she saw him. "Hey," she greeted them warmly. "I didn't think I would see you again today."

He nodded. "Just checking in on your dad—and you of course."

But the concern in his gaze made her heart swell. "I'm fine. I was just having that conversation with the doctor, you know, about how hard it is to sleep now."

"Nightmares?" Trey asked.

She nodded. "Yes, nightmares, … nightmares where I can't quite reach my father, where I can't quite ever get him out of the trouble he's in."

"That's to be expected," Trey told her, "considering what you went through. As he improves, then that will as well." She looked over at Jackson, to see that he had stepped out into the hallway to talk to somebody. "I guess I didn't realize that you and Jackson were related."

"Jackson's my brother," he reminded her. "I told you,

but maybe you were too out of it at the time."

"Obviously I knew it on some level, but it just didn't click. … I don't know. Maybe I've been more confused than I realize, given the situation."

"It stands to reason, and that's why people keep asking you how you are. You have waved off any effort to get treated yourself or to help you. Dehydration, exhaustion, fear, fatigue, exposure, and trauma all can create confusion, and you've had all of that and more."

"Jeez, it's sounds terrible when you put it that way."

"It is terrible, but back to Jackson. He's my brother, which makes Elizabeth my sister-in-law."

"Now she is a lovely lady," she replied warmly.

"She is," he agreed, smiling at her, "and everybody is hoping for the best for your father."

"I'm glad to hear that," she muttered, "because it's been a couple rough days. It's one thing to have him unresponsive out there in those terrible conditions with no medical attention or anything, but having him still that way, here in the hospital, after surgery, where he's warm, dry, and hydrated, is almost worse."

"But you two are safe now," Trey reiterated, "and that is what you need to remember. And Schooner is doing fine at the house with Elizabeth, Jackson and me."

"So everyone keeps telling me, and I'm so glad to hear Schooner is doing okay," she admitted. Then she frowned at Trey. "Did you have another reason for coming here?" He stared at her steadily. "Okay, what am I not seeing?" she asked, her heart sinking. "I don't like the look in your eyes."

"It's nothing to worry about," he replied. "However, out of courtesy, I'm here to tell you that I'm heading back out with Rob. You know Rob?"

"Yes, I know Rob," she confirmed. "So what are you doing?"

"We'll try to retrieve the boat."

Her cheeks sucked in as she stared at him, and her breath caught in her chest. "Right," she muttered, when she finally could. "I should have thought of that."

"You have enough to think about right now," Trey said. "Your concern, and your one and only priority right now, is your father." She glanced back down at her dad. "If nothing else," Trey added, "and I don't want you to take this the wrong way."

"I understand," she said in a low voice.

"If there's any way to get her back into working condition, that is something we would very much like to make happen. It was your father's boat that he loved and adored."

"And his father's before him," she agreed. "It would be absolutely wonderful if that was a possibility, … even if we could save something of it. But I remember the poor shape it was in, so I'm not sure that anything can even be done."

"I didn't take a close-enough look, once I realized that you guys were there and that we might have a chance to get out before the weather got really ugly."

"As I recall, it did get really ugly, but you still got us out," she said warmly.

"With a little help from the Coast Guard," he noted, with a smile.

"We were very lucky that they were out there," she pointed out. "I was wondering about that. How come they were so close?"

"Oh, I can help you with that. Once I heard you on the radio, and we knew you were alive, I got ahold of Jackson. He was able to pass on to the Coast Guard what you had told me about where you were before it all went bad. That got them headed in the right direction. Then, once I was able to find you, I tried to pass along another location. So, by the time we got out of there and turned toward home, they'd been heading in our direction for quite a while. Then eventually we could communicate directly, and they were able to come meet us."

"Which I'm incredibly grateful for," she declared, taking a deep breath. "You don't realize how important all of these connections are, until you're in need, and life gets even more complicated."

"And life can always get complicated," he stated. "That's a given. It's all about making the best of what we have at any given moment."

She smiled. "There's that eternal optimism. You're quite different from your brother in that way."

"Am I?" he asked, tilting his head and glancing back around to see where Jackson had gone.

"He's not a big optimist like you are," she stated. "I think sometimes he's probably quite the opposite." She could see that she had surprised Trey with that comment, but she shrugged. "It's what an outsider sees," she explained immediately. "It doesn't mean it's a fact."

"Of course not," Trey said, but he still gazed at her steadily. "We've had a few rough years."

"Haven't we all?" she said, with spirit.

He chuckled. "At least it's looking like maybe you'll have a happy ending with your dad."

"I sure hope so," she replied fervently, as she stared down at her father's still body. "I just really want him to wake up. I'm finally back from my university days and ready to do my residency with him," she muttered, wincing as she looked back down at the prone figure. "At least I'm hoping to."

"You will," Trey said confidently.

She studied him. "What? Are you some psychic now?"

"Nope, not at all, … but I'm somebody who learned that wallowing doesn't get us anywhere, and projecting positivity—even in bad circumstances—helps us to get through the rough times."

"It might help us get through rough times," she conceded, "but it still isn't an answer."

"No, but it can buy us some time, and that can be important too. Now, back to the boat. I just wanted to double-check with you, to confirm you have no objection to our going out there and trying to salvage the boat."

"No, of course not," she replied, "particularly since you're doing it for my father's sake."

He nodded. "Okay then, in that case, we'll head out first thing in the morning and see what we can find."

"At least now you have a location," she noted, half joking.

"We do, and, with any luck, it will still be there."

"It was up on the rocks at one point," she pointed out, "but the storms can be pretty rough out there."

"That's why we're heading out as soon as we can," he shared. "Just no way of knowing what'll be left of her, if she's even still there."

Missy winced. "That is a reality to be prepared for. I sure hope she's still there, although I'm not sure you'll bring her back. She was bashed up pretty badly."

"We'll start by doing an assessment to see if we can stop further damage from happening, while we come up with a plan. That's why I'm going with Rob."

"Ah." She nodded in understanding. "That is something he does, isn't it?"

"He salvages," he confirmed, with a smile. "In fact, he's gotten a bit of a bad name for mostly salvaging for money, instead of helping people, although a guy has to make a living somehow."

She winced. "I really hope that's not the case in this instance."

"We've already talked to him, and apparently your father helped him out of a spot at some point, so Rob's more than willing to pitch in."

"Oh good," she said in delight. "That would make it a lot easier."

They talked for another moment or two, and then he left, though Jackson never did pop in to say anything further.

She wasn't necessarily surprised. Jackson wasn't somebody she was close to by any means, just somebody she would see out on the streets and would know from high school. They were in the same graduating class.

As she settled back into her vigil, sitting with her father, she watched as almost a grimace of pain shifted across his face. She raced to his side and picked up his hand. "Hey, Dad. I'm here. It's okay. You're fine now. We're safe."

No other acknowledgment came, but just even seeing him respond on a pain level made her feel so much better. He was feeling pain so he was more conscious, right? She didn't want him to suffer by any means, but to think that he was here and was potentially responding to something was huge.

With that frame of mind, she settled on her cot to wait until he woke up.

THE TRIO SET out in the early morning. Trey had Schooner at his side in Rob's boat. Rob had a huge recovery vehicle, not a tug and not a ship, just something that he had bastardized somewhere in between. It did the job, and, for that, Trey was damn grateful. It was interesting to see just what a beast Rob's recovery vehicle was. When Trey questioned him about it, Rob just gave him a toothless grin.

"She's my Mary," he replied, with a big laugh, "and she's the only reason so many of you *younglings* survived out there."

"Any idea how many rescues you've been involved in?"

He shook his head. "Too damn many," he muttered. "Wasn't sure anybody would survive, as I was heading out there so often. … Everybody's got this punk attitude that the world will save them, and unfortunately I seem to be there on the spot to save a lot of them. I should have let a lot of you drown."

Trey wasn't sure if he was being pinpointed directly or if the man just had a gripe with all of humanity. That was the problem with somebody like Rob. He saw a lot of the worst of people doing the stupidest things. If there was ever anybody who could judge the others, it would be Rob. As Trey contemplated the number of rescues he himself had been involved in with Rob, he pointed it out. "I guess I'd forgotten just how many that I know about. I can't imagine how many you've done in all this time I've been away."

"Too damn many," he muttered, "just too damn many. I don't understand why people have to be idiots when it comes to their lives." Rob shook his head. "Somebody like me? … I do an awful lot to get an extra ten or twenty good innings in," he shared, "but so many of the young ones are just out there, risking their lives, and don't even seem to know or to care."

"They just think the world revolves around them and that they'll live forever," Trey suggested.

"Sure, until reality hits, and they find out there is no forever," Rob noted, with a hard cackle.

There was certainly enough truth to his words, but it's not as if anybody had ever been successful in convincing the young to take care of their lives because there *was* always that sense of ownership to the world around them, that they would live forever and would enjoy everything that their parents hadn't done.

Maybe Trey was no better, but then his and Jackson's lives had been a whole different kettle of fish, since their mom had been sick so much of the time. Trey checked his bearings, and then pointed out a change in direction was needed.

Rob nodded. "I hear you, but, with the winds right now, we need to come in from the north, and then angle down that direction," he explained, as he pointed off to the side. "Otherwise we won't make it very far."

"Have you ever been to these parts?"

"A couple times," he said, with a nod. "I don't remember being up here with Silas though."

"Did you go out with Silas much?"

He shrugged. "We both love the water, but we were both loners. Silas? … He got out here to get away from everybody, particularly with his clinic. He used to tell me how stressful it was sometimes and how he wasn't sure he should keep doing it. He was really hoping his daughter would come take over and make the load easier for him."

"And now she's here," Trey pointed out, "and he's unconscious in the hospital."

"That's what I'm saying about not waiting for a better time or a better thing in life," he declared, "because, as soon as you wait for something better, often the situation's just worse." He shrugged. "She's sitting there, waiting for him to wake up, and, all this time, he's been waiting for her to get here."

There was a lot of truth in that statement, although Trey could see that it was hard all the way around, waiting for the training and the education to be complete in order for her to join Silas. But it was also easy to understand how Silas may have gotten overwhelmed sometimes with the volume of work he was doing. Silas's biggest problem had been to put down many animals. Even when done to save the animal pain and a diminished quality of life, it took an emotional toll on the humans. When a bark came at his side, Trey looked down at Schooner, nudging his hand. "It's okay, boy. I know this isn't your favorite place to be."

"I'm surprised he came back so willingly," Rob noted, as he gummed away at some chew in his mouth. "I've seen some good sea dogs in my days, but, after a scare like this one had, I've also seen good sea dogs become land dogs. Yet this guy seems to be quite happy to keep going."

"I think he was probably happy there, not necessarily upset at the change in their circumstances," Trey suggested. "I looked into his training and his service record, and he's done an awful lot of survival work with the military teams, and sometimes that's just what these War Dogs are geared for."

"In this case it's a good thing because Silas didn't necessarily have much luck with his rescues."

"It sounds to me as if his big heart made him take home some of the worst cases because he couldn't let them die alone," Trey offered in a low tone.

Rob looked at him sharply and then nodded. "That goes along with the man I know. … I hadn't considered it that way before."

"No, and he didn't really let a lot of people into his inner circle."

"And he let you in?"

"I think at one time he was hoping I would become a vet myself. I was an eternal disappointment to him when I ended up going into the military … to him and a good share of my family, it seems."

"There's no appreciation for the military anymore," Rob grumbled, looking at him. "I'm surprised any young person goes out into that world."

"Maybe, but I wanted to do something in a big way," Trey shared, with a smile. "I wanted to help, you know? If nobody ever helps, then nothing ever changes."

"Yeah, but let me then ask you something," Rob began with a snort. "Did you see anything change?" And, with that, he headed to his navigation maps, leaving a very quiet Trey in his wake.

CHAPTER 6

MISSY HEARD FOOTSTEPS stopping nearby and looked up.

"Go home, Missy," the nurse ordered, her tone severe. It had to have been the sixth time she'd said something along those lines.

Missy asked her, "Would you leave him if it was your father?"

The other woman sighed. "You're not doing him any good if you wear yourself down sitting here, just waiting for him to wake up. He may or may not wake up, but it won't be impacted by whether you're here or not."

Since that was more or less in direct contrast to what Missy personally believed, as well as what she thought the doctor had told her earlier, she remained, growing even more stubborn. "I'm staying," she stated immediately.

The nurse glared at her and shrugged, then walked out, leaving Missy staring at the doorway. What did it matter to anybody else if she stayed?

After all, it could be the last few hours she spent with her father. If that were the case, she wanted every hour she could get. The fact that this particular nurse didn't believe Missy's being here made a difference also made her sad. There was considerable research proving that having a loved one around, whether the patient was aware of their presence or not, helped to keep alive the person trying to recover, even encouraging the patient to work harder and to heal faster.

That this nurse apparently didn't believe any of it was disconcerting to say the least. And yet she was entitled to her opinion and had probably seen more things in the hospital than most people ever did. So, if her attitude was a little bit jaded, maybe that just came from years of working here.

Yet it didn't mean she should continue working here, and that was something Missy had to wonder at. Why stay in this field if that was how she felt about it? On the other hand, the woman was older, and maybe that's all she had left in her life. Maybe quitting wasn't an option or she was fearful of doing something different. That was something that everybody had to come to terms with in their own way.

Missy was young, looking forward to a career that would bring her and her father closer, and she absolutely refused to believe anything different than that would happen. She'd worked long and hard to get to this point—both of them had. So now she wanted to ensure she had that opportunity to work with her father at her side.

And, with that thought, she sat back down again beside her father and kept talking to him, telling him, "It's okay. I'm here. Come back to me, please."

"THERE IT IS." Trey pointed off in the distance.

Rob peered through the bright sunshine and muttered, "I can hardly see it."

"I didn't see it easily myself."

As they got closer, Rob looked ahead and snorted. "I don't see how you saw it at all."

"Just caught it by luck, I guess," he muttered because, even now as he stared at it, it was really hard to imagine how he had managed to spot the boat and that he'd spotted Schooner first.

As they pulled slowly into the small inlet, Rob killed the motor, and they sat and studied the boat ahead of them. She had, indeed, been battling the waves, but everything was super calm at the moment. So she was just cresting, riding the wash from their own boat.

"She's still floating, sort of," Rob noted, as he eyed it critically. "I don't know what our chances are to get her out of here, but she's in better shape than I thought she might be."

"She's pretty much what I remembered and why I was thinking we could do something with her."

Rob nodded. "It's a little bit odd to see her this way, but I've seen worse." They drifted in closer. Then Rob turned on the motor and pulled in as near as he could, before killing it and dropping anchor. With that, they launched the Zodiac and quickly headed to shore. As they got closer, Rob navigated around Silas's boat from several different directions, trying to get a good look at just how much damage there was. He shook his head. "We'll have to go ashore to see the rest of her." With that, he pulled up alongside the shore.

Trey hopped out and brought the small craft farther up out of the water. As soon as they were safe and the Zodiac was secured, Rob hopped off, and together they studied Silas's boat. They found a good-size hole in the hull toward the front. With each wave, water rushed in, and water rushed out.

"That'll be a bit of a bitch," Rob muttered to himself.

That was one way to put it. As far as Trey was concerned, that hole in the hull was one of the biggest issues, but he also knew that, when it came to these problems, Rob was by far the best person suited to handle it.

By the time Rob had circled the boat three times, he turned and nodded. "I think we can do this," he said, now smiling.

"That's what I thought you would say."

He snorted. "You mean, that's what you were *hoping* I would say."

"Yeah, I sure was," Trey conceded. "I also have an ulterior motive."

At that, Rob looked at him and chuckled. "You mean, the fact that you're sweet on his daughter?"

Trey shook his head. "No, that's not what I was thinking of."

"Then you're not being very honest with yourself."

"Honestly, I hadn't even considered it, but, hey, you do you."

"Don't worry. I will," Rob declared, with another snort.

"What I was thinking about was what Missy told me. While they were out here, Silas mentioned that he thought the boat had been sabotaged."

Silence came from Rob, as he frowned, looking at the damage again. "Now that's an entirely different story. ... I'm not sure what sabotage would end up like this though."

"It wouldn't have to be this, would it? It could just as easily be the fact that something happened to the engine, plus Missy said no lifeboat was on board, no backup radio, no first aid kit."

"Now that's just foolish, but we also know that lots of people do foolish stuff all the time."

"And yet Silas wasn't one to make those mistakes."

"No," Rob replied, thinking about it, "he wasn't. He always had a Zodiac with him. Hell, we used to argue about which one of these was better." He stood here on the rocks, staring down at the boat. "I'll have to get some equipment for this," he muttered.

"I figured you would. I was hoping the pictures would help, but they didn't really show enough."

"No, but I wouldn't have gone forward without seeing her for myself anyway," he shared, with a nod, "but now I have a good idea what we're up against."

"Looks as if we've got clear weather for a couple days, but then we're into rough seas again. So that's our time frame."

"Sure." Rob glared at him. "You paying for it?"

Trey winced and then nodded. "Seeing as I'm the one who brought you out here, I guess so."

At that, he gave a loud cackle. "I ain't saying I'll charge you much, but, for some of the stuff, you know, there is a price."

"There's always a price," he said, with a note of humor. "If nothing else the price of fuel isn't cheap."

"God no." Rob shook his head. "Yet Silas was my friend too, so I'll do what I can. … I'm just not saying I can cover all the costs on my own."

"I got it," Trey replied, "and I appreciate your helping me to see if we could do something about her."

"Oh, we can do something about her, but I ain't gonna say what all the damage is until I get on board." And, with that, and the agility of a man half his age, he quickly clambered onto the broken and battered vessel and disappeared down below. When he popped back up again, he nodded. "We can do this. It won't be pretty, but we can float her again and bring her back. There'll be a certain amount of expense involved. I have some big floats that we can inflate on the inside, but I'm not so sure it'll be enough. She'll be a heavy weight if we don't close up that hole."

They both stared at the big hole at the front of the keel. Rob continued. "We can start by doing our best to patch that hole."

Trey nodded at him. "That's a good thought."

Rob laughed. "You didn't call me out here for my looks." Then he went off in a high cackle that made Trey laugh. "I brought a bunch of gear with me," Rob shared, "but it'll take some time, and it'll be a pretty ugly job. Still, let's see what we can do."

Four hours later, Rob sat back and nodded. "Now, that's about all we can do for the moment. We'll come back out here tomorrow with the pumps and ropes and see if we can get her moving. Then I guess we'll find out if we can tow her back home again."

"That would be absolutely amazing if we could," Trey murmured.

"As long as you don't tell me that you're just doing this out of the kindness of your heart."

"Of course I am," he admitted, frowning at the man. "Since when did you become so jaded that people never do nice things for each other?"

"It's not that I think we don't do nice things for each other. I just think that, all too often, people get their motivations messed up."

"I'm all for helping Silas, who took me out more than a few times back in the day. He spent quite a few hours with me out on the water."

"That's true enough," Rob conceded. "So maybe you

were one of the lucky ones after all."

"Maybe so," Trey agreed. "I certainly appreciated the time I spent with him, and one of the hardest things was telling him that I was going into the military. In a way, … I think he almost saw me like a son. As such, I was also a bit of a disappointment when I made choices he didn't agree with." When Rob made no response to that, Trey looked over to see Rob staring at him.

Finally Rob nodded. "That sounds to be a wind of truth there." Looking up at the sky around them, Rob announced, "Time to go."

Not arguing—because the man had one of those innate senses of weather, direction, and timing—Trey hopped into the Zodiac with Rob and Schooner and managed to get back out to Rob's salvage ship without incurring any damage. As they approached the big boat Rob had aptly named Mary, Trey noted, "Interesting name."

"She started off as a beauty, but I've made so many modifications that she became Big Mary. But don't you get any ideas," he declared, giving him a glare. "She's a good un."

"Hey, I wouldn't say anything," Trey admitted, with a smile. "I'm very aware that, when you do operations like this, you do it for good reasons."

"I've been rescuing folks off this water for a long time," Rob muttered, "and, if people would just smarten up and would not do stupid shit, I wouldn't have to make all these trips."

"On the other hand," Trey pointed out, his tone cheerful, "it gave you a good reason to do this."

They laughed, and together the two of them, along with Schooner, headed home. Just as Trey was leaving the marina, Rob called out to him, "I can't do it alone."

Trey stopped, looked back, and nodded. "No, and you shouldn't have to. I'll be here. What time do you want to leave tomorrow?"

"Crack of dawn," he replied, "and plan for all day—and that's only if all goes well."

"Right." Trey winced, knowing full well that all kinds of things could go wrong. At this stage of the game, they desperately needed to get her back in one piece, before anything else could go wrong. "I'll see you in the morning." And he walked back home.

As he neared his brother's place, about ten minutes away, a vehicle pulled up beside Trey. It was Sheriff Woodley.

"Hey," he greeted Trey. "Haven't seen you in a while."

"I haven't been here in a while," he replied.

"I hear you found Missy and her father."

He nodded. "I was just out with Old Rob to see if we can bring his boat back in."

"Oh, crap," Woodley muttered. "I didn't even think that would be a possibility."

"Not sure it is, but we'll give it a shot."

"Good," Sheriff Woodley said. "I know Silas really loves that boat. I'm sure Missy would like to keep her for that reason alone."

"No doubt, but I wouldn't write off Silas just yet."

"Not writing him off at all. Silas is one of the good ones, and I'm just thankful you gave it a go and found them."

Hesitating a moment, Trey walked closer to the driver's side door, leaned in, and shared, "You may want to talk to Missy about this. I don't really know what shape Silas's boat is in now, but, according to Missy, Silas was adamant that the boat had been vandalized."

Sheriff Woodley stared at him. "What?"

"Now we don't know if that happened or not," he began, "because, of course, Silas isn't talking right now. He is still in pretty rough shape and, worst case, may never talk again."

"I hope like hell that didn't happen and would prefer to think it didn't."

"We won't know until I can get the boat back in tomorrow."

"You let me know when you get that boat in," he stated, his voice hard, "but I'm pretty sure it'll turn out to be the troubled ranting of a fevered mind."

"And that's possible," Trey admitted, "absolutely possible. I just don't know yet."

"What does the boat even look like now?" the sheriff asked.

"Rough, with a good-size hole in the side from banging up on the rocks," he shared, "and, of course, she was taking on water. We did some patchwork today, and, if it holds, we will use some underwater epoxy or floats tomorrow. Rob's got an airbag thing he's been using, if she's still taking on water," he added, with a nod down toward Rob's place.

"I've seen something he's been working on," the sheriff shared, with a nod, "and it looks pretty sketchy, but, if it works, hell, I'm all for it. I have to admit he has spent many hours over the years helping us bring back people and boats that have gone missing out there. So, if he has any technique or trick to make it work, I'm right there with you," Woodley stated. "Do you guys need any help out there tomorrow?"

"I don't think so, but you may want to ask him," he suggested. "Rob's pretty set in his ways."

"Yeah, you're not kidding." The sheriff laughed. "I'll

pop by and talk to him tonight if I can." Just then his radio squawked at him, and he sighed. "Or maybe not." And, with that, he picked up the mic to respond, even as he drove away. He honked the horn as he disappeared from sight, and Trey, Schooner at his side, finished the walk back to Jackson's house in contemplative silence, wondering if there could possibly be anything to Silas's suspicions.

Retrieving Silas's boat tomorrow would be one way to find out, but it might also confirm the ugly suspicions. That wasn't good for anybody.

CHAPTER 7

THE WARM TONGUE lashing her cheek woke her first. As soon as Missy knew that Schooner was in the hospital room with her, she chuckled and gave him a big hug. She looked over to find Trey standing in the doorway, his arms crossed, as he leaned against the door jamb, smiling at her. "That's a hell of a way to wake up," she muttered, as she struggled to calm down the dog.

"He seemed to need to come in and see you guys," Trey shared, with a smile. "These animals have feelings too."

She smiled over at him. "They sure do, and he and my dad have one heck of a bond." Almost in sync with her wording, Schooner headed over to the side of the hospital bed and licked her father's hand several times. It broke her heart to see the dog waiting there, waiting for some reaction, any reaction at all, and getting nothing.

She slid off the cot, wincing at the chill that had settled in, then walked over to give Schooner a cuddle. "Give him time," she whispered. "He'll be back. Give him a little more time."

The dog woofed, more of a whine than a woof, but it was enough to reinforce that he knew exactly how much trouble her father was in. She looked over at Trey. "How did the trip go?"

"You mean the second trip?" he asked, with a smile. "We

got the boat back," he announced, with a shake of his head. "Rob and I started the patch work yesterday, and it was plain luck that the boat was still there when we got back today. He used an inflatable airbag inside the cabin that put pressure against the damaged hull, so we could bring her back in again."

"That sounds pretty amazing. I know they do things like that for submarine rescues, to lift it to the surface, but …"

He nodded. "I don't know that there's anything on the market like this for civilians, but I think Rob is more or less determined that, if anybody else goes missing, he'll have something to help them."

"You would like to think these situations just wouldn't happen," she muttered with a wry smile, as she stretched. Then she bent over to cuddle Schooner again. She was pretty sure the dog wasn't allowed in the hospital, so gave him an extra hug in case he got kicked out.

Trey nodded. "Yet in reality we know that it's quite likely to happen again."

"I do know," she stated. "It's just so upsetting to think that so much can go wrong in what should be a simple, enjoyable trip, but then everything goes to hell."

"That's just life, I guess." He sent her a smile.

She couldn't argue that because he was right. It was one of those things about life that always got to her. She sat back down on the cot and frowned. "What's this?" She pointed at his hands.

He looked down self-consciously at the knitted blanket, then shrugged and held it out for her. "You looked cold when I was here last."

Stunned at his thoughtfulness, she reached out and accepted what appeared to be a very soft blanket.

"It's one of the ones that Elizabeth makes and sells," he explained. "I figured maybe you could use a little extra warmth in here, when you're tucked up, waiting for your dad."

Surprised and touched, she hugged it close and whispered, "Thank you. They gave me a blanket but it seems the opposite of warm when I'm trying to sleep."

"Part of it's the stress," he noted, "and part of it's the trauma. All kinds of things can go wrong at this stage in life, and all you can do is hang on for the ride and hope he pulls through."

"Honestly, it frustrates me to no end that, with all the medical knowledge I've gained in my studies to be a vet, I really don't know a single medical tip that can help him."

"No, but you have the one thing he really needs."

She looked over at him with her eyebrows raised. "And that is … what exactly?"

"Love, silly," he said. "It's your love, your voice that's keeping him fighting. If there's anything left he can fight for, you know that you will be the thing that keeps him going."

She nodded as she looked over at her father. "I thought I saw him shift and fight for a moment yesterday," she shared, "and he seems to be much calmer today."

"That's not necessarily a bad thing," he pointed out. "Being calm is probably a whole lot better than trying to fight his own healing. We don't want him to have nightmares or to think he's still fighting to save you. That would put him struggling against his own healing resources."

"Agreed," she murmured, "but that's easier said than done. … So, back to the *Forget Me Not*. Is she fixable?"

"That I don't know," he admitted, "but I would imagine so. Rob is bound and determined to get her back up and running again, just for Silas and you. I just don't know what the extent of the damage will be at the end of the day."

"What about the bill?" she asked, with a wince. "That sounds expensive."

He gave her a noncommittal smile. "You and I both know that's quite possibly an issue, but it's also the boat that your father loves, and it's been in your family for generations. Now that you two are rescued and safe, that matters to Silas."

"Of course it does," she agreed, with a smile. "Rob and my dad have always had this competitive off-and-on relationship," she noted. "I never really understood it, but I guess I don't need to understand it to know that Rob was always there for Dad, especially when it came to the boat."

"Of course." Trey walked inside and stopped at the foot of Silas's bed. He studied him for a long moment and then nodded. "He looks better."

She bounded to her feet and joined him, staring down at the prone figure. "Do you think so?" she asked anxiously. "I keep thinking to myself that he does, but then I'm afraid it's just wishful thinking."

"Keep it up," he urged her. "I'll never be somebody who denies the power of thoughts. Honest to God, we could all do with a whole lot more hopeful dreams and prayers."

"I've been praying a lot," she said. "It's not something I normally do, but ..."

He smiled. "It's one of the things that people instinctively do the minute they run into trouble. They don't really know why they're doing it, but they feel the need to have somebody's help, and that somebody usually takes the form of the divine, ... especially when we're desperately hoping for an answer."

"I just never know if there even is such a thing," she admitted. "My father wasn't big on religion or faith of any kind. He was more about faith in himself and in his ability to handle things," she shared, as she stared down at the quiet figure. "I've no idea what he would think about this right now."

"He would tell you to get on with your life and to stop moaning and groaning about it all."

She gave a startled laugh. "Wow, that sounds exactly like what he would say. I forgot how well you knew him." She turned to face Trey. "You did go out fishing with him all the time, didn't you? My memory is messed up, I swear. I feel as if I am zoning in and out of reality most of the time."

"Yeah, that happens to the best of us at some point. However, in your case, you've also been through a lot. So give yourself a break. I did spend a lot of time with Silas, but that was a long time ago. I'm pretty sure he was disappointed that I decided to go into the military, in my case the navy," he noted, with a smile. "It had to be the navy, because you know me and water."

She smiled. "Yeah, you should have been born a duck. Dad too. He couldn't join, you know," she added, looking over at her father. "He really wanted to and tried hard, but he had some spinal condition when he was younger that kept him out. It's not something he really talks about, but I do know that he didn't pass the physical, and it crushed him."

"I didn't know that." Trey frowned at her, before he looked down at Silas. "Look at you, man. I'm still finding out things about you that I didn't know."

She smiled. "You're not allowed to tell him that I told you either."

He laughed. "I might tease him about it, when he comes

out of this and is back in good form, and I highly suspect he won't mind."

"No, probably not," she agreed, "particularly since you're now out of the military. He lost a really good friend to the military service, and I know that was always a bone of contention for him."

"Sure, but we can lose friends walking across the road too," he argued. "My family used that on me too but—"

"Yet you still don't have a whole lot to do with them, do you?"

"More with my brother than anyone. My dad no longer knows who I am. That's tough." He shook his head. "They wanted me to move back when I got injured, and, well, … I felt as if I needed to heal first and to get to the point that I could be on my own—you know, independent and not a burden. I'm stubborn that way, or so I'm told."

"I don't know about that. I don't think being stubborn when it comes to independence is all bad. It's one thing to be close with friends and family. It's another thing entirely to depend on them. And the longer you don't heal inside, the more you end up relying on others. Then the harder it is to stand on your own. And that just feels like unfinished business or something to me."

He seemed to hear her but didn't make a comment about that. Then he said, "I'm heading down to take a look at the boat, now that we've got her in the dry dock. I'm guessing Rob is probably already working on her."

"Of course." She glanced at the clock and winced. "Good God, I had no idea it was so early."

"It's one of the reasons I snuck in because a couple people here won't let me bring Schooner inside."

"I don't get that," she muttered, "because he's hugely

important to my father. Still, rules are rules."

"Exactly, but now that the hospital is beginning to stir, I better sneak him out again," he shared, with a big smile. "Try to get some sleep, and hopefully now you'll be warmer." He gave her a brief wave and was gone.

She leaned down, gave her father a kiss on the cheek, then walked back to the cot, wrapping the special blanket around her shoulders. With a smile on her face, she went right back to sleep.

KNOWING IT WAS early but that Rob would be up, Trey drove toward the marina. Rob had a big shed just off to the side across the road. He worked on multiple boats for various people all the time. It was his passion. He needed just enough money to keep going, and rarely charged people as much as he should. He had a good heart, a good soul, but not everybody realized or appreciated it because he could be rough around the edges. He was abrasive as hell and definitely the person who would call a spade a spade. If you happened to be on his shit list, he had no problem calling you out for anything you may have done wrong.

That bluntness wasn't welcome in so many circles. Yet, when people needed help, they were right there looking for Rob to give them a hand, particularly if no cost was involved. Trey parked at the end of the main parking lot to the marina, let Schooner out, calling him back as he immediately raced down to the wharfs. Trey had to call him back several times before the dog really listened.

"Sorry, buddy. We're here for work. Let's go talk to Rob first." Clipping the leash on Schooner, Trey headed over to

Rob's shop. Trey went through the gate and headed around to the back. Sure enough, there Rob sat, his cap turned around on the back of his head, scratching his temple, a big thick ceramic mug full of coffee in his other hand.

He looked up, but no surprise was on his face when he saw Trey. "I wondered how long it would take you to get here," he muttered, with a smile.

"Stopped at the hospital first and checked up on Missy and Silas," he added.

"And?"

He shrugged. "No change in Silas's condition, and Missy? … Well, she's hanging in there."

"She's a good 'un," Rob noted, returning his gaze to the boat sitting on the dry dock in front of them.

"Any thoughts on this mess?" Trey asked.

"She's not as bad as she looks. Once we repair what Mother Nature did, that won't be much of an issue. Now repairing what man did? … That's a different story."

Twisting, Trey turned to Rob. "What does that mean exactly, Rob?"

"It means that Silas was right. Looks as if the plug was drilled, and then was secured with something dissolvable," he explained, getting up and pointing to the hull. "So, when the plug started to fail, they took on water but slowly. When in bad conditions, Silas might not have noticed right away. Then the plug would have given way completely, and, by then, the boat would have been very heavy with water, which steered them off their route."

"And yet Missy didn't mention anything about that."

Rob smiled over at him. "I doubt Silas would have figured it out himself until it was too late, and then he wouldn't have necessarily told her why the problem happened either."

Trey stared at him and then nodded. "He would have wanted to protect her, I guess."

"Yep, that was Silas, through and through."

"That *is* Silas," Trey corrected him sharply.

Rob gave a sage nod. "Let's hope so. The other thing is, his fuel tank gauge read half full when we got there, but she's totally empty. So somebody could have tampered with that. I don't know that Mother Nature would have had anything to do with his fuel gauge not working correctly, but I do know that Silas would have never left shore without a full tank—or believing that's what he had."

"Meaning that they would get way out there, start taking on water, and be stuck out there, with no way to save themselves?"

"Unless they had a working radio, which they also did not have," Rob pointed out. "Silas always carried a spare handheld shortwave radio with him, and I'm assuming that's what Missy was able to answer you on. Do you know where that ended up?"

"She gave it to the Coast Guard when they picked her up, but I know one of the guys there, and he returned it to me, to give to Silas and Missy."

"Considering it's how you knew she was alive and still out there, she might just want it."

"Silas would want it for sure," Trey added. "Are you saying that the ship's radio was damaged?"

"I'm saying that the battery failed on the ship's radio, which is odd considering the fact that Silas had really good radios, with a redundant setup that could be charged with solar, electric, and a third option I didn't even recognize, but none of that was working either."

"Would he have known that as soon as he headed out?"

"He might have but might not have thought anything of it, thinking he would get out a ways, and then he could stop and fix it. He was really good at tinkering with that stuff and wasn't one to cut corners where safety was concerned. There's absolutely nothing in that boat that's the same as when his father had it. Silas was always tinkering and making upgrades. His dad did the same thing when he had it. There have been considerable changes over the years, made by both of them."

"Right, so not only are these changes that he made, but there are also changes his father made?"

"Exactly. When Silas wakes up, we can ask him about it. In the meantime, we know that we have a radio that wasn't working, and we have a gas tank gauge that was not accurate, and we have the drain not working, and a bilge pump that I can't get to work."

"Any one of those is an issue that could conceivably happen," Trey noted, "but, when you look it all together, it was a mess of problems."

"I would say it's much bigger than that. There are too many issues for this to be coincidental. One maybe, two possibly but not this many. Which means that not only did somebody not want him to come back, but they also wanted to ensure it."

With that, Trey sat beside Rob with a hard *thunk*. "That begs the next question. ... Who hated Silas enough to make that happen?"

Rob shook his head. "Oh, he had enemies. I won't lie. He did have enemies but mostly because of the fishing tournaments. Some people thought he cheated. Some people thought he had a little spot where he was feeding fish and tracking them, had them penned up or something. I don't even know what the hell people thought. It just boggles the mind to think that anybody would care that much about a damn competition," he muttered.

At that, Trey agreed. "Yet we know that it happens, and people can get a bit fanatical about it."

"Not a *bit* fanatical," Rob corrected, "but all-out crazy. It absolutely blows my mind how spun up people can get, but they do, and that's the bottom line."

"So, you're thinking that's the reason for sabotaging the boat?" Trey asked.

"It doesn't make any sense to me because it's just a game, but I don't really know how much money we're talking about. Maybe that was a factor, but again, no matter what it is, it's got to be a pretty inconsequential amount for somebody like Silas, who makes big money."

"But it's all relative, you know? It might not be inconsequential for somebody else," Trey pointed out. "I don't know what kind of money we're talking about, but pick a number. Ten thousand to guys like you and me isn't chump change by any means, but it's not the end of the world either. Yet it may mean absolutely nothing to a guy like Silas. But to a lot of people, especially someone in a financial bind, it could be everything. And, if Silas always came out on top, time and time again, that could rub somebody raw. So, in that case, we would have a fairly obvious list of suspects, but I don't really see them as suspects at the moment because they would need access to his boat to sabotage it four ways to Sunday. So has to be somebody nobody would notice or would care about. Yet it would need to be somebody who understood what he was doing."

"Not necessarily," Rob argued. "You can sabotage all kinds of shit and be an amateur at it. But whoever did this may not have known that Silas is pretty decent at fixing things himself."

"Which goes along with the fact that it was sabotaged in multiple ways, just to ensure he couldn't fix everything, which is a hell of a thought," Trey muttered.

Rob nodded. "Agreed, but there's always the chance that we're completely off our rockers, and this is something else entirely."

"As much as I want to say, *I hope so*, I don't see it. Just too much is here that you've already found. It would be one thing if Silas was a guy who does things half-ass, but he's not. He's the proverbial Boy Scout, all about being prepared."

Rob gave him a hard look, shook his head, and stated, "Agreed. The question is, do we bring the sheriff in on it?"

Trey winced. "I tried to get the sheriff to come talk to you, but he got pulled away on a call, even while we were talking."

Rob shrugged, along with a smirk. "He's not really a water man anyway. He would avoid all kinds of watercraft, if he could."

"That's unusual for this location."

"Might be unusual, but he likes his job just fine. That doesn't mean he'll let somebody get away with murder."

"No, but that's another thing. He's not likely to have any murders around here for him to gain any experience with. This is a very small-town sheriff, with very little experience in sabotage, and almost no experience in this level of crime."

"What are you calling the level of crime in sabotage anyway?"

"To me, it's a crime of passion, not romantic passion but emotional, you know?"

Rob smiled. "So speaks a young man who still finds passion all around."

"Of course I do," Trey admitted briskly, "and so do you. More than that, this deal is a no-go for you. With all the people you've helped out of bad spots on or around the water, you would do an awful lot to stop anybody capable of doing something like this," he pointed out. "You might hide behind a gruff exterior, but you absolutely detest injustice."

Rob gave a slow nod. "I don't know what the hell blew my cover on that," he muttered, "but you are correct. So we'll have to find out what the hell happened here."

"The other thing is," Trey added, bending down closer, "we'll have to do it alone. Whoever did this was prepared to kill Silas and his daughter. So they really won't want to get caught."

"Too damn bad." Rob snorted. "I'm old and don't really give a shit about my life anymore, but nobody gets to ruin this beautiful boat like they did." He shook his head. "That's a crime in itself in my book." With that, Rob put his coffee cup down and stated, "Now, let's get to work."

Surprised and not quite sure what Rob meant but happy to help, Trey followed Rob inside the *Forget Me Not*. "What are we looking for?" Trey asked.

"I know it sounds foolish but fingerprints."

Trey frowned. "Even after all the seawater?"

"Even after all the seawater."

"So, do you feel like telling me what you used to do in real life?" Trey asked Rob.

He snorted. "Catching assholes, but that seems like a very long time ago."

"You were a cop?"

He nodded. "I was a cop, but, if you tell anybody, I'll

deny it. Then I'll kick your ass."

Trey laughed. "Is there a problem being a cop in this world?"

"No, but I don't really like the memories it drags up. So save us both some trouble and don't bother repeating it."

"I won't. I'm just happy to hear that you've got skills that go along with mine."

At that, Rob faced him and asked, "Did you do this in the military?"

Trey nodded. "Something like this, yeah."

"Good. In that case we should solve this in no time." He brought out a pad and pen from his shirt pocket. The notebook was at least three inches long. He handed both over to Trey. "You'll keep the running notes, just in case."

"Just in case what?"

He glared at him. "Just in case somebody doesn't like me poking around."

"It's not just you though," Trey pointed out. "We have to keep Missy safe too."

He nodded. "That will be your job too."

Trey frowned, but he also nodded.

"And you're right," Rob added. "She has to stay alive through this. That's your number one priority."

CHAPTER 8

MISSY WAS SURPRISED to see Trey, as the end of the day rolled around. She welcomed the immediate greeting she got from Schooner, then looked over at Trey intently. He seemed tired and worn out. "Did you get approval to bring him in?"

He shrugged. "Had a talk with the doctor about how Schooner and Silas were best buddies, and I suggested that Schooner might be a really good option to help bring Silas back around and pull him out of this."

She smiled, agreeing it would be a good option.

When they walked over to the bedside, he saw that her father had curled up on the far side of the bed. At that, Trey looked at her. "He's moved."

"He has moved," she confirmed, with a beaming smile, "I'll take it as a good sign."

"I would. I would definitely take that as a huge good sign."

With Silas curled on the far side of his hospital bed, there was room for Schooner, who immediately jumped up and curled up with his back along Silas's. It brought tears to Missy's eyes to see the two of them together. "It's so nice to see how much Schooner cares."

"They bonded in a way that not everybody under-stands," Trey pointed out. "Hopefully Schooner can help, because, even when Silas gets out of this, he'll need a lot of recovery time."

Missy nodded. "We have the same issues with animals, yet animals tend to do better than humans in many ways." She sat down on the edge of the bed, rubbing Schooner's head. "And this guy, I don't know what'll happen with him."

"Nothing," Trey claimed, "because you need him. You need him for Silas to come back to."

After a few minutes, she looked over at him and asked, "And?"

"And what?" he muttered, not taking his gaze off Silas and Schooner.

"Did you find anything?"

"We found a bunch of things," he shared, "but we can't yet tell for certain how much of it may have been sabotage and how much was Mother Nature."

"*Right,*" she grumbled.

"Think back to the beginning of your trip. Was he surprised about the radio?"

She looked over at him and nodded. "He was and mentioned that one of his parts must have broken down, but it didn't seem to be too bad. He told me, when we got out a little way, he would go down and fix it. Plus, we always had the extra shortwave radio, so he wasn't too bothered."

Trey just nodded at that.

"So, I gather you're wondering about sabotage, but did you find anything?"

"It's definitely possible. Your fuel gauge was broken, and the tank was empty."

"When you say empty," she asked cautiously, "what do you mean?"

"You mentioned that the tank was half full, and that's

definitely what the gauge says, but the tank was completely empty."

"So, we ran out of fuel too," she muttered, "but we still had the sail."

"Exactly, so not the end of the world," he noted.

She nodded slowly. "I know he was starting to get very concerned at that point in time, and we were trying to head back home again, but nothing seemed to be working. We started taking on water, and she just wasn't cooperating. She wasn't handling right. She was sitting too low in the water," Missy explained.

"Right, and that may have been due to someone potentially replacing the plug with some material that would dissolve over time."

"What?"

"So, in that case, the next thing would be to radio for help, while emptying out the water yourself, limping it back home again."

"Right," she agreed, "which in this case we couldn't do because we didn't have the fuel."

He smiled at her. "Exactly."

She grimaced and stared at him. "So, we're really thinking that somebody did this?"

He shrugged. "Let's just say it's a major concern right now. Too many things went wrong, and I don't believe in coincidence."

"No, especially for someone as careful as my dad," she pointed out, as she sank onto the cot, wrapping the knit blanket around her shoulders, now curling up against the wall. "Never in my wildest days did I think something like that could ever happen here."

"I don't think it's so much that it happened here. I think

it's more that it could happen anywhere, and, if you hadn't been found, nobody would ever have been the wiser."

"But you did find us," she declared.

"Yeah, which may have made me a target too," he suggested, with half a smile, "but I would like to think not."

She stared at him. "What do you think the chances are of somebody wanting to complete the job?"

"I think the trick at this point is to ensure nobody knows how your father is doing, and, if he does improve, … you need to keep that news to yourself."

She stared at him in shock as the meaning settled in. "You think somebody might come back and try to finish the job, don't you?"

"I think the problem is that somebody is likely to be afraid that, since you've been rescued, either your father will say something about it, opening an investigation, or he already knows exactly who did this. You're sure he didn't mention any names?"

She shook her head. "He was swearing a blue streak, and I didn't necessarily understand everything he was swearing about," she admitted, "but he was obviously very perturbed about a lot of what was going on."

"Of course. That's to be expected, but you didn't hear him name any names?"

"No, of course not," she muttered, raising both hands.

At that, Schooner hopped off the bed and walked over, jumping up on the cot and curling up beside her. She groaned, wrapped her arms around him, holding him close. "He's very intuitive, isn't he?" she muttered, as she scratched the top of his head.

"Of course. You're his family, and he knows that one is injured and that the other one is suffering. Schooner will be there for you as much as he can be. And, if I thought that I could leave him here with you every day, all day, I would."

"Why?" she asked. "It's hardly a place for a dog."

"Yet … he would be a great watchdog."

She sucked in her breath at that. "Good God." She stared down at Schooner. "I really don't like the idea that I need a watchdog."

"You may not. … However, if we're correct, and somebody is trying to kill your father, and you are an incidental addition along the way," he pointed out in a calm, flat tone that put a certain sting of reality to his words, "then you have to be prepared for the reality that there could be a second attempt."

She shivered, wrapping her arms tightly around her chest. "Is it a good thing for me to even stay here? Although I don't know where else I would go."

"Presumably you're living at your dad's house, right?"

She nodded. "Yes, I was away at school and home for summers," she explained, "and being in vet school doesn't exactly give you much chance for a personal life."

"No, of course not"—he smiled—"but you're doing something that you've always wanted to do, and I'm sure your father was more than excited that you were coming home to work with him."

"He really was," she agreed, looking over at him, tears in her eyes again.

"Ah, don't even go there," Trey stated. "Your father is a tough cookie. Let's give him a chance to get back out into the world that he loves so much."

"He really does love life. After my mom died, he and my grandfather would take the *Forget Me Not* out for a sail; and it completely changed him. He was so depressed when we lost her, and then again when we lost my grandfather, but somehow the boat just seemed to change everything for Dad."

Trey nodded. "Sometimes it's just a new lease on life. He'd always been an avid fisherman but never felt he had enough time, and the loss of your mom may have been one of those wake-up calls that he needed to push him to get out and to do more."

"I think so," she agreed, "and it was a rough time for all of us. I was young and wasn't doing very well myself. Yet, even as I got older, I felt the same. I really thought long and hard before leaving him alone to attend university."

"He wouldn't have blamed you. Besides, you were doing exactly what you needed to do."

She laughed. "I think you just like giving everybody a pass."

"No, that's not me at all," he corrected, with a smile, "but I do understand that, when life hits you hard, you gotta do what you gotta do."

"Right, and your family wasn't exactly supportive about your decision to join the military or even how to handle your injury, were they?"

"Nope, they sure weren't," he replied, with a smile. "Now that I'm back, one of the first questions that I got from Elizabeth was whether I'm staying."

"It's a good question." Missy focused on him intently. "I've been wondering about that myself."

He stared back at her and shrugged. "I don't know the answer to that. I'm not sure, and I have to figure out a few things for myself. I would like to think that there's more out there for me, but I'm not sure what form it'll take."

"You can always do search and rescue, since apparently

you have a real knack for it," she suggested, with a gentle smile.

"Maybe not so much of a knack for it, as an understanding of the person I was coming to help." He looked over at the dog. "It's really Schooner that I was asked to come out here for."

She frowned at him. "What?"

He nodded. "I didn't even know that Schooner was with Silas, and that was a hell of a surprise."

"You're not kidding," she muttered. "I can't believe that you came out or were sent out for Schooner. Yet, now that you're here, everything might change for you. I know your brother would like to see you living here again."

"Maybe, and that might be nice, particularly now that he's having a family. I think family matters even more when the new generations come along."

"I wouldn't know," she muttered. "We've not had any youngsters in our family yet."

"No, not with your dad waiting for you," he teased, as he turned to look back at Silas. He stepped forward and leaned over. "You hear that, Silas? It's definitely time to get back here. So come back to the land of the living and help us solve this thing. If somebody did something to you or to the boat, believe me that people are here to help you." And, with that, he turned to her. "Did you get anything to eat?"

She grimaced. "You know, hospital food, a little at a time."

"I know you don't want to leave your dad, but can I take you out for a meal or two and get you in a little bit better shape yourself? What do you think?"

"I did run home, grabbed a change of clothes, had a quick shower, and came back," she shared, "but I still feel rough, you know?"

"Yeah, and you will for a while." He shrugged. "I could also pick you up some food." When she hesitated, he shook his head. "Look. You have to eat. You have to look after yourself, because when your dad wakes up, he'll need somebody to look after him."

She smiled. "I like that positive attitude."

"Yeah, and it's more than just a positive attitude," he added. "It's also the truth."

She winced. "You won't let me off the hook, will you?"

"Nope, I won't. So what is it, eat-in food or takeout? It would do you some good to be out of here for a while. I know that Schooner would like to spend some time with you too."

"Oh, that's not fair," she said, as Schooner lifted his head and just blinked at her, then whined.

"We could pick up fish and chips and take it to the docks."

She looked back at her father and frowned. "I just don't want to leave him."

"Do you think something'll happen to him in the meantime?"

"After our discussion on second attempts, yeah. Still, what if he wakes up? I don't want him to wake up alone."

"I'm pretty sure he would be happy to wake up and to know that you're safe, even if you're not right there beside him. You also know that, when he wakes up, he'll get after you for sitting here, waiting for him all this time."

She smiled. "Now that he will do," she agreed, "but it doesn't change what I think and feel."

"In that case, I'll go pick up fish and chips and bring it back for you."

She hesitated and then asked, "Can I ride along? As long as you bring me back fairly quickly, but I really could use a few minutes out of here."

"Good. Do you need to pick up anything or to just get out?"

"Out. Just *out*, out."

"In that case, let me just see if Jackson can fill in for us here. Then let's grab some fish and chips and take them to the docks." He already had his phone out, sending a text.

"You're really after fish and chips," she noted, with a laugh.

"I don't know about that, but it's pretty portable and fast." His phone got a text. "Jackson's on his way. Let's go." And, with that, he motioned at Schooner. "Come on, buddy. Let's get some lunch." Maybe it was the word *lunch*. Maybe it was the word *buddy*, but Schooner whined and rolled over and looked up at her. "See? He wants you to come too."

She got up and immediately Schooner attached himself to her leg. She reached down and grabbed the leash on him. "But you promise to bring me right back?"

"I promise to bring you right back," he stated.

She smiled. "Okay, let's go then."

And, with that, he led her out to the parking lot, even as she kept turning to look back at the hospital. "Thirty minutes," he vowed. "Thirty minutes for you to refresh your brain and to get a chance to smile and to get some fresh air."

"It'll take at least thirty minutes to get the fish and chips," she protested.

"It shouldn't. I phoned ahead."

At the shocked look on her face, he laughed as he took her to his vehicle, helped her inside. He waved at his brother, as Jackson honked as he drove by, looking for a parking spot.

Then Trey took off, hitting the drive-through on the way, where their order was ready and waiting. "See?"

And, with that, he carried on down to the docks and out to one of the big benches, where they could enjoy the fresh air.

She immediately dug into her fish and chips and took several deep breaths of fresh air. "You don't realize just how much your life changes when you come close to losing it," she murmured.

"Oh, I think I do," he quipped, with a gentle smile.

She looked back at him and nodded. "I never realized just what it would mean."

"Of course you didn't. How could you? I don't think anybody realizes it until it happens to them, until they experience it firsthand. Then everything changes. And even though you know that it'll change something, you don't know exactly what it'll change. Still, you will be different forever after."

"Maybe that's a good thing," she noted. "It gives you a better appreciation of what's important in life." She calmly worked on finishing her food. When she couldn't eat the last of her fish, she caught Schooner staring at her with that hopeful look. She sighed. "Okay, buddy. I know it's not the best thing for you, but I won't tell if you don't." He scarfed down the last few bites of fish, then immediately shifted his gaze to Trey.

He laughed. "You think I'm as much of a sucker as she is?"

"Yes," she declared, as he handed off his last bite to the War Dog. "I think you are."

Trey chuckled. "Come on. I promised to get you right back." He sent a quick text to Jackson on the walk back to the truck. As they drove back to the hospital, he asked her, "Has anybody else popped in to say hi? Has anybody checked in on you and Silas?"

She shook her head. "No, and I was half expecting a reporter or somebody to come, but, so far, it's been peaceful and quiet. I suspect that could be due more to the nurses than anything, if they are restricting visitors for him, just because my father's life is still very much hanging in the balance."

"Absolutely, and that's a good thing. The longer we can keep people away, the better."

She smiled. "They're not all bad, you know."

"No, they aren't," he conceded, "but I'm not sure they're all good either." He saw Jackson leaving the hospital, and they exchanged nods, right as Trey pulled up to the main entrance to let her off there. She reached through the window, gave Schooner a big scratch, and then told Trey, "Thanks for dragging me out."

"Go back to your father," he said, with a smile. "I'll check in on you in a bit." With that, he was gone.

She wasn't exactly sure why he was checking in on her all the time, wondering whether it had anything to do with her father's accident or not. Yet it was nice. It had been a very long time since she'd had anybody other than her father give a damn about her. There was something special about that.

She'd been away from town long enough that she'd lost touch with all the friends she had once had. Years of living away would do that, and, now that she was here, she was enjoying maybe finding a friend.

TREY WAITED IN the parking lot until she disappeared, then turned and looked at Schooner. "You ready, buddy?" With that, he headed toward Silas's home and soon stood at the front door. He hadn't really asked permission but realized that he probably should. He quickly texted her, asking permission to go into the house to check for signs of anything suspicious.

She immediately called him. "Do you really think that's necessary?" she asked cautiously.

"Yes, I do."

"Fine, but I was in there yesterday, and I didn't see anything."

"Okay, but I still want to go through your dad's stuff. I know you haven't contacted the sheriff, but—"

"I know. I know," she muttered. "That's not exactly something I want to take on right now."

"Of course not, yet, if something *is* going on, then we need to get it straightened out right away."

"Right," she grumbled. "Go ahead then."

He smiled, and, with Schooner at his side, he opened the front door and stepped inside. Typical small town where no one locked the doors. It was silent inside and should be, since nobody was home, and nobody would be home for a while.

As he stood here in the silence, he looked around the house that he had been in many times, but not recently. It still looked the same. Pictures of Silas's wife were still over the fireplace in the living room. Trey noted even more pictures now of Missy, and some of them made him smile. Schooner immediately headed for his dog food bowl, which reminded Trey that he needed to pick up more for him. He was using everything they had at home, though he had only picked up the one bag of dog food, which was going fast. Trey needed to get more.

When he walked into the kitchen, he added dog food to his bowl, so he could have a decent meal. "Take your time, buddy. We'll be here for a little bit."

And, with that, Trey headed upstairs to where the master bedroom was. As he walked in, he did a quick search through it, not expecting to find anything but knowing it had to be checked regardless. As he walked through the home, he texted Missy, asking if she needed him to pick up anything while he was here.

She immediately replied. **No, I'll go back home again tonight and pick up more clothes.**

He gave her a thumbs-up and sent her a message. **Everything looks fine here.** She gave him a thumbs-up in return, but he knew that she was really curious as to why he felt the need to come. He then headed in to do a quick search of her bedroom to ensure all was well, then went downstairs to look around each room.

He didn't really understand his need to search their home either. It was just that sense of missing something. It wasn't that they were missing a piece of the puzzle. They were missing everything. So far, none of this mess made any sense, and maybe it wasn't intended to. That's the thing that got him. Just because you wanted answers didn't mean there were any, at least not clear-cut and ready for you.

He headed through the living room again, the dining area, then onto the kitchen. On his way to Silas's home office, Trey knew Silas kept his business office at the vet clinic. As Trey considered that, he wondered what had happened to the vet clinic all this time. Picking up his phone, he called Missy, as he walked to the home office.

"What has happened to the vet clinic?"

"Bill has been running it. He is my dad's assistant."

"And he's a full-fledged vet?"

"Yeah, he is. He's been there for quite a while."

"Any reason to suspect that he would be behind this?"

"I can't imagine it. He's terrified of water for starters," she added, with a note of humor. "He was horrified that both of us would go out on the boat together."

"Maybe there was good reason for that."

"I've been thinking about that too, but, no, that's not possible. I don't think Bill would have anything to do with something like that."

"Good enough," he murmured, "at least for now. Did your father keep any important documents or anything in the house?" He had reached the open doorway to Silas's home office now.

"Not as far as I know. He has a safe deposit box, but I don't know that he has anything else under lock and key. The lawyer keeps track of the legal documents and all, so I don't know what Dad would have there at home."

"So, there's no reason why anybody would be in the home office here?" he asked her.

"No, I don't think so. Why?"

He stepped in through the office door and shared, "Because your dad's desk has been dumped."

"What?" she cried out.

He quickly sent her a photo. "This is not how you left it?"

"No, of course not."

"Now, think carefully," he began cautiously. "When were you last in here? In your dad's home office?"

"Oh my. I ..."

He could almost hear the wheels spinning in her head. "You must be sure that whenever you were in here that it was normal."

"I can't be sure," she replied. "Yesterday I raced home, showered, grabbed some clothes, then carried on. You're right. I'm not sure I was in his office yesterday. Damn," she muttered.

"So the break-in could have been even three weeks ago, when you first went missing," Trey noted.

"But how could I have missed it?"

"You had no need to go into your father's office. If it's not a place where you keep anything, there would be no reason for you to go in there."

"Right."

Enough hesitation filled her tone that he had to ask, "Or is there a reason for you to come in here?"

"No, not really, but I'm accustomed to being in there. It's not as if I would avoid it. It's not as if it was a restricted private space that nobody was allowed into," she explained. "It was definitely a room where I was welcome, but I wouldn't have gone in there because I didn't need anything."

"Are there things you sometimes need in here?"

"The printer is there and the scanner," she noted. "So, if I needed that equipment, sure. I certainly have used the printer and the scanner in the past because of school, but, other than that, I have no reason to go in there. Typically I would only have gone in there if Dad was there."

"Okay, so who else has access to your house?" Dead silence came from the other end of the call.

"I have no idea," she replied.

He heard the fatigue in her tone, as she worried about that question.

"I just don't know who would have access."

"The replacement at the vet clinic?"

"I don't think so, no, … but Miranda would."

"Who's Miranda?"

She laughed. "Somebody Dad would tell me that he was *not* sweet on, yet I think a budding relationship was there."

"Have you seen Miranda since you've been back?"

She stopped, then whispered, "No."

"Okay, so would Miranda have had anything to do with this?"

"God, I hope not," she muttered. "I don't know why she would, but, even if she did, that's too unbelievable."

"Everything is unbelievable right now, but we have no choice but to consider all possibilities."

"Of course," she stated bitterly, "but it's terrible even thinking about it."

"Yes, it is," he agreed, "but *not* thinking about it doesn't make it go away."

"Are you sure?" she quipped in a half laughing tone. "Because I would give a lot to have that happen. I just want Dad to wake up and to tell me that everything is fine, and that it was all his own error or something, that the boat wasn't sabotaged."

"And yet in your own heart you don't believe that."

"I don't know what I believe," she snapped, "so don't go putting words in my mouth."

He smiled, happy to see the return of some of that fighting spirit. "Got it. I'm sending you a series of photos, but I don't suppose there's any way for you to know if anything's missing, is there?"

"No. … Will you call the sheriff?"

"I intend to," he said. "I guess the other question I have

is, if this was an intruder—"

"If it's all torn apart, it would have to be," she stated in a dry tone.

"Yes, but we don't know what they were looking for or why they would have done this," he pointed out. "Do you have any suspicion either way?"

"No, of course not, but I'm pretty sure that the sheriff will say, once it became known that we were missing, that would have been somebody's opportunity to break in and to take advantage of the fact that nobody was there."

"Honestly, that's a damn good thought," he noted, as he stared around the small room. "I don't like it, but it is a reasonable assumption."

"Exactly, and you know nobody'll give a crap beyond that."

"I don't know that though," he countered immediately, "and I don't want to believe that."

"Sure, but that doesn't mean you're correct."

He smiled. "No, it sure doesn't, but we'll see what we can get for information. I'll call him now." He ended the call and immediately phoned Sheriff Woodley. When he answered, Trey said, "Hey, Sheriff. It's Trey."

"Hey, Trey. I hear you got the boat back." Hesitating, he asked, "Anything suspicious?"

"Yeah, there sure is. I take it you haven't made your way down to talk to Rob, have you?"

Apologetically he agreed. "No, I sure haven't. Life's gotten a little difficult here. I was thinking to head out there soon."

"It'll get a little more difficult now because Silas's house, at least his home office, has been busted into and tossed. The contents of the drawers are everywhere, as if the intruder was looking for something. I know you'll say it was just an opportunist, somebody who found out they were missing and knew that the house was empty."

"It does happen," the sheriff noted in that same tone as before.

"Sure, except the TV is still here and all the items I would expect to be stolen are here too. I can't tell what might be missing because it's such a mess, with only the office being tossed. So, you'll have to think about another motive because, if they were just here to steal, they would have taken a hell of a lot more than whatever they were after."

"But we don't know that," Woodley argued.

"No, we don't. We don't know who was behind this, and that is something we have to get to the bottom of."

"Sure, and, as soon as I handle a drunk man and the domestic violence call on him, then I'll get there."

"This is an attempted murder, Sheriff, and it could end up being the murder of Silas, if not also Missy," Trey snapped. "So you might want to keep that in mind too."

And, with that, he ended the call.

CHAPTER 9

S HERIFF WOODLEY WALKED inside Silas's hospital
room, his hands on his hips, glaring around the small
room. Missy immediately stood up, then walked over and
motioned him outside into the hallway. He stepped out with
her. "Any change?" he asked, even his hushed voice sounding
loud in the silence of the hospital.

She shook her head. "No, none." He frowned at that,
and she nodded. "I know, not what you wanted to hear, but
it's not what I want to hear either."

He winced. "Sorry, I'm not trying to be insensitive."

"I know. Everybody's walking on eggshells, trying to see
what the end result will be, but we just don't have any
answers."

"I'm sorry for that too," Woodley added. "That's got to
be the worst. Listen. Trey is making some accusations and
stirring up some pretty strong waves so that I do something
here. I'm not sure what I'm supposed to do at this point. He
says your house was broken into."

She stared at him. "Have you been to the house?"

"Not yet. I wanted to stop in and to get your take on
this first. Trey is new in town, and, while I know he's lived
here in the past, he's not somebody I know."

"Yet he came and rescued us and put himself at risk trying to get us in fast enough to give my father a chance," she

pointed out. "So he is somebody I am more than willing to bend over backward for."

"Agreed, but I also don't want anybody coming through town, making accusations of a kind we don't need."

She smiled. "I don't think we need any accusations honestly, but he sent me photos because I haven't been there yet myself." She sighed. Then she pulled out her phone and showed him the photos.

He stared at them, his jaw working. "When were you there last?"

"I was there yesterday." When he looked up, she continued. "I didn't go into my father's office. I quickly went upstairs, showered, and picked up a change of clothes. I stopped in the kitchen long enough to grab some granola bars, then raced back to the hospital. I didn't check his office—or the rest of the house for that matter—because I had no reason to."

He nodded slowly at that. "And that's the thing, isn't it? You had no reason to, so who knows what happened or when? This could have been somebody taking advantage of the fact that you were gone, as soon as you went missing, to see if you had some extra valuables around."

"And, if that was the case, why destroy just the office and not take the TV?" she asked.

"And yet you haven't seen it yourself."

She glanced at him. "No, I haven't seen it myself, but are you really implying that Trey might have done this?"

"No. God no," he stated, shaking his head rapidly. "I wouldn't do that. I'm just concerned that it might not be what we're thinking it is."

"Maybe so you would walk away from it, without having to deal with something?" she asked, a note of humor in her tone. When he glared at her, she smiled. "Look, Sheriff. I've been back and forth on this rollercoaster mystery ride for weeks now," she explained, "and frankly, at the moment, a break-in at the house is the least of my worries. However, if anything happens to my father, or if the boat was, indeed, sabotaged, that person should be brought to justice."

He frowned. "Yet that'll be pretty damn hard to prove," he pointed out. "Trey and Rob have both brought it up to me, but they are apparently looking for proof, which I don't have any to offer either way," he stated. "So that's a big concern too."

She nodded. "As is the fact that you would need to be handling it, should it be true."

"I'm not against handling it," he protested, "but we definitely don't have that level of skills here. I'm a small-town sheriff in a town where murders are nonexistent and where sabotage is rare."

"Which is why Trey and Rob are taking on as much as they are," she pointed out, "because both of them do happen to have those skills." When the sheriff frowned at her, she nodded. "Rob doesn't talk about it much, but he was a cop in his day, and I know that Trey was doing something along that line in the military."

"When you say, *along this line* … ?"

She shrugged. "I don't know exactly, but feel free to ask him."

He groaned. "That doesn't sound like a good idea to me."

"Maybe it's not. Yet, when you want answers, the best thing you can do is go to the source. So maybe you should be talking to them," she suggested. "I don't understand any of what's going on myself, but I've got my hands full right here."

"And your father?" he asked, turning to look at him in the hospital bed. "Did he say anything about this being something other than an unfortunate accident?"

"Yes," she declared, "he's the one who told me that the boat had been sabotaged."

With that, Woodley picked his hat off his head and scratched his hairline. "Well, damn," he muttered. "Silas's always been one of those commonsense type guys."

"Yes, he has," she agreed, "and I highly doubt anything here would have changed it."

"Stress can be pretty rough on anyone, and we all have a breaking point," he muttered. "Potentially losing your life, and knowing that your daughter will die right there beside you are pretty big stressors for a man. A man might have said anything in a situation like that."

She groaned. "He might have, but, chances are, he didn't. I can't tell you anything more than that, Sheriff. You'll have to talk to Trey and Rob."

"And your father," he added, "because that's really the only person I'll listen to."

"I would find it very distressing if you needed his words in order to lend some validity to mine and Trey's and Rob's," she stated, "because there is a very good possibility that Dad won't wake up." He turned to face her, and she nodded. "I don't know who else you'll talk to because, although the doctors have encouraged me to not give up hope, the reality is, Dad's not showing any signs of im- provement, and that is something we're all concerned about."

"That's the worst," he muttered.

"It's very difficult, yes," she agreed, staring at him, "but so is the thought that nobody gives a crap that someone may have tried to murder us and may well end up succeeding with a second try."

TREY WALKED BACK into the hospital, Schooner at his side. The War Dog obviously knew where they were going, and his steps had quickened to get there. Trey stopped at the doorway to Silas's room and smiled when he saw Missy stretched out on the cot beside Silas's bed. Because Trey hadn't moved forward, Schooner looked up at him and tugged ever-so-slightly on his leash.

"I know, buddy," Trey whispered. "I just don't want to disturb her. Missy's resting and really needs it."

"I wouldn't worry about it," she muttered, stifling a yawn. "I haven't been able to sleep for a while."

When she looked over at him, he smiled. "How're you doing?"

She opened her arms for Schooner, who pulled at the leash and raced into her arms. "Hey, buddy," she said in a cooing tone, as he hopped up on the cot. She wrapped her arms around him, burying her face against his chest.

Trey studied her features, or at least the little bit he could see of them. Her movements made him realize something was wrong. He looked around as he walked closer and sat down on the edge of the cot. "What's up?" He kept his voice lower than normal.

She looked over at him, gave him a small smile, and shrugged. "Just life, I guess. The sheriff was here, but he doesn't seem to be too concerned about whether this was a deliberate act or not," she muttered. "It's hard, you know?

My dad has spent his entire life here, helping people in many ways, and now when he needs help, it doesn't seem as if anybody cares."

"Oh, I think people care, but I don't think the sheriff wants to move too quickly because of any number of issues that could come up to bite him in the butt," he suggested, waving his hands. "Let's give him a break for now. He is involved in his own investigation, and you're right. He doesn't like what we're telling him, but he's not ignoring us."

"Maybe that's what he's saying to you, but that's not what he's saying to me."

He nodded, then rubbed her shoulders. "I'm sorry. This is the hardest part. You don't know if your father will wake up. You don't know how he'll be if he does, and it's all just a waiting game, and that hurts. The idea that someone may have done this on purpose is really just too much to consider on top of everything else."

She sniffled back the tears and smiled at him. "Very true," she muttered. "I'm just trying to hold on while we figure out what's going on and what's next. Everything in my life suddenly came to a complete stop, and I can't begin to know how to pick it up again."

"For one thing," Trey began, "I'll come by more often and stay with your dad, while you go home on a more regular basis and come back on a regular basis. Sitting here full-time, just waiting, is not the best thing for your health, physically or mentally. You can also check in on your dad's business to ensure everything is okay there, as well as the things at home, you know? Just getting out of this hospital would really help you in the long run."

She looked at him and slowly nodded. "You're right. I just hadn't really gotten to that point yet. Going to the clinic just reminds me that it was supposed to be something my dad and I did together, something we've planned for my whole life."

"And that's not off the table by any means," he reminded her. "Let's stay positive."

She smiled, wiped away her tears, and nodded. "Sorry, it's just, … some days are better than others."

"And some moments will be better than others," he added. "You really have to take it one moment at a time."

She studied him, then leaned a little closer so she could look into his eyes. "You really do know what it's all about, don't you?"

"When you've been there," he replied, "you never forget. There is life on the other side of whatever this turns out to be. That's what you have to hang on to."

She straightened up, gave Schooner a big hug again, and sighed. "Okay then. In that case, maybe I could ask you for a ride back to my place."

"Sure," he said. "I know the sheriff wanted you to check out your home, just to determine if anything was missing."

"That makes sense," she noted, "though I'm not sure I can tell."

"Let's get you home and get you some food and a shower, then, if you want to come back, … I'll bring you back again."

She looked at him and then nodded. "Maybe that would be best. I sure could use a chance to get out for a little bit again."

"It should definitely be a daily thing," he suggested, "and don't ever feel guilty about it."

"But what if he wakes up, and I'm not here?"

"Then he'll wake up, and you'll see him as soon as you

get back. Plus, I'll ask Jackson to stay with Silas for a bit, while we're gone," he added, with a smile, already typing the text. "Remember that you also have to look after yourself."

"It doesn't feel like it. I really just want to look after him." She turned to face her father again. She walked closer, then leaned over and whispered, "I'll be back soon, Dad. I'll go get showered." As she walked away, she was overcome with emotions. Outside, she stopped and took several deep breaths of fresh air. "What if he never wakes up?" Tears once again choked her voice.

"You'll adapt, but it will be really hard and not the way you want it. Yet you'll learn to survive," he explained, with a nod to Jackson, as he waved to them on his way inside the hospital. "The human spirit takes time to heal, but it does manage eventually." He wrapped an arm around her and gave her a gentle hug. "Come on. Let's get you home."

"Food and a shower," she murmured.

"You should also have a nap in your own bed, where you could get some real sleep. That cot looks uncomfortable."

"I don't want to be gone that long," she said, shaking her head. "That just feels like too much time away."

"Then you do what you can do today and take it as far as you can," he suggested. "Yet your dad would never blame you for looking after yourself."

"No, he wouldn't," she agreed with a smile. "He was always really big on making sure I did that."

"Of course he was because, the bottom line is, he wants you safe. The last thing he would want is to come back to full health only to find out you had wasted away to nothing in the meantime."

She smiled. "That's a little melodramatic."

"Hey, I'm trying to make a point here," he said with a

big smile. "Just think about it. All kinds of things make life worth living, but it all starts with you taking care of yourself. If you don't, nobody else will."

"That's a sad truth, isn't it?" she muttered. "Even if people are willing to take care of you, they can't do it in the way that you need it. People are always all over the place and willing to help, but there's still a certain element that requires you to step up."

He quickly drove her back to her place, which was only a few blocks from Trey's brother's home.

"Are you still staying with Elizabeth and Jackson?" she asked Trey.

"I am." He nodded. "I've got to figure out what I want to do from here on out pretty soon."

"You could stay," she replied, looking over at him. "I would be happy with that."

He smiled. "I was thinking about it, but I don't want that to be the only reason."

"It would be a good one though," she said, with a laugh. "I don't remember us having these kinds of conversations before."

"No, we probably didn't. We were miles apart in school years, and that meant miles apart in life experiences. I was really happy to hear you'd gone to veterinary school though."

"Me too. … Yet, if, if my father doesn't come back, … if something happens to him, I don't know if I would maintain the business."

"Why not? You have somebody—Bill, you said—who's already there. Surely you can intern somewhere nearby, while helping out there as well. And you would pick up the business aspects in no time."

"I don't know," she muttered, looking at him. "I hadn't

considered that, but maybe."

"Regardless, I'm sure there is a solution, one way or another," he noted. "This town definitely needs more people like your father."

"I know. He was ... is," she corrected immediately, "well-loved by a lot of people."

"Exactly."

Back at her house, she hesitated at the front door, and he nodded. "The sheriff and his deputies have been here, though I'm not sure that they did a whole lot. They took pictures at least. If you want to come take a look, then you'll know the worst of it."

"Sure. Why not? I have to do it sometime." As she walked into the office, she stopped and gasped. "Jesus, I wasn't expecting this. I saw your photos but still ..."

Schooner sniffed the entire area going from chair to desk to different areas of the mess on the floor as if searching for her father.

"In a way your reaction's a good thing. I was hoping you wouldn't say it was like this all the time."

"Right." She chuckled at his joke. "But, no, God no," she muttered. "Dad was meticulous with his records."

"What records would that be here though?"

She shrugged. "I'm not sure. Everything businesswise, such as legal matters and things, he kept with his lawyer. As for the actual business, the veterinary practice, he didn't bring any of those records home—not that I ever saw."

"And yet he had a home office. So what is this room for?"

"Honestly, he would work on some of his cases, doing research in the evenings on stuff that he didn't know, people he needed to contact or to consult with, that sort of thing. I don't know that he needed this home office except that it was a good place for him to spend time when he needed to work, but not as draining or as full of interruptions as being at the clinic."

Trey nodded and didn't say a whole lot to that. "So, I'll ask you another question. Did you ever have any serious boyfriends, or did you ever get close to marrying? Or, crap, maybe you're married already," he said, staring at her, his eyebrows raised. "I don't know why I just assumed you weren't, but is there anything like that in your world?"

"No, not at all," she said. "Why?"

"I just wondered if somebody in your world may have been at odds with your dad."

She smiled. "That would assume that I was some sort of femme fatale," she teased, "and that is definitely not the case." He just smiled at her. "You don't believe me, do you?"

"It's not that I don't believe you," he began, still focused on her. "It's just that something has happened, and, until we can rule out suspicions in every direction, we don't really know which way to go."

She nodded. "I hadn't really considered that," she admitted, "and you're right. It is possible, I guess, … but my one and only serious relationship broke up before I went to veterinary school."

"Okay, we'll table that discussion for now."

"Are you certain you're not asking out of interest for yourself?" She smiled at him.

He flashed her a bright grin. "Okay, it might have been a dual-purpose inquiry. So I'm glad to hear you weren't still pining away for somebody else."

"No, absolutely not," she declared. "No pining here. It was very serious at the time, but it didn't work out."

"Lots of things don't work out, particularly when we're young," he said, with a laugh.

"What about you? Do you have a girl in every port?"

"God no," he replied. "That's definitely not my style. I want to thoroughly enjoy each and every one of them." At that, she looked astonished, then burst out howling with laughter. He grinned. "See? Laughter is good for the soul."

"Oh my gosh. You got me on that one. I did not expect *that* for an answer, but thank you. I needed a good laugh."

He shook his head at her. "It wasn't intended to be hilarious, but I was hoping to put a smile back on your face." He was quite happy that he'd succeeded.

As they walked through the rest of the house, she shared, "Nothing else appears different."

"Okay, I'll tell the sheriff that."

"I don't think he'll really care," she muttered.

He patted her on the arm and added, "Don't worry about that now. Just go get a shower. Let me talk to him, and we'll see what happens."

CHAPTER 10

MISSY HEADED UPSTAIRS and stepped into her shower, letting the heat soak into her tired and sore body. She felt compelled to stay with her father at the hospital, and she desperately wanted to go back to him. Yet Trey was right about her not sleeping well. The hospital cot wasn't the most comfortable bed, but she felt guilty for even thinking about comfort when her father was still unconscious.

She quickly finished her shower, got dressed, and put another change of clothing in her carry bag. She walked downstairs to find Trey sitting at the counter, staring out at the backyard, Schooner stretched out on the floor next to him. He jumped up at the sight of her and gave her a greeting that made her love the furry mutt even more. Glancing at Trey, she realized he held a cup of coffee. "Is that coffee?" she asked in astonishment.

He turned to her and nodded. "Yes, I took the liberty of making you coffee."

"Making *me* coffee?" she asked, with a knowing look.

"Making *us* coffee, if you prefer. … I stand corrected."

"Oh, I definitely prefer, no matter what your motivation." She laughed. "There is something to be said for having somebody around who can look after himself."

"Pretty sure I fit that category just fine," he stated, with a smile. "I've never been accused of being too dependent on people."

"I suspect you're the opposite," she noted, studying him. "You probably don't let anybody help, unless you absolutely have to."

"I try not to be that stubborn," he shared, grinning at her as he held out a cup of coffee for her.

She accepted it gratefully, thanking him and sincerely happy to have it. They sat here for a few minutes, comfortably staring out at the backyard. Then she muttered, "I have such great memories of being here."

"I do too," he added. "It's one of the reasons I'm considering staying."

"And here I thought it was all about me," she teased, with mock laughter.

"You are definitely one of the reasons," he agreed, "and Silas. He was always really good to me. We had a hell of a friendship, and I do feel in a way that, … when I left for the navy, I let him down. I knew he would understand, but it's not the same thing. … I sure would give a lot to go fishing with him again."

She stared at him for a long moment and smiled, feeling the tears hit against her lashes. "I'm sure he would absolutely love that. He missed his special fishing partners."

"Who were the ones he was the most competitive with?"

She frowned at him for a moment. "I can't believe you're even thinking along those lines."

"I'm not sure what I'm thinking," he admitted. "We just have to map out clear possibilities." She gave him three names, only one of which he recognized.

"But I'm pretty sure it was a happy rivalry," she noted. "If anybody were to *not* make the derby the next year, it would disappoint all of them."

"Right, those are always the fun competitions."

"Exactly. I can't imagine any of these men having anything to do with hurting Dad."

"I hope not," he said, with a smile. "Come on. Let's get you back to the hospital. I'll tell Jackson that we are on our way."

Quickly rinsing the mugs and putting them in the sink, he drove her to the hospital where they left Schooner in the vehicle again. As they walked into the elevator to go up, she smiled at the other man inside. "Hey, Charles."

He smiled, then grimaced. "I hear your dad is doing poorly. I'm sorry about that."

"He may have been doing poorly, but he's doing a lot better now," she replied, with a bright smile.

"Good," he murmured. "I don't know what happened exactly, but I heard you got lost out there."

She shrugged. "I'm not exactly sure what happened myself."

"You were there though, weren't you?"

"I was there," she confirmed, "but the conditions were terrible, and the memories are not a great thing either." And, with that noncommittal comment, she stepped out of the elevator, waiting for Trey.

"WHAT WAS THAT all about?" Trey asked.

"I try not to speak to Charles that much—or about him for that matter." Missy shrugged. "You were asking about old boyfriends. Well, he would be one of them. He and my dad never got along well, but, no, Charles wouldn't have done anything to hurt us. At least the Charles I know wouldn't. It was so many years ago, he wouldn't have cared to do anything now."

"Oh, I don't know," Trey argued, turning to look back at the elevator. "Lots of people prefer their revenge served cold."

She laughed. "You make it all sound so melodramatic."

"Maybe it is," he stated. "So, who is this Charles guy?"

"Somebody I went to high school with. Then I went to veterinary school, and he went to med school, so just ... different paths all the way around."

Sensing more to it or something else going on, he waited until they got into the hospital room before he spoke up. "This really isn't the time to hold back details."

She turned to him, then shrugged. "Charles is an arrogant jerk, so I try to avoid him as much as I can. He's always thought I went into veterinary school because I couldn't get into med school. That grated on me for a while, but I never attempted to get into med school. That wasn't my plan. He just always had that attitude of superiority to everybody else. I hated that."

"How did your father take to him?"

"How do you think? No, forget I asked. First off, Dad didn't like him because he was dating me. Second, Dad's a veterinarian, so any conversation with Charles includes the idea that Dad's somehow less than because he's a vet and not a human doctor. So, of course, that doesn't go down well."

Trey laughed. "I can't imagine Silas thinking much of that at all."

"Charles is also a lousy fisherman, and I know my father took a great deal of delight in that. However," she added, giving Trey an eye roll, "Charles never would have done or even attempted to do anything to hurt my father. No matter how much of jerk he is, Charles is a doctor, remember? *Do no harm.*"

"Yeah, but doctors are also human," he pointed out.

She sighed. "See? That's the trouble with guys like you. You can see drama everywhere."

"Really?" he asked in a dry tone. "Personally I thought it was the circumstances that made us that way."

She nodded. "Maybe it is," she conceded, "and I probably shouldn't be knocking you for it. So I'm sorry."

He laughed. "Don't even think about it. You have nothing to worry about there."

"Ah, you say that," she began, with a smile, "but I just never quite know. I don't know what I'm even supposed to think right now."

"That's why you're not to worry about it," he reminded her. "Just leave that part to me."

"Sure," she muttered. "Will you solve all this on your own?"

"Maybe," he said, giving her a bright smile. "And, if I do, then what?"

"I have no clue," she admitted, "but it would definitely make me very happy if we could put all this behind us."

"That's the intent," he confirmed, "because it's really important that you do put it behind you, one way or another. And that means we have to solve it." And, with that, he leaned over, brushed his lips against hers, and said, "I'll see you later." He turned and walked out.

She had no chance to do anything but stare at him in wide-eyed surprise.

He quickly headed to the parking lot, and then on down to Rob's. Schooner seemed more than happy to hang out with him on his errands.

As he walked into the back of the workshop, Rob glared at him. "I still don't have any answers. Do you?"

"No, but who is this Dr. Charles guy?"

Rob frowned at him. "Mrs. Roberts's son? Charles Roberts?"

"Yeah, that's the name. He was apparently Missy's boyfriend for a while, but he also likes to mock both Silas and Missy's profession."

"He can mock it all he likes, but that doesn't make him a killer."

"No, but he also sucks at fishing."

At that, Rob burst out laughing. "If we put every person who sucked at fishing on the suspect list," he replied, "you would have half the town or more. Even so, I still think you probably have something there with that fishing derby angle, but it's also a good idea to check out anybody who had Missy on their wish list."

"God, that sounds disgusting when you put it that way."

Rob nodded. "I know, and yet it's true and worth checking out. You know it too, or you wouldn't have brought it up."

"No, you're right. I do know it," he agreed. "I just don't like thinking about anybody treating her as a thing to acquire, an object."

"Ha," Rob muttered. "Too often, that's all men do consider."

"We also know that, in cases of murder, the motives of both love and hate go hand in hand."

"As does jealousy," Rob pointed out.

"What about Miranda?" At Rob's frown, Trey continued. "Missy says that Miranda has a key to the house and that her dad might be *sweet* on her."

Rob shook his head. "Miranda has a key to Silas's house because she cleans it. She cleans the clinic too, if my info is current. I don't see her dating Silas as I think she's been dating Bill, Bill Bedford, the other vet at the clinic."

"Wow," Trey muttered. "The next time I need intel, I'll just ask you."

"True, but I still can't see it over a fishing derby. Yet I've seen it over ten bucks, so I'm not quite so ready to write off the derby just yet."

"I won't argue with you there," Trey replied.

Rob nodded, glaring out at nothing. "It's a stupid world we live in, and that's something we have to consider too."

"Agreed," Trey muttered as he sat down on a couple crates nearby. "Did the sheriff come around?"

"Yeah, he sure did." Rob groaned and sent Trey an eye roll. "He doesn't have anything to offer, and, as long as we don't have anything to offer him, he can't go forward. I've suggested that he bring in forensics from another department, but he doesn't seem to think that's a good idea. He also doesn't seem to think that our theory is really feasible and feels it's more than likely just a case of Silas's fevered mutterings."

"I suppose it's possible," Trey grumbled, "but I can't really see that, or maybe I just don't want to. But, without forensics or a good viable suspect, it'll be hard to determine either way." When another man called out, Trey turned, watching as somebody he didn't know came in, but with the casual manner of someone who had been here many times.

"Hey, Rob. What's this I hear about you salvaging Silas's boat?"

"First off, your source is faulty," Rob stated, spitting chewing tobacco on the ground beside him. "I didn't salvage his boat. I just helped bring her back, so we could work on her."

"*Huh*, that makes more sense."

"Who said I salvaged it?"

The other guy shrugged. "Not sure anybody did, as much as … rumors always make it sound worse than it is."

Rob snorted at that. "Ya think? But, for the record, no, I'm not trying to take the boat from Silas. He'll wake up and come grab it himself."

"He'll what?" The new arrival had an expression of shock on his face. "I thought he was more or less dead?"

"*More or less* isn't exactly the same thing as *dead* though, is it?" Trey asked the stranger, finding it hard to keep his mouth shut.

The man looked at him and frowned. "Who are you?"

"Friend of the family," he said bluntly.

"This is Trey," Rob added. "He's Jackson's brother."

The face of the other man cleared. "So, you're the guy who found them."

Trey nodded. "I am."

"That was a hell of a deal. You go out there and find them on the first pass? That's sick. We were out there for days," he muttered. "That was a pain in the ass, and we didn't find a damn thing."

Rob shrugged. "Now that they're both at the hospital and doing much better, hopefully they'll get a chance to get back out again, but I've gotta work on the boat first," he explained, motioning toward it.

The stranger nodded. "I'm glad to hear you're so positive, since the rumors are pretty negative. Even talked to a couple doctors about it, and they just shook their heads and wouldn't commit."

"Of course not," Rob replied. "Besides, what do doctors know?"

The other man laughed. He reached out a hand and introduced himself to Trey. "I'm Derik, by the way. I know your brother pretty well."

Trey smiled and nodded. "That's the thing about a small town, isn't it?"

"Sure is, we all know and trust each other," he declared, with a nod, "and that makes a massive difference. I'm glad you were there to help out Missy. She must have been terrified."

"She was doing pretty well though," Trey shared. "She's pretty smart."

"That she is. I think we all had a hand in her education and training when it came to sailing the ocean."

He smiled at that. "I knew Silas many years ago myself."

"Really?" he asked, studying Trey closer.

"Yeah, it's one of the reasons I had an idea for where to look."

At that, Derik leaned forward and asked, "Hey, do you know anything about that fishing hole, where Silas always wins the derby?"

Trey immediately shook his head. "Nope, and I wouldn't tell you even if I did."

Derik eyed him in disgust. "We're all supposed to be friends here, remember?"

"Yeah, I remember, but, if Silas gets the chance, ... I want to see him back out on that water, whipping everybody's butt in the next derby."

Rob laughed at that, and even Derik gave a chuckle. "I guess I would be okay with that myself," Derik admitted. "The damn place isn't the same without him. Plus, I've got to get my dog in for her shots, man. Now where do I take her?"

"Take your dog to Missy," Trey suggested. "She was set to do her practicum here at the clinic anyway."

"Really? You know, Silas did say something about that, but I wasn't sure what would happen now."

Trey added, "If nothing else, she should make arrangements with whomever her father practiced with. ... I don't remember his name, but the one who's there now, handling things."

"Ah, Bill's been trying to buy that place off of Silas. Be interesting to see how that goes."

"Really?" Trey asked. "That's odd."

"Why?"

"Because Silas has always had it set up for Missy to join his practice and to eventually take it over. It doesn't make sense that Silas would ever sell it or would even be in a situation where anybody could think they would buy it. Missy's been in veterinarian school for a long time, and that was the plan for many years before that. It's not as if everyone didn't know she was coming back."

"That's true," Derik confirmed. "And hopefully we won't even have to worry about it because Silas will back on his feet in no time." And, with that, Derik waved at the two men and took off.

Trey turned and frowned at Rob. "So, I need the low down on some of these local characters." He waved at Derik, who just walked out the door. "Trustworthy or not?"

"Trustworthy. ... It's just the damn fishing derby fever coming out," Rob pointed out. "I don't think you realize just how insane these guys get about it."

"Yeah, remember me?" Trey asked. "I'm the one who

wondered if they were competitive enough to look at killing each other over it. So, what's the deal with Bill, the vet who's got the business supposedly well in hand right now? Sounds as if he might want it as his own business. That wouldn't be something we would let happen, is it?" he asked Rob, not giving him a chance to answer. "That should be handed down to Missy, as she and Silas planned. The fact that she still needs her practicum doesn't mean it isn't still her business."

"Oh, don't worry about that. I agree with you 100 percent, but we may need to ensure that Bill fully understands that. Maybe it's about time you paid him a visit," Rob suggested, with a chuckle. "Go make yourself even more popular around town than you already are."

Trey stood up. "What do you mean by that? That sounded awfully sarcastic." He stopped on his way out the door to turn and look at him. "What are you suggesting?"

"Missy is a pretty-hot number in town, and I'm sure you've already gotten that angle sewn up for good."

CHAPTER 11

MISSY LOOKED UP from her cot to see two high-school friends standing in the doorway, whispering. "Hey," she greeted them, as she sat up. She'd talked to them a couple times on the phone, but this was the first time they'd come to the hospital. They ran over and gave her a big hug. She wrapped her arms around them and just hung on. When she'd left for college, they had drifted apart. So a slow and very gradual rebuilding of their friendship had been in the works since she'd returned. They still weren't as close as Missy would like, but she had every hope that they would get there at some point.

"How are you doing?" Sammy asked, glancing over at Missy's father, then quickly glancing away with a wince.

"I'm doing okay, and he's doing okay. So that's all that counts," she said.

"Is he though?" Sammy looked back and shook her head. "He's so still."

"That's what happens when you're in a coma, silly," Becky stated with a smile. "We just wanted to stop in to see if you're okay and if you need anything."

"I'm fine," Missy replied. "I'm doing okay."

"And," Sammy piped up, "we also wanted to check out who the hunk is who's apparently hanging around you all the time now."

Missy frowned at her and blinked. "What hunk?"

"Don't be dense. … The guy who rescued you."

"Oh." She laughed. "That's Trey, and he went to high school here too. He's Jackson's brother."

The two looked at each other, then back at her. "Seriously?" Becky stared at her with an incredulous expression.

Missy nodded. "He came back, and I was lucky enough to be the recipient of his wonderful skills and was rescued by him."

"Wow." They both gasped. "We haven't officially seen him, but we've been hearing rumors and didn't realize that's who he was."

"That is who he is, and I, for one, am very grateful that he came home when he did."

"Yeah, talk about good timing. Everybody's amazed that, after weeks of searching, nobody found you. Then *he* goes out, and there you are."

Missy nodded. "Yeah, he didn't know we were lost until a few days ago. So he got here as soon as he could. And I'm so grateful that he came back when he did."

"Of course," Sammy agreed. "There are rumors that the two of you are an item already."

Missy frowned at her friend. "I'm not sure where that's coming from, since we've barely had time to do anything, considering the condition I was in when we got here, not to mention my father, who was in critical condition," she explained. "But if you're asking if I see him a fair bit, then yes. He's been hugely helpful and considerate."

"I'm sure he has," Becky quipped, winking.

Missy groaned. "You guys see romance everywhere. You should be finding somebody to hook up with yourselves."

"We're trying," Sammy admitted, "but part of my question was to see if he's available or if you've already snagged him up."

The instant pang of jealousy surprised her. "I don't have any claim on him," she said. "I don't think he would take kindly to anybody thinking they had some claim on him either."

"Not that anybody has a claim," Sammy clarified, "but that doesn't mean the folks around town aren't talking about who may or may not be the one to snag him."

"Snag him?" Missy shook her head. "Man, I've been gone way too long if that's still the talk of the town at our age."

"It is still the talk of the town," Sammy stated, and Becky nodded in confirmation. "Remember that it's all about who you're dating."

Missy groaned. "I've been in school for a long time and didn't have time for dating or any of that nonsense."

"It's hardly nonsense now, after being missing for so long that everybody thought it was a lost cause, then suddenly you pop up out of nowhere."

"I hardly popped out of nowhere," she protested. "This is my hometown. Then I went away to college. Now I'm here for my practicum with my dad. For the last couple weeks, I was quite busy doing my best to keep us alive. So any suggestion otherwise is insulting." Both women just looked at her and shrugged. "It doesn't matter," Missy muttered, as she smiled at them. "It is good to see you though."

"Is there anything you need? Can we bring you anything?"

"No, I'm fine," she murmured. She really just wanted them to go. It was hard enough to conjure up any enthusiasm for ever seeing them again, after how everything in their world seemed so shallow and immature. Missy felt as if she didn't even know how to relate to them anymore. She suspected it had probably been that way since she got back from vet school, but she didn't really notice, just happy to have the beginnings of friendships again. But now, after what she had been through? Their adolescent behavior stood out—and not in a good way.

When they left, Missy sagged back onto her cot and groaned out loud. When one of the nurses popped her head around the corner of the door frame, Missy waved her off and muttered, "I'm fine, honest."

The nurse laughed. "As long as you're doing fine, that's what counts. … Yet it sounded as if you were about ready for them to disappear. So I planned to come in and interrupt in a few minutes."

"Did it sound that bad? I thought it might just be me, but everything else seems so meaningless after you've been through something like this."

"And that's something to understand as well. Very few people have been through your ordeal, so it'll be hard for them to relate. Better for you to adjust and to move on."

"Right, but I still have nightmares when I close my eyes and fall to sleep."

"And you probably will for quite a while," she stated calmly. "This kind of trauma does not go away just because you want it to."

"Are you sure?" Missy asked, with half a laugh. "That doesn't sound fair to me."

"You mean, now that you're rescued, it should all go away?"

"Wouldn't that be nice?" she murmured.

"You can get PTSD from the events you've just experienced, you know?"

"I don't even want to think about that," she muttered. "That sounds pretty rough."

"It's all about your point of view, but you must be willing to work through the trauma, and getting help when you need to."

"Maybe," she muttered, "we'll see."

"Don't leave it too long because dealing with trauma is best done while it's still warm. After it goes cold, it's like grease. It gets thick and congealed and harder to plow through." And, with that, she was gone.

What an unexpected image, and yet it worked for Missy. She wondered if she should be talking to somebody, but had no real clue who that would be. What would she say now versus if her father didn't make it? That was something she couldn't even bear to think about. Yet obviously it loomed right here in front of her, and she might not get the choice to think about it at all.

She collapsed back on the cot, and then, warning herself to not get too moody, she hopped back up again and walked over to sit beside her father.

"Dad, is there some way I can coerce you to come back? If so, please let me know what to do. Can you hear me? I hope so. It would be so very nice to know that you will pull through this. Sitting here, hour after hour, waiting for you and not knowing whether you'll come back to me or not is deadly, and it hurts in a big way. You've always been my best friend, and the thought of losing you just isn't something I even want to consider."

She stayed here at his bedside, talking with him for a few more minutes, and then got up, went to the bathroom, and wondered if she should get some food. Just then the door opened again, and there was Trey. Instead of thinking, *Oh God, more people*, her immediate reaction was *Thank God, he's here*. Not overthinking it, she walked over, and he just opened his arms. She burrowed deep inside, hugging him back and just letting herself relax.

He whispered against her hair, "Tough day?"

She leaned back, looked up at him, and nodded. "I don't know that I would even call it a tough day," she explained, "but one of those increased awareness things." She explained about her girlfriends having been here and how hard it was to deal with their immaturity, as if Missy had changed somehow and had grown in a way that she couldn't explain.

He nodded. "I do get that. You had a different experience than they did, by leaving your hometown and going to college elsewhere, not to mention your latest adventure."

She smiled and nodded. "See? That's one of the things I like about you. You get me. You do understand. Everything that's happened in your world has helped you get to the point where you can understand what I'm talking about, and that is, … well, huge," she shared. "I don't want to depend on you, but it is really nice to know that you're there ahead of me on this journey."

He smiled. "You'll do just fine," he murmured. "Remember that all of this will change. It may take some time, but it will get better."

"I hope so," she said. "Where is Schooner?"

"I left him in the truck but told him that we would be out soon to get him." He cheekily grinned at her. Then getting serious, he asked, "Have you had any other visitors?"

She nodded. "There's been a steady stream of them to-day." She named off a few, who he half remembered, and then she got stuck for moment, before she relented. "Charles showed up. He was polite, friendly even. I appreciated that he was checking in on me."

"The doctor ex-boyfriend?"

She nodded. "Yes, the doctor."

"How did your dad feel about that relationship?"

"I already told you that he wasn't exactly thrilled."

"But would he have been unimpressed enough to have maybe done something that would have hurt the doctor's feelings, enough to make him want to do something like this?"

She stared up at him and winced. "God, I hope not because, if this has anything to do with me, it'll just make me feel even worse."

"We're not dealing with levels of guilt here," Trey pointed out. "We're just trying to get to the truth."

"Maybe, but that's a truth that would be pretty rough. I don't want to think of anybody having done something to my dad because of something I did."

"It's not even something that you did," he clarified. "It would be more about something your father had done, maybe to stop a relationship."

"I don't think he would do that," she replied. "My dad and I were good friends, and he was generally content to let me learn whatever lessons I needed to learn when it came to relationships. Sometimes they weren't easy lessons. How does anybody get through their teenage years without getting a few scars and some hurt feelings?"

"I don't think anybody does," Trey agreed with a smile, "I just want to ensure that your dad wouldn't have stopped somebody from coming into your life, only to have that person be angry—angry enough to hold a serious grudge."

"I don't think so," she muttered. "I don't even like the concept."

"I'm just checking," he said, giving her a reassuring smile, "because we do need to find out who could have done this. … As far as access to his boat, I gather that could have been anybody."

She nodded. "Especially the way the marinas are set up, and the way this town is. Everybody knows whose boat is whose, and everybody is open to sharing. They use each other's boats a lot of the time. Obviously they ask ahead of time, and safety measures must be followed, but, in most instances, everybody is quite happy to take people out on their boat when they want to go," she explained. "So I can't even imagine that being part of the issue."

"Okay," Trey muttered, frowning. "So what could possibly have gone on that would bring so much—I don't want to say, *hate*, but I guess in a way it has to be hate—to have done something like sabotaging Silas's boat?"

"I've been racking my brains over that too," she said, staring up at him. She stepped back and wrapped her arms around her chest, not so much because she was cold but was shivering inside at the thought of somebody willfully doing this to them. "All I could think about was that it might be because of me, or maybe it was against me, not because of me," she corrected. "Maybe somebody wanted me dead."

"I've been considering that too," he noted, staring at her. "The question really is tough though, and I want you to think hard."

"Is there somebody in my world who would have done this? … I have no idea."

"I know you don't want to think that there could be someone, but we're not children anymore," he added, making her question everything she knew. "The reality is, sometimes people are shitty."

She snorted at that, giving him an eye roll. "Sometimes I feel as if I've had more than my fair share of people who fit that category."

"Okay, and that's maybe a good place to start. Where and what would require somebody to do this to you? Obviously it's not an ideal scenario to contemplate, but …"

She nodded. "I hear you. If somebody did this, the question really becomes why and who were they hoping to hurt?" She sat back down on the cot and went silent.

He faced her and added, "Look. Why don't we get out, go for a walk, shake up your brain a little bit, and see if something comes to mind? We'll talk about some possibilities and just try to get you out of your head a little bit. Maybe we'll pick up a coffee and walk around the water a bit."

She smiled up at him. "You do realize that one of the reasons my girlfriends were here was to find out more about you?"

"Why?" he asked, his brows furrowing together.

She laughed. "They wanted to know if you are on the market."

He started to laugh. "I'm not too interested in being considered on the market or off," he declared, with a shudder, "particularly if they are as immature as you say. I'm still not even sure what my own plans are."

"Yeah, I know," she agreed, with half a frown in his direction, "but you should stick around. My dad would really appreciate it."

"I know he would," he replied, his gaze going over to the hospital bed. "Honestly, I would like nothing more than to take him out fishing, or, better yet, go against him in a derby," he noted, with a chuckle.

"Oh my gosh, you've got to be careful there. Those fishing derbies are pretty rough."

"Are they rough enough?" he asked, turning to look at her.

"Meaning?"

"Meaning, are they rough enough that we have to consider that as a potential motive?"

She frowned at him. "God, I hope not. … I haven't been back here all that long myself, but that's a horrific thought."

"I know, and maybe I'm barking up the wrong tree on that idea."

"I hear you," she muttered. "My dad would probably say it definitely was enough of a motive, and that's a little disturbing in itself."

He smiled. "Your dad is very special in so many ways, and, if he would say it's enough, then I'm half inclined to agree with him."

"Maybe," she replied cautiously, "but that's still a long way away from understanding who it could be. We get people in here from hundreds of miles away, you know?" When he frowned at her, she nodded. "These derbies can be pretty big, really feisty, and definitely something that people would complain and argue about all the time," she shared. "Enough to kill over it? I don't know, but you'll not likely get any argument about how fierce the competition can get."

"The influx of people from out of town wasn't something I considered," he murmured.

"Yep, now that you know, you need to consider that. Dear God, I hope my dad's secret fishing spots aren't the reason for all this."

"So, how does that work? If he headed out, … can't somebody just follow him?"

"Sure, but you would also have to find him, and he's pretty good at hiding, when it comes to things like that."

"You're kidding. That's a part of it too?"

She nodded. "I haven't been here for the last several derbies because I've been in school," she reminded him, with a shrug, "but they are definitely really competitive, and people can get pretty feisty."

"Right." Trey smiled. "I hadn't really considered that, since fishing poles aren't typically the dueling weapon of choice."

"Twenty paces, right?" she said, with a laugh. "Okay, so we'll have to consider competitive fishing as a motive, but then again, in a practical sense, it would still need to be somebody local who had access to the boat and who knows their way around it, somebody who understands my dad's system."

"Yes, but not enough to realize that he also takes an extra radio with him."

She frowned at that and then slowly nodded. "That's true," she muttered, "and there are a lot more fishermen than radio buffs in town."

"Right, so, in a sense, we're back to ground zero again."

"Which isn't where I want to be," she grumbled, with a sigh.

"Come on. Coffee will help."

"Yeah, you keep saying that, yet we're still standing here. Are we waiting for Jackson?"

Trey shook his head. "Nope, he and Elizabeth are at a doctor's appointment, but don't worry. We won't be gone long." He grinned and led her to the elevator.

She asked, "What if I want to take the stairs?"

He stopped to look at her.

"I'm fine," she replied, but he watched her closely. She glared at him and snapped, "Quit doing that."

He shrugged. "I just don't want to wear you out by taking the stairs."

She moaned and said in exasperation, "Stop it. I'm not wearing myself out by sitting on a cot all day long."

"Fine," he said, as he pushed the elevator button and stepped inside with her. "Let's go get a coffee. Obviously you need some."

She glared at him. When she saw the corner of his mouth turn up into a smile, she groaned. "You're right. I do need some, and I didn't realize how bitchy I was being. I'm so sorry."

He laughed. "It's all good."

"You're just too nice for your own good, you know that?" He stopped to look at her in horror. She rolled her eyes. "It's true. You're one of the good guys."

"Don't tell anybody that," he warned her. "I'll never hear the end of it."

"What? That you're a nice guy?" She snickered. "Pretty sure everybody already knows that."

"They shouldn't," he declared, mock-glaring at her, "unless you told them."

"I might have," she quipped, enjoying the banter. "There's absolutely no reason not to. After all, you're apparently part of the famous commodity market around here. So I can tell any interested party whatever pleases me in the moment. Just a little firsthand knowledge to sweeten the pot."

"Oh God," he groaned as they exited the elevator and

headed outside. "None of that, please."

"Too late," she said. "I already heard how you're at the top of the eligible bachelor list right now."

"Yeah? Did they also ask if you had any interest in that little game?"

"They did," she admitted, still laughing.

"Next time you just tell them that you've got it all sewn up."

"Really?" she asked, her lips twitching.

"Yeah. That might keep them off my case."

"Oh, but you won't know what you like until you try it."

He gave her a suggestive smile and said, "I'm all for trying it, honey."

Her cheeks flared bright pink, but she laughed out loud in spite of herself. "Oh my gosh, I hadn't realized how little there's been to laugh about lately."

"That's another reason to get you outside, where you can get a little bit of fresh air and a fresh perspective," he murmured. "Plus, we need to grab Schooner." And that's what they did. The War Dog was so happy to see them both. After jumping around and getting licks in and hugs shared, Schooner settled down and quietly walked beside them.

They walked toward town, where the main coffee shops were gathered. The hospital area always had coffee shops, but he seemed hell-bent on getting Missy farther away than that. They stopped at the first one and ordered their coffee to-go. Soon they were back outside, and she realized just how fast she was walking, yet heading nowhere in particular. Trey was just letting her churn up the pavement. When she slowed down, he was right there beside her. When she came to stop, she looked at him and asked, "Are you always right?"

"Nope." When she glared at him, he smiled. "It was pretty obvious you needed to get out, to let off some steam, and to just feel better about life. Don't hold it against me that I could see it."

"I can't hold anything against you," she muttered. "You've been nothing but kind to me."

He rolled his eyes again, and she glared at him. Yet he smiled back at her. "I know, and I'm happy that we have these few moments amid all the chaos around your father. Your dad is one of the good guys, and I am very grateful for the opportunity to help in some way."

"I can't believe rescuing us took as long as it did," she muttered. "We were out there for so long." He nodded but didn't say anything. She halted abruptly. "I just had a horrible thought." When he remained silent, she frowned at him and saw it all over his face. "Oh my God, you've had that thought too."

He winced and nodded.

TREY STARED DOWN at her. "I was hoping it wouldn't occur to you."

"It's horrifying if that's what happened."

Nobody had come right out and said anything about it yet, but she was looking at him with that glint in her gaze that said they were on the same track. Still, he needed her to be careful. "The thing about assumptions," he began, "is that all kinds of issues come up. We don't know which way to go in this investigation yet. So I don't necessarily want you to think that this happened, but I don't want there to be any misunderstandings either."

"Oh my God, the search was deliberately waylaid," she muttered. "The search was waylaid because … someone really didn't like the idea of us surviving. They wanted it delayed, … so we wouldn't be rescued. The longer it took, there was a much better chance for us to die out there."

Trey nodded. "Yeah, that thought crossed my mind. I don't have any solid reason to believe it though, and we need to keep that in mind."

"But every day that passed, where we couldn't be rescued," she explained, "was another day in favor of whoever sabotaged the boat."

"I agree with that," he said, "but it also could have nothing to do with any of it. Maybe it was just lucky timing on their part."

She snorted at that. "Lucky timing, my ass."

He hooked an arm around her shoulders, careful not to spill the coffee they each carried, and he tucked her up closer. "Promise me that you won't say anything about that to anyone."

She twisted to look up at him and then groaned. "Does everything have to be on the down low?"

"Everything has to be on the down low for now," he confirmed. "We don't dare take a chance on anybody getting wind of this. The fact that you're alive and survived with as few injuries as you did is absolutely amazing. We want to ensure your father gets the chance to survive too."

"What do you mean?"

"It means we don't dare give anybody an idea that we may be on to them. If so, that might prompt them to make a second attempt."

She shuddered at that. They found themselves down in front of the marina. As she stared around at the ocean in front of them, she shook her head.

"It's not Mother Nature's fault," he pointed out, "so don't blame her."

"I won't," she said, her voice thickening. "I'm not sure how interested I am in going back out there, though."

"You don't have to," he noted. "Certainly not for any set time period and especially not in a rush to do it. Only when you are ready to get back on that proverbial horse. Other than that, don't worry about it. Don't let yourself be rushed by other people's choices." She nodded, and he could tell that she wasn't convinced. "Maybe you have other friends who don't boat all the time," he suggested, "and, if not, maybe it's time to cultivate those kind of friends."

"I don't even know what *friends* are anymore. Listening to Sammy and Becky today, I feel so out of it. I haven't been back in town very long, and they were my childhood friends, but, wow, I'm just not where they're at anymore."

"And you don't have to feel guilty about that either," he stated, looking at her. "The last thing we want you to do is to take on more guilt."

She groaned. "Here we go again. You're always a nice guy."

He sighed. "Nope, I'm so not, but I am a realist," he declared, "and being a realist also means that I want very much for you to just give yourself a break, to not always have to be the one who does everything, to not always have to be the one who's perfect."

They continued to walk a little bit farther, as she looked out around at the harbor. When she waved at someone, Trey turned to see Rob out there.

Rob lifted a hand and walked over. "Aren't you a sight for sore eyes," he greeted Missy, smiling broadly.

She laughed. "It's good to see you. For a while there I wasn't sure I would see anybody anymore."

"And yet here you are," he said, with a beaming smile in her direction, "and all because of Sir Lancelot here."

Trey jerked at the moniker. "Good God, where the hell are you getting all these terms and concepts from?" He rolled his eyes at them. "I was just doing search and rescue, nothing more."

She laughed. "Nothing more? Maybe for you. I'll have to think about how I feel about *Sir Lancelot*," she said, smacking him lightly. Turning to Rob, she added, "Good one."

"But listen up, Trey. … For everybody else, you rode into town and immediately accomplished what they couldn't, and that is something they won't forget," Rob noted carefully.

"As long as they don't hold it against me," Trey said, with a shrug, "it's all good."

"I don't think they would," she replied, looking at him. "Yet probably a few people are pissed off that they stopped a little too early, and then you come in, and there we were. For my part, I'm just so grateful that you did."

He nodded, then looked over at Rob. "Any news?"

Rob shook his head. "Nope, not yet." He looked over at Missy. "Have you got any clues?"

"No, I don't. I keep hoping that it was just my imagination and that maybe Dad didn't say anything about sabotage."

Rob eyed her steadily with a gaze he didn't use much these days. "Do you really think that's possible, considering everything you now know?"

She winced. "You could allow me an illusion or two."

"That ain't keeping you safe in this world, gal," he stated, with a long look, "and you know that."

"I do know that," she muttered. "I just don't know what to say about this whole nightmare. I already lived through it, so I don't really want to analyze it now."

"No, maybe not, and I get that. However, until we know what's going on," Rob pointed out, "you aren't safe."

Hearing it stated so clearly, she half gasped.

Trey reached out and held her close. "He means well, but his delivery is a little rusty."

"Oh my God," she whispered. "I hadn't considered—as in really considered—that surviving the fight of my life was putting my life in danger all over again." Her gaze went from one man to the other. "What kind of a world do we live in?"

"A sick one," Rob noted darkly, "and don't you forget it." With that, he turned and walked toward his shop.

Trey wanted to call out to him, but it was not the conversation to have right now, not in public. He looked over at Missy, but she was stunned into silence. "Hey, it was a warning. Take it as a warning, and let the rest go."

"He sounded quite adamant," she whispered.

"Yes, and clearly he is adamant that you are in danger, and that is something you need to be aware of," Trey murmured. "I just don't think he needed to scare you to that extent."

"No doubt he would disagree with you on that entirely," she stated, her breath coming out shakily.

He frowned and held her close. "Look. I don't want you so terrified that you'll be looking at everybody sideways, wondering if they were the one behind this," he said. "It's bad enough that we have to suspect as many people as we do."

"I know," she agreed, "and that's half the problem.

It's … I don't really want to be in such a state that I spend every moment focused on people who might be out there, trying to hurt me," she whispered. "Up until now, I had no reason to believe that I was anything other than a long-time member of the community, settling back in after years away at school. I don't want to be a target in my own hometown."

"You don't have to be," he replied. "You absolutely don't. Rob gave you a warning, and he's not wrong, but don't let this change who you are and how you feel about being here. Just because there could be one bad apple in town doesn't mean all the townspeople are bad," he murmured. "That is something we have to remember." She nodded, but he could tell she wasn't convinced. "I guess bringing you out here wasn't exactly a good idea, was it?"

"What, you mean terrifying me a whole lot more, then sending me back into my father's hospital room again, ensuring nobody is looking at me sideways?" she muttered. She shook her head. "Sorry, it's not your fault. I really did need to come out, and I was hopeful that maybe, with a little bit of time, somebody would have found something. I guess in my heart of hearts I'm not allowing any other alternative in my mind. So I feel as if this has to be a stranger, somebody who did this for God-only-knows what reason. Yet it just befuddles me to think that this is personal."

"It could be."

"And yet," she added, nodding in his direction, "I get it, and I don't know how it can be anything else, but I'm still hoping we come up with a reasonable explanation for all this."

"I hope so too," he agreed. "I really do. Until we find out what that is all about, you need to stay safe."

"And staying safe means staying in the hospital, staying

at my father's side, protecting him." She winced as she thought about it. "And yet we left him alone."

"Do you want to go back?"

"Yes, I do," she declared, turning to look back in the general direction of the hospital, where they just came from, "especially after what Rob just told me."

"Right," Trey replied. He moved her a little faster along the lane, feeling an odd little prick of concern himself. He grabbed his phone and quickly texted the doctor. **Can we get a welfare check on Silas please?** The doctor sent him a question mark back. And Trey replied, **Please don't ask, just move.** When the phone rang a few minutes later, Trey answered it with a question. "What happened?"

"He's fine," the doctor replied, an odd tone to his voice. "Where are you?"

"We're just walking back. I convinced Missy to come out and get a bit of fresh air, get a few minutes away from there, which she really needed, but now she's worried."

"I'm glad you did that. Looks like her father might have had a visitor."

"How do you know that?"

"Because he was on the floor and not necessarily in good shape. We've got him back in bed, but it seems somebody may have tried to wake him up or otherwise disturbed him in some way. I don't even know what to say," he admitted. "We thought Missy was already in there with him. So, when I got your text and headed down there, I really didn't expect any trouble or to find Silas on the floor."

"We're on the way back right now. So give us ten minutes. We'll be there as soon as we can."

"I'm standing here in his room, and I think you better hurry."

Trey looked over at her and said, "Now we need to hus-
tle." Using every bit of energy that he could muster, he
moved her quickly back into the hospital and up to her
father's room.

CHAPTER 12

M ISSY RACED INTO her father's room to find him in
bed, in a completely different position than before.
"What happened?"

"He was on the floor," the doctor stated. "I don't know
if he had help getting there, but all his IV lines had been
pulled out. I'm in the process of getting everything put back
and straightened away."

Just then came a loud groan from her father. She raced
to his side. "Dad, Dad, wake up. Wake up, Dad."

"Give him time," the doctor noted. "He'd been in rough
shape, and his recovery won't be quite so fast."

"As long as there is a recovery," she stated, looking up at
him.

He smiled. "I don't see any reason why there wouldn't
be, but I can see that we're definitely not out of the woods
yet."

She sighed but grabbed her father's hand and gave him a
gentle hug. "Any time you want to wake up, it'll be really
good to see you."

Another half groan came, but he didn't do anything
more than that.

She watched, worried, as the doctor checked him over
and worked to get his IVs reestablished. "Please don't knock
him back under again."

"We're only keeping him lightly sedated for the pain. When he's ready to wake up, believe me that he'll wake up, and nothing we're giving him would stop that."

"I just don't know that he'll wake up."

"Everything is good here," he shared. "He just needs time, and hopefully that's all he needs." The doctor looked around and asked, "Where did your partner go?"

"I have no idea," she muttered, looking around for Trey. "I don't know where he went." She was filled with a sense of disquiet at the thought of his not being at her side, and yet she had no claim on him. She'd gotten used to Trey being here for her so steadily.

The doc added, "I did hear him muttering something about the cameras, so I imagine he's off trying to get a hold of the security camera footage."

She stared at him and then nodded. "I can see him doing that, and I knew about them, but it never even occurred to me."

"It occurred to me, but that doesn't mean anything right now," he said, with a smile. "I'm a little on the busy side, but it would be great if we can see if anybody came here and disturbed Silas—even better if that didn't have anything to do with it. Maybe Silas heard something, or maybe he was lunging around in his sleep, thinking he needed to do something. Just no real way to know yet."

"Right," she muttered, hating the sense of despair that always seemed to take over whenever she considered her father's condition.

"What is important," the doc reminded her, "is that your dad is still fighting. He's still here, and he needs every chance to wake up and to know that he can be just fine."

"I hope to God you're right," she stated fervently.

"I'll go check on the cameras myself now. You stay here and look after your father." He stopped as he approached the door, then added, "What about this dog? Will he let me leave?"

She looked over to see Schooner, standing in the open doorway, staring at the doctor with a suspicious gaze. She walked over and placed a hand on Schooner's shoulder. Immediately Schooner sat down and focused on Missy. "It's okay now," Missy said to the doctor. "You'll be fine."

"I'm glad to hear that. Maybe you should consider leaving him here on guard the next time you decide to step out for fresh air."

It's not that he said anything wrong, but the fact that she had stepped out made her feel horribly guilty. She groaned as she sat back down at her father's side, Schooner right there with her. "I really need you to come back, Dad. You have no idea what craziness has been going on, and it's getting worse. I really need you back. But here's the thing. I don't want any more of these crazy suspicions every time I turn around. I don't know who to trust anymore, and just hearing the wrong word, the wrong sentence at the wrong time, makes me so mistrustful. I'm looking at everybody as if they could have done this to you, and yet that's not fair. It quite possibly was nobody from here. I hate this, Dad. Please, please come back to me."

She kept talking to her dad, pleading for him to come back to her, and finally, when she went silent, she moved over to her cot and sagged onto it, wondering just when this nightmare would be over. Of course, with that came the horrible thought that the answer to that was never. There was always the chance that her dad could remain in this vegetative state for the rest of his life.

And what would that do to her life?

Schooner came closer to give her a nudge with his wet nose. She hugged him, glad to have him here.

She tossed off that other thought. "It doesn't matter, Dad. It does not matter. Schooner and I will always be here for you, and it doesn't make a damn bit of difference. You were there for me all these years, and I will be there for you no matter what," she vowed, and, with that, she settled back onto her cot to wait.

TREY GRABBED HIS phone and immediately called the sheriff, explaining what the issue was. "I'm here at the hospital in the security office, but they won't let me see any of the camera feeds without some official request from you guys."

"Of course not," the sheriff replied smoothly. "There are all kinds of privacy laws."

"Maybe, but Silas was attacked in his hospital room while we were out having coffee, and it's still fresh, still in the camera feed. We need to see it."

After a moment of hesitation, the sheriff said, "I'll get right back to you." With that, he ended the call.

Trey turned to look at the hospital's IT team, still sitting at the monitors, waiting to hear how it would go. "He'll get back to me," he explained in frustration.

At that, the younger man nodded. "That's pretty typical. He's got to go through the hospital board first."

"That's ridiculous. So, in the meantime, this guy's getting away."

The other man didn't say anything.

Trey asked, "What about your own security procedures? Do you not focus on things like that, strangers moving patients, and send out security to pick up these people?"

The two men looked at each other and didn't say anything.

Frustrated beyond belief, Trey pinched the bridge of his nose. Then, with a brainstorm of an idea, he immediately stepped out of the security room and called Badger. Within seconds, he explained what was going on and the stumbling block he was up against.

"Of course. Give me a second." And, with that, Badger ended the call.

Trey groaned as he stared down the hallway to see the doctor who'd been working on Silas coming toward him.

"No luck?" the doctor asked sympathetically.

"No, apparently not," he snapped, glaring. "Everybody's more concerned about privacy than the lawsuit that'll come out of this."

At the word *lawsuit,* the doc's eyebrows raised, and he pondered it. "I guess in this case, there would be some justification for it, wouldn't there?"

"Absolutely there would be." Trey snarled and then shook his head. "Sorry, Doc. I'm not angry at you. It's the damn red-tape bureaucracy." However, the words had barely come out of his mouth when the door to the security room opened.

The older of the two men motioned them to come in. "We have clearance." With an odd expression on his face, he told Trey, "You have some friends high up in the federal government."

Trey didn't look a gift horse in the mouth and immediately stepped into the room. "What do you have?"

"What we have is somebody tall and slim entering, but he's hiding his face," the tech noted. He quickly led Trey through the few minutes of footage they had gone through. It's almost as if, as soon as Trey and Missy shut the door on Silas's hospital room and entered the elevator, somebody opened up a door to the stairs nearby, then stepped out and walked straight to Silas's room.

"So, they already knew where he was," Trey muttered to no one in particular.

The men just nodded and then pointed. "Watch."

The man, if it was a man, walked into the room and within minutes was back out again. He quickly returned to the stairs again.

"So, you see," the IT guy shared, "it's not as if we had anything to offer."

"Yes, you absolutely did because you should follow this trail all the way back outside again."

The younger man was working on that, just as Trey suggested it. "He goes to here, and then we lose him."

"No, you didn't lose him. He's taken off the disguise."

"What disguise?" the older man asked.

"That's a wig," Trey declared, immediately pointing to the same slender build he noticed on the guy in the hallway, "and he was wearing a white lab coat. So now we're looking for anybody in this time frame who is tall and slender but walks out of the hospital without the wig and the lab coat." It didn't take them long, and they quickly had somebody going out a side door, moving at a rapid pace.

Trey froze the frame, while they assessed what they were looking at.

"It's pretty-damn hard to see who it is though," the older of the two IT men noted, as he studied it.

"Maybe, but we also know that's who it is now. Do you have cameras out in the parking lot?"

"No," the older man said, sliding his gaze away. "After the budget cuts happened, that one went down, and it was just one of those things that never got fixed again."

"Of course it was," Trey grumbled, staring at him and shaking his head. "How about now? What do you think about the need for that camera now? Do you think it's worth having a security camera?"

The doctor reached out and gave Trey's shoulder a squeeze, making him realize that, once again, he was attacking the wrong people.

"Sorry," Trey muttered. "I know you don't run the budgets, and you probably would do them in a very different way if you did." Trey shook his head. "It's just incredibly frustrating to think that somebody walked into the hospital, attacked a patient, walked back out without his disguise, got in a vehicle, and left, while you guys had no idea."

The two men stared at each other for a long moment.

"Look," Trey began. "Can you give me any details off that footage? Can you get me the height of him or any side feature, anything at all?"

They went through the films a couple more times, and Trey grabbed a couple images, a little bit of a profile on the one. Armed with those images, he headed down to the rear parking lot, looking for anything that might be helpful.

He knew that the chances of the guy being around were more than a long shot and was nothing to hope for. The stranger had done what he'd intended to do, and now he was leaving, but, if Trey could at least figure out where the wig and lab coat had disappeared to, they might get DNA, which should at least help get them some evidence. But, of course, that was a long shot too.

He went to Silas's room, grabbed Schooner, and started to check every garbage can on the way. He walked past several cans, but nothing was here at the parking lot, or, even if there was, he couldn't see it. Swearing and pissed off at the entire scenario, he called Badger back. "I'm out in the parking lot, but there is absolutely nothing. This guy just slipped in, did this thing, and slipped out again."

"The disguise has to be somewhere. If he's smart, he took it away with him. Yet, if he's not so smart, then it'll be somewhere nearby."

"I was hoping he would have just ditched it, and that would have been a lead in terms of finding out who and what," Trey muttered, "but I didn't find a thing. I did see on the video that he took a bag outside with him, so it's quite possible he's got his disguise, but it's also quite possible he dumped it somewhere else."

"I'll contact the sheriff and let him know to look out for a bag holding a wig and a lab coat."

"Yeah, you do that. I still highly doubt the sheriff will do anything to help me."

"I don't know about that," Badger argued. "Their hands are often tied in this scenario. They can't piss off the hospital too much, even though I'm sure he would go running in there, guns blazing, just to look like the big hero. Still, in these cases, there just is no hero."

"I'm beginning to realize that." Trey groaned. "I don't think I can do law enforcement."

"Are you sure?" Badger asked. "You would be really good at it."

He snorted. "I haven't got a new career choice figured out yet, but I can't really say that being a cop will be at the top of my list."

"You might change your mind by the time this is over. That's how change happens, when people want something better, and they have to create it themselves."

"Okay, enough of the sales pitch," he muttered. "Is this what you end up doing? Get everybody retrained?"

"As you said, you're not sure what you'll do next. We try to help. Besides, have you thought about staying over there?"

"I've thought about it," he admitted. "I was also thinking about coming back to New Mexico."

"*Hmm*, not sure that'll happen," Badger said with a laugh.

"Why is that?" Trey asked, puzzled. "It's nice over there."

"Sure is, that's why we settled here," he confirmed.

"*Nah*, you settled there because of Kat."

Badger burst out laughing. "You've got that right, and I suspect you'll stay where you are for the exact same reason." And, with that, he ended the call.

Trey stared down at his phone in confusion.

CHAPTER 13

MISSY TEXTED TREY when he didn't return after taking Schooner out. In fact nobody came back. She'd been sitting here, waiting for what seemed like forever, trying to figure out if anybody had gotten any information.

Trey responded immediately to her text with a phone call.

She asked, "I shouldn't bug you, but did anybody find anything? Everybody took off, especially you," she noted in confusion. "I wasn't sure what was going on."

"I'm almost to your room again. Give me a minute."

She ended the call, and, sure enough, a moment later Trey popped through the door.

He smiled at her, then walked over to Silas's bedside. Looking down at the patient, Trey asked, "How's he doing?"

"He's doing fine," she replied, "at least as far as we know."

He nodded. "As for whatever happened, we did see somebody coming into this room just after we left. Whether his arrival was good luck on his part, or he was more or less waiting, or he just didn't care if he got caught, I don't know."

She asked, "What do you mean by that?"

"We watched the security videos, and he came from the stairwell almost immediately after we left the room, goes inside here, then goes right back outside, having changed out of the outfit that he wore inside here. He dropped the lab coat, took off the wig, and walked outside, carrying a bag."

"Jesus," she muttered, staring at him in shock. "So, not only was this an attack that I need to be concerned about, this was preplanned."

He stared at her and nodded slowly. "That's exactly what it was, an attempted hit."

She stared down at her father, suddenly finding it hard to breathe.

"I'm sorry. There wasn't an easy way to say it."

She brushed it off. "I'm not interested in easy. I just want to keep Dad safe, and apparently that's something I can't even do here," she wailed, looking around helplessly. "Dear God, what is going on that this is even happening?"

"That's what I'm trying to get to the bottom of," Trey declared, "and again I have to apologize. We haven't gotten very far."

She stared at him, then shook her head. "This isn't your fault," she said immediately. "I'm the one who sat in the middle of nowhere, wondering what I could do and how to get him back here. Still, even now that we're here, look at the shit we're dealing with." She shook her head. "This isn't about you. This is about somebody who is after my father. It's one thing for us to wonder if this truly was what was happening, but another thing entirely to know for sure."

"I guess that is the one thing we can count on now," he pointed out. "I hate to say it, but now that we know your father was attacked again, then somebody did target the two of you."

She winced. "You still think it's both of us?" she asked cautiously.

He hesitated and then slowly nodded. "I don't know what to say about the two of you versus one of you," he clarified, "but, if you had still been here, alone with your father, I don't know what the stranger's reaction would have been."

She stared at him in shock and then swallowed. "Meaning that, if he had come in here and found me too, he might have done something to both of us?"

"It's quite possible, yes. Maybe he was planning on taking out two birds with one stone. … That would explain why he came here dressed as a doctor. He didn't care whether anybody was here or not, or whether you were here or your father was alone. Or maybe he came on impulse and lucked out to find Silas alone."

She just nodded but stared at Trey. "This is incredibly unnerving," she murmured. "I don't even know what else to say."

"Of course you don't." He walked closer and sat down beside her. "However, it reaffirms the fact that you can't be alone."

"And neither can Dad," she pointed out quickly.

Trey nodded. "I know. And I doubt that the sheriff has any interest in putting security in place for Silas. Of course the hospital will only allow for liability of a certain amount, so they can't just pay for a security guard either."

"Of course not," she muttered. "That would be too expensive, wouldn't it?"

Hearing the disdain and the anger in her tone, Trey smiled and nodded. "It's also the facts of life."

She let out her breath slowly. "I guess it is. I'm just not used to dealing with this side of life. Who the hell is?"

"We'll deal with it. You being here obviously won't be

enough now."

"I'm not leaving him again," she snapped. "You can count that out."

"I know that's how you feel," he replied. "I want to take over some of these shifts, so that you can go get some rest. Of course Schooner would be with you all the time that I'm not with you."

She stared at him blindly. "What?"

He reached out a hand and squeezed her shoulder. "I'll relieve you of half your shifts here. So long as somebody is here at all times with Silas, we have a better chance of keeping your father alive."

"You don't have to do that," she said immediately.

"No, I don't have to," he agreed, with a smile. "I want to. I've also known your father for a long time."

"I didn't know you very well back then."

He waved a hand. "Because we were always out fishing. I don't think you were into it much back then."

She winced. "I was into my friends at the time, … but, hell, all of that just seems so frivolous now."

"That's not what you'll focus on now," he stated. "None of that has anything to do with what's going on right now."

"Are you sure about that?" She stood up and started to pace the small room. "I still can't get past the idea that maybe this all has something to do with a friend or somebody who had an argument with Dad that involved me somehow. I can't even think of anything that would cause all this, but the guilt is eating me up."

"It's not guilt. You're just worried, … worried that something you did caused all this to happen. It's the very idea that all this trouble could be something you're somehow responsible for. Remember that, whoever tried to kill you is responsible, not you. You can take on as much guilt as you want, but that doesn't change the fact that somebody out there is targeting Silas and may be targeting you."

"I think I'm just collateral damage then …" She stopped, shook her head. "That completely eradicates what I was saying a minute ago."

He smiled. "You're grasping at straws right now, trying to make anything make sense, but the trouble is, nothing is making sense, which just makes it all that much harder."

She blew a strand of hair off her face and stared at him.

He nodded. "I get it, and I'm sorry that this has become such an issue. What we never really expected was that somebody would come here to the hospital to go after your father."

"No, God no. How could that possibly have crossed anybody's mind?" she asked in a whisper. "Of all the things I might wonder about, that's what I end up with?" She shook her head. "My father was so well loved."

"*Is* so well loved," Trey corrected.

She flushed, then walked over and sat down beside her father on the bed. "*Is* so well loved," she whispered. "I just can't imagine why somebody is doing this."

"Does he have any business partnerships?"

She looked over at him. "I have no idea. Why?"

He frowned. "I'm just tossing this out there, but, if your father did die, I wonder what would happen to his assets."

"They would come to me," she said, "at least that's what I assume. But have I seen a will? No."

"A business relationship can be different. If it's not specifically stated in the will, the business partner could end up getting everything based on a separate business contract. Plus, if there is life insurance of the business-related kind, the partner could get that too."

She sat back and stared at him. "What?"

He nodded. "Certain things are a little bit more delicate when it comes to death, and that might be something we need to look into to understand better."

She swallowed. "You're thinking about Dr. Bill, his assistant who runs the clinic?"

"My understanding was that Bill wasn't a full partner but was just an assistant, correct?"

"Yes, he's not. My dad had the business himself, with the idea that, at some point, it would become mine."

"But did he always have the business himself? Is there any chance that some old business partner is around who maybe wants to come back into the business, but your father was against it?"

She stared at him, then slowly shook her head. "I don't know. I really don't know. It's possible, I suppose. I don't quite know when or how he started the clinic. He's been a veterinarian forever, but, along the way, who's to say that things didn't change at some point or go in another unexpected way."

"Exactly. I'll get some friends of mine to do some digging to see if we could come up with some answers."

When a sharp bark came at the door, Trey turned to see Schooner standing there, glaring up at somebody in a white coat at the door.

"If this dog can't be controlled," the doctor snapped, "he's not staying here."

"He's staying," Trey snapped right back. "If he'd been here before, her father wouldn't have been attacked."

"We don't know that he was attacked," the doctor retorted in a testy voice.

"Then you haven't seen the security video, have you?" Missy snapped.

He froze, frowning at her. "Seriously?"

"Yes," she exclaimed loudly. "Somebody in a white lab coat came into this room as soon as we left, was here for all of a minute, left, took off a wig and the lab coat, then quickly disappeared out the rear parking lot."

The air left the doctor's lungs immediately, as he blinked several times. "Wow, that is not a good thought."

"No, it absolutely is *not* a good thought," Trey declared. "So the dog stays, and I will be staying from now on too."

The doctor glared at him, and Trey glared right back. "Whatever," the doc muttered. "It's not as if you'll listen to me anyway."

"No, I sure won't," he muttered cheerfully. "I'm all about keeping Silas safe. He's been to hell and back already, and that somebody is still trying to kill him in this hospital is absolutely ludicrous."

"Still?" the doctor repeated, confused.

Trey nodded, not sure that he should say anything more, but they had to share their thoughts with some people. "We believe that their boat was sabotaged, and that's why they were marooned out in the middle of nowhere."

He stared at them for a long moment. "Jesus. I've been in this town for a very long time, and I sure as hell hope you're wrong."

"So do we," she declared, as she stepped up beside Trey. "So do we." She reached out, placing her fingers in his, and squeezed his hand. "It's been a rough time. My father told me that the boat had been sabotaged long before he went unconscious. I didn't tell anybody but Trey. However, now, with *another* attack on Dad, right here inside this hospital, that says it all."

"YOU'LL HAVE TO get official hospital approval to keep the dog here," the doctor, a different one than before warned. "I'm not against it, if it keeps my patient safe. It's hard enough dealing with these cases, without having somebody mess up my patient's recovery." He glared at them both.

"Agreed," both of them replied immediately.

He looked from one to the other and frowned.

"I'll arrange clearance for the dog," Trey clarified.

"Yeah, good luck with that," the doctor muttered, rolling his eyes. "The hospital will be all about legal BS and avoiding lawsuits."

"Yeah, they sure will," Trey agreed, with a wry smile, "but, with the lax or failed security around here, they may very well be involved already."

The doctor stared at him and then nodded. "Understood, but just remember that the hospital isn't actively trying to harm him."

"No, but they're not doing anything to actively protect him either," he pointed out.

"I'm not going there," the doctor admitted. "I just want to keep my patient safe."

"Understood, and, as soon as we get some clarity as to what's going on, we'll let you know."

"Do that," he stated, glaring at them. "It's complete BS that this is happening."

Trey smiled. "You won't get any argument on that point, and we're doing all we can to not cause any trouble. We just want to keep Silas safe, when the hospital alone can't seem to do that."

The doctor sighed. "I do have some good news for you on that end. It seems as if he's slowly starting to come around. Now that he's stable again, we'll continue to lighten up the dosage on the meds and see if we can get him to wake up."

A gasp came from Missy, and she looked at the doc so hopefully. "Do you really think that's possible?"

"Yes, I do think so," he confirmed, with a smile. "I didn't want to say anything until I could see the latest results, but it seems he's potentially taken a turn for the better." He turned and glared at Trey. "All the more reason for you to ensure nobody's in here messing things up."

Trey agreed, but he also found it interesting that he was now marked as the person in charge. Not something he thought the doctor would have done, but what did Trey know? He waited for the doctor to complete his exam, and, when he turned to walk out, he gave Trey a warning look because Schooner still sat at the doorway, glaring at the doc again.

"It's okay, buddy," Trey said to Schooner, refusing to go quite so far as to say the doctor was a friend because, at this point, Trey had no idea who their friends were and were not. Still, as long as Silas was here, Schooner needed to let in the medical personnel. Schooner stepped back and let the doctor out. The doctor shot the War Dog a hard look as he disappeared down the hallway.

"Oh my God," Missy gasped, as she walked over to her father, leaning over and kissing him on the cheek. "This is the best news."

"It's great news for sure," Trey agreed, "but we've got to figure out the rest."

She turned and looked at him. "What do you mean?"

"I want to know that he'll be safe when he comes out of it," Trey explained. "I don't want him to get this far, only to be in even more danger the minute he wakes up again."

CHAPTER 14

MISSY KEPT TRYING to resist Trey sending her home. Finally she glared at him and asked, "Why do you want me to leave?"

"I want you to leave so that whoever is after your father will think Silas is alone and unprotected."

Her jaw dropped. "What?"

He nodded. "I just didn't want to tell you that."

"Yeah, … no kidding." She stared at him. "So, what now? You're planning on leaving Dad alone and unprotected?"

"Of course not," he said, shaking his head.

"So you'll stay here and use him as bait?"

"More or less. I'll appear to walk you and Schooner out of here, but I'll double back inside and hide somewhere. I'm not exactly sure of the details yet," he admitted. "I've been thinking about setting it up so that anybody who wants to come in can potentially come in."

"And attack my father."

"And *try* to attack your father," he corrected her.

She stared at him. "You're trying to protect me at the same time."

He gave her a ghost of a smile. "To a certain extent, yes."

"It sucks," she announced.

"Maybe so," he agreed cheerfully, "but you also know

that you're tired, worn out, and would certainly benefit from some good restorative sleep."

"Yes, and yet my father has just been attacked, so I don't find myself in any mood to leave him defenseless," she shared, as she glared at him. "Nor am I prepared to leave you here to get attacked by this guy."

"What makes you think I'll get attacked?" he asked, looking at her. "I am setting a trap for him, remember?"

Her jaw worked as she thought about it. Then she sighed. "I would feel much better if Dad had better protection than just us."

"The trouble is, we don't know who we can trust, even if someone was available to stand guard," he pointed out. "So the sooner we solve this, the better."

"But that means catching them in the act."

"It does, presuming that whoever is doing this is the same person who wants him dead."

Confused, she stared at him.

Trey nodded. "See? You're not thinking straight because you're so tired, but what if somebody else hired the guy to do this?"

"Oh shit," she muttered, sagging down onto the cot. "I don't even want to think about that."

"No, you may not, but that doesn't change the fact that it's a possibility."

"It shouldn't be," she declared, glaring at him.

He hid a smile, but she saw it anyway, immediately causing her anger to flare, only to die off almost as quickly. She just stared at him again. He continued. "It also means, if he's attacked again—and I know that sounds absolutely horrible, but—what if you're here and what if the attacker comes after you?"

"Yeah," she conceded, throwing up her hands, "and that makes me feel crappy too."

He shrugged. "You're not wrong about that, which is another reason I want you to go home."

"Why?"

"Because we don't want you attacked either."

"I don't want it to happen, but neither do I want somebody to come up here and attack you. This is such a mess. Why is this even happening?" She glared at him. "It shouldn't be happening at all."

"No, it shouldn't, but that hasn't changed, and we don't want anything else to go wrong."

"No, I don't want anything to go wrong," she agreed, "but it still feels very much as if it will."

"And that's also why we need to put a stop to this."

She groaned. "I'll go grab some sleep, but I'm coming back as soon as I wake up. If I can't sleep, I'm coming back even sooner."

He smiled at her. "That's fine, as long as you take Schooner with you."

She got up, grabbed her purse, motioned for Schooner, then marched to the door and stopped. "What about your brother? Don't you need to be with them?"

"Why?" he asked, looking at her curiously.

She frowned and shrugged. "I don't know. Maybe to maintain family relationships?"

"I don't think Jackson will be upset if I'm not there from time to time," he noted with a smile. "He doesn't know all the details of this, but he isn't a fool either."

"But he'll get the wrong idea if you're spending all this time with me."

"What's the wrong idea?" he asked her.

She flushed and shrugged. "Never mind. I just want all this to go away." She turned to face him. "Thank you for letting Schooner stay with me. He's such a source of comfort and security, even if it is far-fetched."

"It's not far-fetched at all," he countered, looking at her. "He's a trained War Dog, so he's certainly trained to attack anyone, should you be in trouble."

"Then maybe we should leave him here for my father."

"As long as I'm here with your father, Silas will be fine. I do have an awful lot of training myself, you know?" he reminded her.

She smiled over at him. "Sorry, I forgot about that. No offense intended."

He laughed. "None taken. You and Schooner go get some rest. I'll see you both when you come back."

"Okay, he needs to go outside anyway."

"He does, indeed."

When the dog stopped beside her, she clicked on his leash and headed out. Schooner stopped at the doorway and turned to look back at her father. "Do you want to say goodbye?" she asked Schooner.

When she let go of the lead, the dog walked back over to the bed and stretched his nose up to check on her father. It brought tears to her eyes to see how gentle Schooner was. "I really need him to wake up," she whispered from the doorway.

"Give Silas a chance," Trey noted. "He's not down and out yet, so you have to give him a chance."

"I know," she whispered, brushing the tears from her eyes. "I'm just so tired."

"I know you are. Go home and rest, and we'll see you in the morning."

"Or you'll see me in an hour when I can't sleep at all," she muttered.

"You might be surprised," he replied. "An awful lot of stress has been in your system, and it'll be good for you to get some sleep."

"Maybe, but just because you say so doesn't mean it'll work that way."

"No, of course not," he agreed, with a smile.

She nudged Schooner along, and they walked the few blocks to her house. As she got to the house, she stopped, just now remembering how it had been broken into. At that point she realized just how much she didn't want to be here. She picked up her phone and called Trey.

"Problems?" he asked immediately.

"No, but now that I'm standing outside my home, I just remembered it got broken into."

"Right," he replied. "So do you want to go somewhere else?"

"Yeah, back to the hospital."

"You can't just stay here the whole time."

"Why not?" she asked, as she stared up at the house. "I don't really want to go inside."

"Then grab yourself a hotel room," he suggested immediately.

"They won't take dogs."

"Some will," he stated.

"No," she said stubbornly, "this won't work."

"You need sleep."

"Not as much as I need to know that my father is safe. I'm coming back." With that, she ended the call and walked back in the direction of the hospital. She was almost there when her phone rang. It was Bill Bedford, from the clinic.

"Any chance you can come in tomorrow and give us a hand?" Bill asked, fatigue in his tone. "I don't know if it's because your father's out of commission for the moment or what, but we've just gotten slammed with so much business."

"Ouch," she muttered.

"I know you're probably standing watch over your father, but I just wondered …" Bill added, not sure how to end the sentence. "I've called around, trying to see if we could get a temporary helper brought in for a few days, but it's not looking good."

"No, I hear you," she said. "You're right. I do need to get back to the land of the living."

"I wouldn't ask if it wasn't major, and I know that you're not fully credentialed yet, but, honest to God, I could use some extra hands."

"Right, I'll see you tomorrow," she agreed. She ended the call and stood outside the hospital, wondering what her options were for sleeping now. She turned and looked down at Schooner, ever quiet at her side. "What should we do, buddy?"

Schooner just looked at her, silent.

In all this mess, the indecision was killing her. She wanted to go back in and look after her father, but she was also rather desperately in need of sleep. Trey was right on that point, particularly if she also would go to the clinic and help out there.

She turned as one of the nurses just starting to come off shift called out to her, "Hey, are you all right?"

"Yeah, I'm okay," Missay muttered. "It's just life, you know?"

"It absolutely is life," the nurse Celia agreed in a gentle

tone, "but you must look after yourself."

"How do I do that when everything else is going to pot?"

"Listen. If disaster strikes, and you should lose your father, or even if he has an extended recovery, you still need to pick up the pieces of your life. So making some balanced decisions right now will help you then."

"And yet—"

"I get it," Celia interrupted. "You don't want to even consider such an option, and it likely won't come to that. All I can say is that, right now, you look exhausted, and you desperately need some sleep."

"That bad, *huh*?"

"Yeah, that bad," Celia confirmed, with half a smile. "I would love to see you go home and just crash."

"I would love to, but my house was broken into," she shared. "So, as much as I would love to go to my place, it doesn't really seem to be a good option right now."

Celia hesitated and then nodded. "We do have some places to sleep in the hospital." When Missy stared at her, Celia nodded. "It's for the nurses mostly, but I don't think anybody would necessarily mind."

"And yet I have the cot in my father's room."

"But, after what you've already been through and now the attack on your father, I can see you are not getting any sleep there either."

She hesitated and then sighed. "You heard about that, *huh*?"

"Oh, yes," she said, with a grimace. "All the staff did, and believe me that it didn't make us feel very good. Security isn't something that we've ever really had to watch for or to address here, so it's a very disconcerting concept."

"Of course," she agreed and didn't add anything.

"Come on in and bring the dog with you. Let's grab you a place to sleep for a few hours. Then you can go back to your dad. Honestly, I'm surprised you've left him unattended," she noted, looking at Missy sideways.

"I didn't. I left Trey there with him."

"Ah, that makes sense," she noted. "That's a good thing. None of us want to be in the way, and we don't want anything to go wrong. Yet we don't have the extra time to look in on Silas, outside of our usual checks."

"Of course," Missy said.

In the hospital, Celia took Missy to another area and opened a door, where all three cots inside were empty. "Go ahead and crash. We don't have that much staff on overnight duty anyway, but I'll let everybody know that you're in here, so they won't come in and disturb you. I doubt that anybody would be welcomed anyway, since you've got Schooner with you."

Missy smiled down at Schooner, who just looked at her. There was no greeting in his gaze, just that *checking and looking at her* thing. "I don't know how much of a watchdog he is," Missy conceded, "but we wouldn't want anybody to accidentally open the door and surprise him."

"Right, I can appreciate that," Celia agreed.

With that, Missy stumbled over to one of the cots and sat down. Schooner was right at her side and stretched out on the floor beside her immediately.

"Good," Celia noted. "Looks as if he approves. You'll feel quite a bit better if you can grab even a little sleep." And, with that, she turned and walked out the door.

With Celia closing the door behind her, Missy now felt she just might sleep. Nobody would know where she was to interrupt her. Then she suddenly realized how that was a problem. She quickly called Trey and told him what had happened.

"Good. I like the idea of your being somewhere safe and sound. Now go to sleep. I'm here, and I'll keep watch over your father."

And, with that, she curled up on the cot and closed her eyes.

TREY WONDERED ABOUT a hospital that gave up its sleeping rooms for exhausted family of the patients, then realized that maybe it was just a kindness on the nurse's part. Anybody coming by Silas's room would see that Trey was here, and it would make sense that he'd sent Missy home and that he was now standing guard over Silas. Still, this hospital attack made him uncomfortable.

It did help to know that Missy was somewhere on the grounds, and, if he needed to find her, he was sure he could. Plus, he and Missy and Schooner all seemed to get along just fine.

Trey stayed in the room with Silas and updated Jackson and Badger on the case. Badger called and asked him how he was doing personally. Trey smiled and replied, "It's not exactly what I thought would happen here, but, considering all the issues we've been going through, I'm doing fine."

"Good. What about any evidence of sabotage from the boat? Any more progress on that?"

"I'm out of touch on that," he admitted. "You need to talk to Rob." Then he quickly gave him Rob's number. "I'm on guard duty at the hospital," he explained, "and, if I can grab some sleep, I will. Otherwise I'm waiting for Missy to come back."

"How is that going?" Badger asked, a note of amusement in his tone.

"You mean with Missy? It's going fine. Why?" he asked.

"Oh, just checking."

"Are you trying to be a matchmaker or what?" Trey asked as he realized what Badger was implying.

"I'm not, but Kat is always trying."

"I'm not against the idea," Trey admitted. "It's just definitely not on anybody's radar right now."

"Right, and Kat would say that's the way it should be." With that, he ended the call.

Trey stared down at his phone in confusion. A few minutes later Jackson called.

"I'm coming up to visit," he announced, then abruptly ended the call.

Jackson didn't give Trey a chance to say yay or nay. Regardless it would be good to see his brother, good to talk to him and to catch up. Trey had arrived in town and then had been busy elsewhere ever since. It took about twenty minutes before Jackson appeared, and, when he did show, he had coffee in a travel cup and a brown paper bag for Trey.

Trey smiled and asked, "Did Elizabeth send you?"

"She hardly sent me," he replied, "but, once I told her where I was going, she packed you some things."

Trey smiled and thanked him. "I would never say no to that."

"Who would? She's one hell of a cook," Jackson boasted with a smile. "It would be good if you settled down and found yourself a good woman too."

"That would be nice," Trey joked, "though it would be pretty tough to find one as great as Elizabeth."

"Oh, you might be surprised," Jackson muttered, with a knowing smile. He walked over to stand at the foot of Silas's hospital bed. "God, it's terrible to see him like this."

"I know. He's always been so vibrant and alive—always just a little bit larger-than-life."

Jackson shook his head. "He hadn't calmed down much either, still the bragger when it came to the fishing derby."

"That is sure a theme around here. Does it bother people enough to be a problem?"

"I don't know," he said, turning to face Trey. "What makes you think it's anything?"

"I don't know if it is anything," he stated, "but comments about the fishing derby keep coming up, making me wonder if that's what's behind all this."

"It would blow me away to think that anything to do with fishing would be enough to kill somebody. … Are you sure you've checked out all the other avenues?"

"Of course. I've checked as many as I can," Trey replied with a groan. "We're still waiting on information on a bunch of them."

"Of course," Jackson agreed. "It does take time, doesn't it?"

Trey nodded. "Have you ever known Silas to get upset about anything?"

"Only about his daughter, if anybody would bad-mouth her or would doubt her abilities, anything along the line of somebody saying something crude or disrespectful. As any good father, he wouldn't tolerate that."

"We did wonder if she could be part of or even all of the issue here, but we don't have any way of knowing that. Plus, we haven't found anything to support it."

"She was going out with that one doctor here."

Trey nodded. "Charles. Right. We talked to him, checked him out, but I don't really see him as being a viable candidate."

At that, Jackson looked over at him with a note of amusement. "Maybe you should look at it as a jealous boyfriend, and you might see things differently."

"Meaning?" Trey asked, a challenge in his tone.

"If you look at all the men as just suspects, it's one thing. However, if you allow yourself to understand what it would be like if Missy were going out with one of those men, you might understand her father's side of it a little more."

"I'm not trying to *not* understand that," Trey said, frowning at his brother, clearly puzzled.

"Let me just say that everybody seems to think that you two are sweet on each other."

He stared at his brother and shrugged. "I like her a lot, but it's not as if I've had ten minutes to even consider anything past the chaos right now."

"Right, and I think that's probably why people are smiling about the whole thing," Jackson shared, "because it seems as if you just arrived in town, and already there you are, with the belle of the ball."

"What do you mean?" Trey asked.

"She's considered quite a prize around here. Not only is she a vet, but her father is a vet with a busy clinic. I don't know whether they have any money or not, but people seem to think they do. Apparently Silas also inherited quite a bit from his wife when she died."

Trey frowned at him. "Do you know that for sure?"

"No, I sure don't," he admitted cheerfully. "It's just ... rumors."

"Rumors can be deadly."

"They sure can," he agreed, pointing at Trey. "You need to keep an open mind."

"Do you really think that Silas would say or do something that would upset somebody enough to do this?"

"I don't know," Jackson replied, "but, should Silas die, who stands to inherit all the money that everyone thinks he has? Think about it. Odds are, Missy does, and, if Silas is gone, and if she's got the practice to take on, she also gets not only the house but the clinic and also the inheritance from her mother, plus the inheritance from her father on top of that."

Trey stared at his brother. "I wonder if that could be what's behind all this," he murmured.

Jackson shrugged. "I don't know, but you may have to dig a little deeper. Just ensure you really find out what's going on because, whenever money is involved, … we both know it can get ugly really fast."

"I understand," Trey muttered, turning to stare at Silas. "And often in a very devious way."

"I prefer that greed concept to the idea of a fishing derby gone wrong," Jackson noted cheerfully.

Trey rolled his eyes at that. "I would really hate to think it had anything to do with a fishing derby too. Yet this is all so criminal at this point in time that there could be multiple layers of crimes. And the inheritance theory doesn't quite work, since, if Silas has no business partner, and he dies, Missy inherits."

"It does clear the road though, doesn't it? There would be an awful lot of people knocking on her door, and, if you're sitting there, waiting in the wings—"

"People will just look at me suspiciously," he pointed out.

"I'm not so sure that they aren't already," Jackson murmured. "You weren't even here when they turned up missing, so that's in your favor. Yet you somehow miraculously found them," he pointed out, his tone thick with irony. When Trey sat back and stared at him in shock, Jackson shrugged. "No, I'm not saying that's what people are saying," he clarified, "but you also know what people in this town are like."

"Christ," he muttered, as he stared at Jackson. "I hadn't expected that comment."

"Nope, and I'm only bringing it up because, while you're looking at all kinds of options here, I want to ensure my brother isn't the one getting skewered at the end of the day."

"Jesus," Trey muttered, "no way anybody could think I'm behind all this. I just arrived in town."

"And you have that alibi, which is a good thing," Jackson noted, with a shrug. "But still, the fact is, after all the days and days of searching, suddenly you turned up and went out one day and brought them home, as if you knew exactly where to go. … Anyway, I just wanted to keep you informed as to what's been playing on the local jungle drums."

"Keep me informed? Don't you mean, me keeping you informed?" he teased, with a headshake. "Although it does sound as if the gossip mill is working overtime."

"The gossip mill is always working overtime around here. Small town, remember?"

"And, in this case, a prominent figure, missing people who suddenly get found, and now another attempt on Silas's life," Trey recapped.

"I just don't want anything to happen to you. I would

love it if you would consider moving back home again," Jackson shared, "and I don't want this mess to tank your view of our town. I don't know who's doing this shit, and, as far as I'm concerned, it's complete BS. Still, I do want you to feel comfortable enough to come home and to stay home. Especially now with Elizabeth pregnant, there isn't anything quite like family. Ours has had some issues to deal with, and it sure would be nice if we could pull it together and be a close-knit family for a change." With that said, Jackson turned and walked out.

Trey thought about his brother's words. It's not that they didn't have a close-knit family, but Trey had been gone a lot. It was hard to be very close if you were never in town, missing the big milestones in other people's lives. At the same time, they'd missed out on the milestones in his life too.

He would potentially consider staying here, and, with that, he returned his gaze to Silas, his eyelids still closed. "You would be one of the reasons for me coming home again," he muttered, "but, for that, you have to get your ass out of that damn bed." It almost seemed as if Silas had shifted at his words. Trey smiled and walked over to the edge of the hospital bed, then stared down at Silas and asked, "What the hell happened, man?"

"What are you doing so close to him?" a nurse snapped, glaring at him from the open doorway.

Trey crossed his arms over his chest and glared right back at her. "What are you doing here?" he asked in a snappish tone.

She frowned at him in astonishment. "I am one of the nurses."

"Sure, and what is it that you think you're coming here

to do?"

"What? You'll stop me from doing my job now?" she asked in a testy voice.

"Maybe. I'm not sure where that attitude of yours is coming from, but you can bet I don't like it."

"I don't like yours either," she stated, glaring at him. "This used to be a nice quiet hospital."

"Until when?" he asked, puzzled at her hostility. "All I'm seeing from you is a whole lot of anger."

"Sure, I don't like dogs. I don't like anything about this scenario." Her face softened as she looked at Silas.

Then he realized that was the problem. She had feelings for him and didn't like to see him this way, but nobody likely knew all that. "If you're so sweet on Silas, why are you being so ugly about it?" he asked, bringing it right out into the open. When she immediately glared at him, he shrugged. "It's obvious from the look on your face that you don't like seeing him this way."

"Of course I don't like it. He's a good man. He deserves more than being struck down like this."

"I agree," Trey noted, "but that still doesn't match your anger."

She stiffened and shrugged. "It's none of your damn business either."

"Maybe, but I won't let you have anything to do with him if I think you'll hurt him."

She stared at him in astonishment. "You think I'll hurt him?"

"I don't understand why you come in here with that chip on your shoulder. After two attacks on Silas already, you can bet that I won't let another one happen."

"What do you mean, *another* attack?" she asked, the fear

in her gaze obvious, as she turned to look at the man in the hospital bed. "What do you mean? What do you mean by attack?"

"An attack," he repeated calmly, studying her and wondering at her reaction. She backed up several steps. "Maybe you know something about it, considering the expression on your face."

She gave him a terrified look, then turned and raced from the room. Curious, he stepped into the hallway to see where she went, and, sure enough, she headed to the nearest staircase, the same one the attacker had used. So, was she a nurse or not?

Just as he weighed his options to stay or to go after her, another nurse walked toward him. "Did you see her?" he asked.

The nurse frowned at him, surprised. "Who? Mildred? Yeah, I sure did. She looked upset. What happened?" she asked, turning to eye him suspiciously.

He groaned. "I don't know what happened," he said. "Mildred looked pretty upset at seeing Silas here on the bed, and I mentioned the attack that happened recently."

"Yeah, don't worry about it. She's pretty sweet on Silas and always has been. I'm Celia, by the way."

"Trey."

"*Aah*, the one everyone's been talking about."

Trey rolled his eyes, as he steered the discussion back on topic. "So, back to Mildred, that's interesting." He turned to face Celia. "She bolted out of here, as if she would be accused of the attack. What's up with that?"

"Chances are she's thinking about her damn son," Celia shared. "*Keith*. That guy's a piece of work."

"In what way?"

"He's got a record longer than my arm," she shared, as she walked into the room with Trey.

"And, if you're here now to check on Silas, why would Mildred come here just a couple minutes ago?"

Celia shook her head. "I don't know. Did she come in?"

He nodded. "She did and was instantly mad because I was here."

"Honestly, I have no idea. I'm here doing rounds. I don't know why she would be in here, especially since she was off shift." She frowned, then checked her watch and shrugged. "I think she was off shift about an hour ago, but she's been sweet on him for quite a while. Maybe she just popped in for a visit, saw you were here, and wasn't sure what to do."

"I wonder if she's popped in before."

"Oh, she has been here often because I've come in, found her sitting at his side—only if his daughter wasn't here, though Missy could very well have been sleeping at the time. We're used to moving through the night in a stealthy way, so we don't wake up people," she explained, with a bright smile in his direction.

He filed away that information because that made sense, and it wasn't their intention to wake up every sleeping family member who might be here. Still, it was definitely not something he had really considered. When Celia was about to leave, he asked casually, "What do you know about her son?"

"Not a whole lot, just that he's got a rap sheet that's supposedly pretty long. My boyfriend is a deputy in town here, so I get tidbits of information, but not much," she shared. "I don't really want to know much. I live on the healing side of life and don't want to hear the details of all the shit people do to each other. I see the results day in and day out."

"I can understand the need to distance yourself."

"It's one of the reasons I moved here," she said with a smile. "It was a small town, a lot easier pace, and a whole lot less violence. I used to live in Chicago, and I don't want to go back there." And, with that, she was gone, leaving him with something else to think about.

Not long afterward, he heard a *woof* from the door and turned to see Schooner racing toward him. Schooner jumped up on him and gave him a hero's welcome. Trey laughed and tucked him up close, but it was impossible to hold the wiggling mass. Trey turned to see Missy standing there, holding what could be food. He smiled at her. "I'm not sure whether you look better or not."

"Right, and I appreciate the fact that you didn't lie about it," she noted, with a grimace. "I know I look like shit."

"No, you don't look like shit, but you do look as if you've had a difficult few days. You could use some more sleep and some real rest."

"Yeah, that's code for *I look like shit*," she declared.

He just gave her a frown and shook his head. "You're always beautiful, so don't even go there."

She laughed. "I'm not fishing for compliments, and I tried to sleep. I did get a few hours, but then I was awake again, and that was it. My mind was up, wondering if everything here was okay."

"It's okay," he said. "I did have one question that escaped my mind before, but did your father have any relationships, any girlfriends, past girlfriends, anything like that?"

She shrugged. "Not now. He did at one time, but it

didn't work out."

"Who was it?"

Missy stared at him curiously. "You can't think she had anything to do with this."

"I don't know who may have had anything to do with this, but, if you say Mildred, we need to talk a little more."

Her eyebrows shot up, and she nodded. "It was Mildred. Why?" He explained about the visit and the woman taking off in a rush. "Well, … I know my dad was pretty upset about it, but I don't know all the details. I just know that they did break up and that he was the one who initiated it."

"Sounds as if she still may be in love with him."

"He's a good man," she said, her gaze turning to her cot, even as her feet carried her in that direction.

"So, maybe we're not looking in the right direction," he began. "Is there any chance that Mildred might have had something to do with this?"

Missy immediately shook her head. "Mildred can't stand water and doesn't know anything about boats. However, if you are talking about her son, Keith, that might be a different story."

Trey stared at her and asked, "What about her son?"

"I just know that he has a criminal record of some sort," she replied. "Yet I can't imagine that he would have anything to do with this."

"Why not? Why do you say that?"

Missy frowned at him and then sighed. "I guess I don't have an answer for that. Feel free to talk to him."

"I will talk to him, so thanks." He got up and took a lazy stretch. "The nurses were just here, both of them," he noted, with a laugh. "Are you okay if I go out and do a little bit of reconnaissance?"

She checked her watch. "It is seven in the morning. So you are good to go."

"My brother's been here, not to mention a bunch of other people."

"Sure, go ahead, but I brought some food, if you want something first."

"Maybe." He stared at the bag. "What did you bring?" he asked, with a cheeky grin.

She laughed, opened it up, and said, "Muffins and coffee."

"I'll take both," he replied immediately. Smiling, he accepted the goodies.

"You don't really think this has something to do with my dad's love life, do you? It feels as if we're just fishing now."

He swallowed the muffin in two bites. "That's exactly what we're doing," he admitted, "because, somewhere along the line, something happened, and it's something that none of us know about. So, whoever is doing this isn't even worried about getting caught because, as far as they're concerned, they're completely under the radar. We need to shine a light on it and figure out just who is doing this and what it's about."

"If you can figure it out," Missy replied, with a shrug, "more power to you. I've racked my brain until I gave myself a massive headache, and I still have no clue."

CHAPTER 15

MISSY WATCHED AS Trey left, his cup of coffee in hand as he headed out. She wasn't sure where he would head to first, but, considering the hour, she hoped he got a shower and maybe a few hours of sleep. She heard her father, restless, mumbling in his sleep. She raced to his side, laced her fingers with his, and whispered, "It's okay, Dad. I'm here."

Almost immediately he calmed down, and she smiled, patting his hand. "Keep coming back to us, Dad. Keep coming back. I'm here, and I'll stay with you. It's all right."

She wasn't sure what it would take to bring her dad all the way back to consciousness, but it wasn't very long afterward that the doctor she'd seen earlier came through on his rounds. She quickly told him about how her father had been acting, and he smiled and nodded.

"That's good," he told her. "It might get a little rough while he surfaces, and he could immediately be wiped out with pain. So, as soon as you see him show consciousness in any way, you call out for help. Understood?"

She nodded. "I hear you."

With a wave of his hand, the doctor was gone.

She beamed as she turned to look back at her father. "Hear that, Dad? It looks as if you might be coming out of this after all." It was the best news ever and gave her complete and total hope. She quickly sent Trey a text, telling him about it.

He phoned her right back. "Now that is great news."

"It is," she murmured.

He hesitated, then said, "But don't tell anybody else, okay?"

"Why not? If people know he's alive and waking up, they won't see him as simply a victim they can come and prey on. What's wrong with that?"

"Because then they might try harder," he explained, "and I can't be there right now."

"Do you really think they will?" she whispered.

"I'm afraid they will, yes. So, let's not put it to the test. At least not before I get there."

"No, of course not," she muttered.

"Besides, waiting a day or two won't matter, will it? Everybody thinks he's a miracle at the moment anyway."

"He is a miracle," she declared warmly. "A miracle I care very much about."

"I know, and let's just not cause any more chaos before we get where we need to be with him."

"No, no, of course not." She put away her phone, completely sobered by the thought that this good thing may not be a great thing. It was a great thing for her father, but maybe not if anybody else knew.

Several other doctors came through over the next few hours, and she was always protective after Trey's words. Yet they all seemed to be harmless, only caring about her father's condition more than anything else. There had been no change in his condition, but she kept hoping, so much that she jumped at every sound, then walked over to see if it was him. She knew Schooner would alert her of any danger, but still…

Finally she heard another sound, then looked over to see her father slowly opening his eyes. She raced over, tears in her eyes as she picked up his hands and whispered, "It's okay, Dad. Take it easy. You're here in the hospital."

He had both eyes on her, staring in confusion.

"We're in the hospital." He blinked several times, as if trying to understand what she said. She immediately hit the Call button for a nurse to get somebody to come help them. "Take it easy, Dad. I know you'll be in a lot of pain," she whispered. "It's okay." He gave her half a smile, then closed his eyes and seemed to drift a bit.

Just then, one of the doctors raced in. Schooner bolted to the bed as if to defend her father. She immediately reached out for him, pulling him back out of the way.

"He just had his eyes open," she cried out. "He was just looking at me."

"That's a good thing." He came over and spoke to her father in a sharp tone of voice. Her father opened his eyes and stared at him. And that was it. She was quickly moved out and asked to back away from the bed, as several other medical personnel came in. Silas was immediately run through a gambit of tests, as all of them spoke to him in calm and muted voices. She could barely even see her father through the sea of people, and finally she heard his whisper.

"My daughter?"

"I'm here, Dad. I'm right here," she said, elbowing her way back to him. She smiled at him. "Here I am."

He looked up at her with such relief and love in his expression, the tears filled her eyes all over again. "I thought we were done for. I thought my enthusiasm had killed you."

"No," she whispered, "I'm fine, way better than you in

fact."

He groaned and whispered, "My head."

"Yeah," one of the doctors replied, "you've got a nasty head injury. We had to open you up, drain some of the bleeding, and release the swelling inside your scalp."

He blinked several times at the doctors, as if trying to process what he'd just been told, and then his eyelids drifted closed. Within a few minutes her father fell back asleep.

The doctor turned to her with a big smile. "No need to worry. Now he just needs to sleep. Regular old sleep," the doc clarified, with a beaming smile. "It looks as if he'll pull through and will come out of this relatively unscathed."

Tears in her eyes. she thanked him profusely.

He shook his head. "Hey, he's come back for you as much as for anything we did," he pointed out, with a smile. "Sure, we've helped his body get through some of the worst of it, but it's that emotional fight to come back to you that makes the big difference, so keep it up."

Just then her phone rang. She looked down and realized it was Bill Bedford. "Oh my God," she cried into the phone, "I forgot I was supposed to come in."

"You forgot?" he snapped. "How the hell can you just forget? I told you how we were slammed, and I even asked you specifically if you could help out today."

"I know. I know. I'm so sorry. My father has more or less woken up, and things got out of hand here."

"He woke up?" There was complete and utter shock in his tone.

"Yes, isn't that wonderful?"

"Absolutely it's great," he replied, "especially when I'm so overwhelmed."

"I know the struggle you're in, so I'll get somebody to

come stay with him. I should be there in about forty minutes."

"Good because, in about forty minutes, I'm about to walk." And, with that, the phone went dead.

She winced and quickly phoned Trey. When she got no answer, she sent a text message, and then sat down to wait.

TREY DOUBLE-CHECKED THE address before he got out of the car and walked up to Mildred's house and knocked.

She opened the door and glared at him. "What are you doing at my home?" she snapped.

"I came to talk to your son."

Immediately fear filled her eyes. "You've got to no reason to talk to him," she declared, trying to shut the door.

He reached out a hand and asked, "So, does he live here or not?"

"Ma, what's the matter?" The shout came from the living room.

When she hesitated, Trey called out, "I'm here to talk to you, Keith."

A snort came from inside, and a tall, skinny, gangly character arrived at the door, looking at him sideways. "Who the hell are you, and what do you want?"

Trey smiled at him. "I just want to have a talk, that's all."

"I don't want to talk to you. I don't even know you."

"No, but your mother's afraid you may have had something to do with the attack on Silas at the hospital."

Keith just stared at him, his expression turning stony. He looked at his mother and asked, "What's he talking about? What the hell is this?"

She gasped in shock. "I didn't say anything." She turned and pointed at Trey. "He's just making up stuff."

"No, you took off like a bat out of hell from the hospital," Trey stated. "So it was pretty obvious what you thought."

"I didn't say anything," Mildred cried out, falling back.

"You didn't have to," Trey replied, "and now I need to know for sure if Keith attacked Silas or not."

"Who the hell are you? A fucking cop?" the son asked, crossing his arms over his chest.

"No, I'm not," he muttered, "but I am the guy who rescued Silas and Missy, and I'm spending a fair bit of time trying to ensure that whoever tried to kill them in the first place doesn't get another chance."

"Another chance?" he asked, his eyebrows raised.

"Yes, their boat was sabotaged, which is why they ended up stranded out there in the first place," Trey explained. "I brought them back in, after search and rescue stopped."

"I was out with the search and rescue team," Keith declared. "We didn't find any sign of them."

"But if you had something to do with their going missing, you would have been pretty happy to misdirect all the search efforts, wouldn't you?"

His gaze grew cold as he stared at him. "That's a hell of a thing to accuse a guy of."

"I'm not accusing you, just checking your story to ensure you didn't have anything to do with it."

"I don't fucking have to talk to you," he yelled. "You ain't nobody from around here. I don't give a shit what you think, and I'm not talking to you."

"That's fine. The sheriff's office is my next stop anyway.

We've had plenty of talks over these last few days because we're looking for a motive."

"Yeah? What motive could I possibly have?" Keith asked.

"Silas broke it off with your mom, so maybe that upset you, maybe you want to protect her." The son snorted at that. "Maybe you just wanted revenge, who knows? It didn't take very much to dredge up your criminal records, and you seem to enjoy breaking and entering. And we found an intruder had been in Silas's home. So maybe you had something against Silas from the beginning. I don't know."

Keith was completely nonreactive to anything going on around him, which was an interesting trick in itself.

If this guy was involved, he wasn't involved emotionally. "I can see that maybe this isn't something you really give a crap about," Trey pointed out, with half a smile. "So, as far as motives goes, that would be interesting to figure out."

"I don't have a motive," Keith declared, adding a sneer. "And I didn't have anything to do with sabotaging the boat. Christ, around this place that's a death warrant."

"Exactly," Trey agreed, "and that was the plan. Then somebody went into his hospital room and sabotaged his IV and monitor lines, somebody who had access to doctors' jackets and things, somebody who knew the layout of the hospital. Silas ended up on the floor, so we're not certain just how bad the attack was, but the good news is that he's slowly coming around."

At that, Mildred stepped forward. "Is he?" she whispered, with hope in her tone.

"Oh, Jesus, give it up, Ma. If he wanted anything to do with you, he wouldn't have broken it off in the first place."

She turned and glared at him. "He broke it off because of you."

"He isn't much of a man then, is he? Of course I'll give him a shakedown to ensure he'll treat you right."

"Instead, all he did was break up with me," she wailed, "because he didn't want a hoodlum hanging around all the time."

"I've been clean for a long time," he snapped, swinging his arms out, "so that ain't got nothing to do with me. If he broke it off with you, that's on you."

"Not hardly," she snapped, glaring at him. "If you weren't in the picture, he would never have broken up with me."

"So, what now? You're trying to get me in trouble, hoping that maybe I'll disappear, so you can go back to your happy little world with him?" he asked, with a snort. "That ain't happening, Ma."

With that, she crossed her arms over her chest and glared at him.

He shook his head. "This house is as much mine as it is yours. Remember that."

"How could I possibly forget?" she snapped. "You bring it up every chance you get."

"Dad left half to you and half to me, so I would always have a home—because he knew."

"Yeah, he knew how much trouble you were always in," she added, glaring at him. "No way this is how I want to live."

"You can move out then."

"Or we can sell and split the money," she stated, still glaring at him.

"I ain't selling. I like it here, and this is my home." He turned back to Trey. "Now, if you haven't figured it out already, the only problem between my mother and me is this home we were left. I have every right to be here. She just happened to like having it to herself, while I was in jail."

"Interesting," Trey murmured, his mind immediately triggered to consider something else.

"But I didn't have nothing to do with any of that, so don't even think about it."

"Maybe not, but rest assured that I'll be figuring out who the hell is after Silas. Of course there's always the chance they're after the daughter," Trey mentioned, casting another glance at Keith.

"Now you're really fishing. I've got nothing against her or for her. I don't give a shit either way. I'm not looking to get into any trouble. I'm still on probation, and no way I'm going back in the slammer. We all know it wouldn't take much at all for the cops to crawl all over my ass and to railroad me over any crime that came along, especially if they couldn't solve it." Shaking his head, he declared, "I'm staying away from any trouble because I'm not going back."

"You want to tell me what happened in the first place?" Trey asked.

"No, I sure as hell don't. I want to tell you to fuck off, so why don't you just take a hike? My ma's got to work soon enough, and you can talk to her there. Otherwise this is my house, so you can back the fuck off." And, with that, the door was slammed in Trey's face.

Almost with perfect timing, he got a text from Missy, about needing to go to the vet clinic. When he read it, he shook his head, and muttered, "Never a break for any of us."

As he headed back to the hospital to keep watch on her father, he was hoping they got Silas fully back … and soon.

HURRYING INTO THE vet clinic with Schooner at her side, Missy smiled as she was greeted by several women, who all rushed over to give her a hug and cuddle Schooner. "Heard you've been swamped. I'm so sorry I haven't been in at all."

"Hey, we understand. We're just so happy you made it back okay," Patty exclaimed. She was one of the older employees and had been working with her father forever. "Things have been a little hairy all of a sudden."

"So I hear," Missy noted, with a grin. She quickly shifted to the back office, grabbed her lab coat, and walked over to see Bill working with a patient already. When he looked up, she saw the relief on his face. She nodded and offered, "I'll take the next one." For the next couple hours, she was buried in the work she had trained so hard for.

When lunch came and went, she didn't even notice, until one of the receptionists stopped her. "Have you eaten?"

Missy blinked several times as she thought about it, then frowned. "I think I had breakfast."

Patty laughed. "Come on with me. We have a few things in the breakroom."

"Good." Missy checked her phone and found nothing from Trey. She quickly called him, as she took a break. He answered as she was pouring coffee. "Hey," she greeted him.

"How's my father?"

"Maybe you should ask him that," Trey said.

The next thing Missy knew, a soft voice came on the other end.

"Baby?"

"Dad," she cried out, tears in her eyes. "Oh my God, it's so good to hear your voice."

"I'm feeling a little rough, but I'm here."

"Thank God," she muttered. "I'm at the clinic right now."

"Are you okay?"

"I'm fine. I'm absolutely fine, particularly now that I know you're okay."

"I will be too. It's just a little rough right now."

She heard the smile in his voice, even though she knew he was feeling the pain right now.

He continued. "I won't be leaving here any time soon, according to the doctor."

"No, you're not," she declared. "You need to stay right where you are. Is Trey still there?"

"Yes, he's here. Apparently you've picked up a watchdog," he teased, "and I couldn't be happier."

She raised her eyebrows at that. "He's been here since we were rescued. In case you don't know, he's the one who found and rescued us."

Silence came on the other end for a moment. "No, he didn't tell me that. That figures though, but he is—"

Trey interrupted Dad and took over the phone just then. She was ecstatic. "Oh my God, when did he wake up?" she asked.

"Just a few minutes ago. We were just getting ready to call you."

"Thank you," she muttered. "I've been so busy all morning at the clinic that the time has flown by."

"Good. That's probably been a positive change for you, something to take your mind off everything else," he suggested. "At least Silas is now sleeping and resting normally, so he should be improving markedly over the next few days."

"Yes," she whispered, "and I'm so damn glad. I can hardly believe it." The tears gathered in the back of her throat, and she couldn't even begin to hold them back. "I'll come up as soon as I'm finished here," she muttered.

"Take your time. He'll be right here. He's going back to sleep now, but, according to the doctor, he'll wake up a lot more frequently. Then he'll eventually get into a normal sleep pattern. Just know that he'll be here."

"Yep, and he'll probably be sleeping when I get there," she grumbled, yet followed by a laugh.

"Maybe not, he was pretty damn glad to see me and to hear that you were doing fine, but he does need to rest a lot."

She hesitated and glanced around, before asking, "You won't leave him alone, right?"

"No, I won't leave him alone," he vowed, "and he hasn't mentioned anything either."

"Damn," she muttered, "because that would help a lot too."

"Only if he has any ideas," Trey added. "However, we also don't want him worrying about it or thinking that you'll be in danger because none of that will help him get better."

"I know," she agreed, scrubbing her face with her free hand. "God, I sure wish I didn't need to be here right now, but I really do. The clinic is swamped."

"You do what you've got to do because that's also your

father's world, and I know it makes him feel better to know that you were stepping in and taking the heat off the clinic."

She laughed. "That's one way to put it. Anyway I've got to go. I'll see you as soon as this calms down." And, with that, she ended the call and turned back to the others. "Dad's awake. He's talking, smiling, and looking for all intents and purposes as if he'll pull through," she announced, brushing away her tears.

"Thank God for that," Patty declared with joy, everyone buzzing with relief.

"So, the clinic can get back to normal sooner than later," Bill stated, glaring at her.

"Absolutely," she murmured. "Sorry, I didn't realize things had gotten so bad."

His gaze softened for a moment, then he shrugged. "I'm not sure what the hell happened, but it's as if everybody and their dog came out to support you and your father by coming here to the clinic." Bill shook his head. "I'm not sure how they thought that would work out."

"It might just have been curiosity too," Missy suggested. "People being people, you know? They do that. *Let's go down to the clinic and see what's going on,*" she quipped, with a smile. "Who knows? Anyway, I'm back, and the sooner I'm done here, the sooner I can get to the hospital."

And, with that, she quickly disappeared into the next exam room to deal with a dog who had met a porcupine. Groaning, she settled in for what would be a long appointment. By the time the business day was done, she was able to escape with well wishes from all the staff and with her promises that she would let them know when they could come visit her father. Right now she headed to the hospital and took Schooner with her.

As she walked into his room, her father was talking with Trey. Immediately she raced over and gave her dad a big hug. "I'm almost jealous," she told Trey. "He's been sitting here visiting with you, while I've been hard at work."

Schooner seemed to agree with that sentiment as he jumped his front paws onto the bed to greet Silas with ecstatic barks, licks and a full on wiggling body. Silas looked just as happy to see him and her.

Silas smiled and patted her cheek. "Yet that's the way our world is, isn't it? Thank you so much for stepping up at the clinic."

She laughed. "Considering it's our family clinic, it only makes sense. Of course I would help out even if that wasn't the plan."

Silas nodded. "Apparently I'll need to take it easy for a while, so I'm hoping that you'll be okay to pinch hit even more."

"Of course, and, yes, you do need to take it easy."

"I thought I would probably go to the clinic and sit around doing nothing," he shared, with a smile. "It'll feel good just to get back there."

She glanced at him, tears in her eyes. "I have been through so much to get you here. ... I don't ever want to go through that again."

He reached out his hand, and they clung together for a long moment. "I didn't think I would make it," he admitted. "Honest to God, I really thought I was done for."

"Yeah, me too," she admitted with a sigh. "I wasn't sure I would make it either, but first I had to watch you slowly die in front of me. If it weren't for Schooner here," she reached down a hand to gently stroke Schooner's head, "I don't want to think how that would have ended."

"Never again."

"You're right, never again."

Silas looked at her, then back at Trey. Silas settled into his hospital bed, smiling the whole time at them.

Missy walked over and sat down beside Trey.

He hooked an arm around her shoulders and gave her a hug. "How was work?"

"It sucked," she shared, "yet it was good, except the part about wanting to be here with Dad. Still, I needed to help out, so we got through quite a few patients today," she added, with a smile. "Bill's at least a little bit happier."

"He's grumpy most of the time," Silas noted with a smile. "Yet he's been talking about a partnership. I just wasn't sure I wanted to go in that direction again."

"Again?" she asked, looking at him. "Did you have a partnership?"

"I did originally, way back when, but it ended up ugly," he told them, "and cost me money to buy out the other party. Once that was done, I swore I wouldn't ever do it again. I did think about it when your mother was ill because it was just so much of a load to bear all on my own, but I made it. Now I have my daughter with me," he proudly stated, "so that will be even easier."

"Of course," she agreed, with a bright smile. She looked at Trey, who seemed to be deep in thought, and she shook her head.

"What's that for?" her father asked with a testy voice. "What are you keeping from me?"

"It's not that I'm keeping anything from you," she replied, facing him. "However, while you were getting sick out there, trying to figure out how to get us back home again, you mentioned something about the boat being sabotaged."

He slowly nodded. "I remember that. Since nobody said anything about it today, I wasn't sure just where we were on that subject." Then he looked at Trey. "I guess I lost the boat, didn't I?" He sounded sad and resigned.

"You lost her out there, but I went out with Rob, and we brought her back in again."

Silas looked at him in shock but with a glimmer of hope. "*Forget Me Not* is in the harbor?"

"She needs a bit of work. She got damaged pretty well when she was powerless, getting slammed up against the rocks," Trey explained, "but we brought her back in. I haven't talked to Rob about the repairs, so I'm not sure what we're up against there."

"If anybody can put her back together again, it'll be Rob," Silas declared as he sank in the hospital bed with a sigh. "Good God." He looked over at his daughter. "I am so sorry. I would have done anything to save you from this nightmare."

"The worst part," she replied, as she walked over and sat down beside him on the edge of the bed, "was watching you deteriorate and not being able to do anything to help you."

He nodded slowly. "I hate that and wouldn't have done that, especially since, … well, you're my daughter, and I'm supposed to protect you. I would have done anything to save you."

"Hence the same problem I had," she noted, with a teary smile in his direction. "It was rough, but then this guy"—she turned to look back at Trey—"pops into town, looking for Schooner no less." Schooner lifted his head and gave a *woof*. She bent down, cuddled him, and cooed, "Yeah, you're the one who kept us alive out there."

"In what way?" What do you mean by that?" her father

asked. She told him about the rabbits Schooner brought her. "Good God," Silas muttered, "maybe he's a good hunting dog too."

When her father looked at the dog with added interest, she groaned. "No sir, you're not taking this dog hunting. Never. I already promised Schooner that he gets to live on Easy Street from now on."

Trey smiled in her direction. "Sounds as if you get to be on Easy Street too," he teased.

"I wouldn't disagree with that, but Dad and I both know that having our own practice will be demanding, and there probably won't be anything easy about it."

"You're right," Silas declared. "Easy it is not." Yet he smiled broadly. "We'll have to decide if we want to let Bill go or if we want to keep him there to ease up on some of the work ourselves."

"I think we should probably wait on making a decision on that just yet," she suggested, "especially considering that we still need to figure out who's behind the sabotage."

"I was really hoping when you woke up that you would tell us," Trey shared.

"Did I say anything about it while I was out all that time?"

She shook her head. "No, you didn't, and that was so hard because I didn't know who to trust and who not to trust."

"Apparently you did good by trusting this guy." Silas motioned at Trey.

She smiled. "It's not hard to trust a man who risked his life to come look for us, long after others had given up, even dragging your sorry ass back to town."

Silas laughed. "Isn't that the truth?" He looked over at

Trey. "So, tell me. Just how the hell did you find us, when everyone else had failed?"

Trey smiled. "Let's just say that I had a couple of your favorite fishing spots in mind that you showed me a very long time ago."

Silas looked at him in alarm. "Good God, you still don't remember those, do you?"

"Of course I do, and I'm pretty happy about it now that I've heard you're pretty much the fishing derby king around here."

A crafty look came in his eyes. "But you don't know if that's where my fishing derby spots are."

"No, but I don't have to," Trey replied, "since your panicky expression is already telling me. But don't be sad, as I already had a good idea where they were. You just get back on your feet, and we can either be on the same team or we can go against each other."

"Oh come on, Trey. Let's not get him started on that yet," she muttered, giving him a smirk.

Her father looked at him, and a big smile crossed his face. "Son, I'll enjoy having you on my side." Then he looked over at his daughter. "I'm pretty sure I'll have to, since I do remember showing him those damn places and more, way back when."

She burst out laughing. "I'm not sure what to even say to the two of you right now," she scolded. "But can I at least remind you that there are much more serious issues at play here?"

"There are," Trey agreed, with a smile, "but, if Silas doesn't remember or have any clue who could have done this, we're back to square one again."

"I didn't say I didn't remember. I do remember most of

it, although obviously not when I was unconscious," he noted. "I was thinking about it during the time we got shipwrecked. I just don't know if I came to any conclusion," he admitted.

"We've gone through a ton of people. I'm just not sure that we've come up with any answers." She looked over at Trey.

Trey shook his head. "No, we don't have any solid leads. We're pretty much back to square one, but I did go talk to Mildred."

At that name, Silas frowned at him. "Why did you talk to Mildred?"

"Because I wanted to know if her son was involved."

"Ah." Silas nodded. "In a way that makes sense, but I also know that Keith would do an awful lot to avoid jail again."

"Yet did you break up because of him?"

"Who, the boy? No, I didn't break up because of Keith. Why?"

"That's what Mildred told him and me."

"No, no, no," he countered. "I broke up because of Mildred. She was getting very, very clingy and very ... stifling, maybe? I don't know the right word or exactly how to explain it. She's just very intense, and I found it hard to be peaceful around her."

"But she doesn't know anything about boats?"

"No, she doesn't know anything about boats," he confirmed. "I can't see her behind it, at least not ... If she was behind it, then she most definitely would have somebody else help."

"But not her son?" Trey asked.

"No, not her son. ... No, no, not her son."

"But you were just thinking about something."

Silas opened his mouth, then closed it. "I can't just say things that don't have any factual bearing on this."

"But you need to," Missy stated, walking closer to her father, as Trey came up behind her. "We've been considering this from all different angles and don't have a clue. Yet what you don't know is that you were attacked while you were in this hospital."

His gaze widened. "No, no, please not."

"Yes, and our house was broken into. Your office was trashed."

He stared at her and then winced. "Oh God," he muttered.

"So you need to tell us what you're thinking," Trey urged.

"But I could be wrong."

"Good, go ahead and be wrong. At least it would be somebody we could take off our list."

Silas stared at them, his gaze going from one to the other. "But …"

"No," Trey declared as he wrapped his arms around Missy's shoulders. He tucked her up tight, her arms automatically going around his chest, waiting instinctively for bad news. Trey grabbed her father's hand and continued. "Listen. The time for protecting anybody is past because now we're afraid that somebody will come after your daughter."

"Oh God," Silas gasped, trying to straighten up in the bed, but Trey pushed him back in place.

"No, don't try to get up," Trey said, "but you need to tell me what's going on in your mind."

He winced. "I don't know. I can't be sure, and all my memories are a mess. I do know that some things fit, and some things don't." He swallowed hard. "Mildred's brother was my original partner."

At that, Trey turned to Missy and nodded. "That would fit."

"No, not at all," Silas argued. "I don't know why it would. I haven't seen or heard from him in a very long time."

"Maybe not, but that doesn't mean he's dead."

"No, I don't think he's dead at all. Why would you even say that?"

"Because one of the questions we've had fits only when something happened when you were in business together."

At that, her father swallowed, the color draining from his cheeks, as he whispered, "Life insurance on the business partners."

"Yes," Trey repeated, "life insurance on the partners of the clinic. So, if Mildred's brother is alive," Trey added, "there's a good chance that an active life insurance policy is still in place. It could very well be all about that."

"Oh my God," Missy exclaimed.

Trey asked Silas, "So, who is Mildred's brother, and where would he likely be right now?"

"I don't know. I lost track of him after I bought him out. Mildred and I were together back then, after my wife died, but we never really talked about her brother. Mildred wanted us to marry, but she and I were together off and on, plus I was raising Missy, so that didn't suit me. Mildred knew things had gone bad between me and her brother, but she didn't seem too worried about it, and neither was I. I thought we parted amiably."

"Sure," Trey conceded, "but now that you're totally separated, maybe she has a different viewpoint on it."

"But she wouldn't get the life insurance," Silas pointed out. "It would go to her brother, and that's only if I died. And it wouldn't change if my daughter died too."

"No, but maybe by taking both of you out, maybe all of your estate could potentially go to the same person."

"I don't know," Silas said. "Sounds like a long shot. At the very least he would get the life insurance."

"What about Mildred's son? Would he be in on this?"

"No, I don't think Keith would have anything to do with it. Honest to God, his uncle, the one I was in partnership with, he was the worst of the lot, but I always protected him. We'd been best friends since forever," Silas explained. "I didn't really see that side of him until I was in business with him, and then it was just too late. Things got ugly," he shared. "Yet I really haven't had anything to do with him in a very long time."

"Good enough," Trey replied, as he looked over at Missy. "If you're okay to stay here for a bit, I need to make some calls, get in touch with my boss. I don't know how long this part will take, but I need Schooner with me. Will you two be okay for a while here?" She immediately nodded, and Trey grinned, then leaned closer. "By the way, when this is all over, we'll have to try a real meetup."

She looked at him oddly. "A real meetup? What does that mean?"

He smiled, then kissed her briefly, prompting her fingers to immediately go to her lips. "A date, a real one, not all these halfway stolen moments." And, with that, Trey and Schooner were gone.

She turned to her father to find him grinning, an absolutely huge smile on his face.

He looked at her, then nodded. "You know, there is

something to be said for leaving you to work it out on your own," he muttered, "because, this time, you've found a man I approve of."

She rolled her eyes at that, as she sat down beside him. "Trey said you were upset when he went into the military."

"I wasn't so much upset that he went into the military, more that I was afraid he wouldn't come home again. That was happening to so many other families, and I loved him like a son," he explained. "But I wouldn't try to stop him from making his own decisions. Just like I didn't want to pressure you into going to veterinary school, but you were adamant, so it was for you to decide."

"Of course," she declared, "I wanted to be just like my dad."

His eyes filled with tears, and he reached out, beckoning her to come closer. "I'm glad you're *not* like me because, as it turns out, you're a whole lot better than your old man."

"Oh, I don't know about that," she argued. "I did an awful lot of thinking when we were on that rock out there, and nothing is quite so terrifying as seeing somebody you love dying right beside you."

He gave her a long look. "That's how I felt when we lost your mother. It was the most terrifying journey, spending every day watching her slowly slip away and not being able to do anything about it."

Tears filled her eyes, and she nodded. "And that was a journey that you took on largely yourself because I was so young," she whispered, "but I understand it so much more now, and I feel so much sympathy for you."

"I don't need sympathy," he declared. "When life happens, you just get back on the horse and keep on riding because there's really no other choice. Only after you get some distance do you have a different perspective and then realize how far you've come," he explained. "Right now what I can tell you is that you have become an absolutely brilliant and gorgeous young woman, and I'm so terribly proud of you."

"I tried so hard to get us out of there, but I just couldn't."

"Yet you did get us out of there."

"I didn't do anything," she stated immediately. "That was all Trey."

Silas nodded and smiled. "Apparently it was Schooner too," he added, with a chuckle.

"Yes, it was, and you know something else? He also brought Trey back here to begin with."

"What do you mean?" Silas asked. She explained about the War Dog program that Schooner was part of. "Good Lord, is that what it took to bring Trey back to us?"

"Schooner absolutely loves him, by the way," she murmured.

"Good, because I was wondering if this dog needed somebody with a more physical lifestyle."

"In that case maybe we can just share him," she suggested, with a laugh. "I'm hoping that Trey sticks around."

At that, Silas stared at her. "He's not moved back here?"

"No, he literally came back to search for the War Dog," she admitted. "I'm hoping I can convince him to stay, but I have no idea where his mind is at this point."

Silas winked at her. "Honey, it won't take any convincing. He's clearly smitten, and he's just been waiting for me to wake up, so we can put this all behind us, and so he can make a move."

"*Huh*," she muttered, looking at her dad. "Do you really

think so?"

"I know so." He smiled. "I saw the way he looked at you. He's an honorable man, so he'll ensure that you're safe and sound. He won't put you under any undue stress or pressure. I've always liked that boy."

"Hardly a boy now, Dad, and, in a way, you're right to worry because he did come back damaged." He looked at her quizzically. "He wears a prosthetic on his leg. He hasn't talked about it much, but I think there may also be some steel up and down that back of his, not that he needs a whole lot of steel in his back. He's already seems pretty full of it." When her dad chuckled, she went on. "He's a man's man, you know?"

"He's also a ladies' man, just not the way you think. I don't think any of that is an issue at all," her dad declared, with a nod in the direction that Trey had disappeared. "If the two of you can make a go of it, I can't think of a better match."

"You really like him, don't you?"

"Always did," he said, resting his head on the pillow now. "And not just because he was a great fishing partner," he added, scolding her for the look on her face.

She burst out laughing. "But it doesn't hurt to have him as a fishing partner, does it?"

"No, it sure doesn't," he declared. "I've been thinking a lot lately about maybe trying to find a life partner myself again, but I don't know. You get set in your ways, and then you're not so sure someone else would fit in. So Mildred was always nearby, and we had this arrangement."

"Yeah, I think it's called *friends with benefits*, Dad."

He winced. "Sounds crude when you say it that way, but, yeah, though I guess she always had an expectation of more."

"I don't think so much an expectation but maybe a hope," Missy clarified, "and I know that Mildred is still very much in love with you."

"I don't know about that. … Well, maybe."

Missy smirked. "Maybe wait and see where this all ends up."

"Yeah," he agreed. "I'm a little worried that maybe she did have something to do with this, but I can't quite see it. Anyway, I'm sure Trey will get to the bottom of it."

"And you don't expect him to contact the sheriff?" Missy asked.

"Oh, Sheriff Woodley will have to get on board at some point in time"—he waved his hand about—"but he and Mildred have also been pretty close at different times too." When Missy stared at him, her dad nodded. "Nobody ever sees all the relationships steaming beneath the surface. Mildred and I have been broken up for quite some time, for, … gosh, I don't know. It's been a while," he said, looking at her. "I don't really know how much time has gone by, but it seems like years. I look at you and see how grown up you are, how beautiful and poised, and it all seems like a lifetime away."

"Some of that could just be recognizing you almost lost your life," she noted, with a gentle smile in his direction.

"It's about how much of it is gone, about how fast time goes by. Sure, almost dying is part of it, but honestly, seeing Trey, seeing the man he's become, seeing the two of you together, seeing that blossom, it's really special," he murmured. When she flushed, he smiled. "See? That's exactly what you need, a man who can make you blush."

She shook her head at that. "I don't think one has to do

with the other," she muttered.

"Maybe not. I guess we'll see."

"So, this partner you had. What does he look like?"

"Tall and skinny, similar to his nephew."

"Ah," she muttered.

"Why?"

"Because somebody was caught on the hospital's security camera, and we wondered if he had anything to do with attacking you, but we weren't sure."

"What do you mean?"

"You were attacked here in the hospital. On the security cameras, we saw someone leaving the area after you were attacked, but we couldn't recognize him, yet the person was very tall and skinny."

"Really?" he asked, his gaze widening. "That's not good."

"That was just one of the things we had to consider while you were out cold, while we were trying to go through all the people who we knew, trying to find someone capable of doing all this. Of course Trey is out of the loop because he hasn't been here for so long. I'm pretty sure he has been talking to his brother and the sheriff," she clarified.

"Yeah, I'm sure he would have. It would be hard not to at this point, especially after multiple attacks." At that came a clearing of a throat behind her.

She turned to see the sheriff standing there, glaring at them. She smiled. "Hello, Sheriff. As you can see, my father is awake."

"I see that. From the conversation that you're all trying to wrap your brains around, you are trying to figure out who may or may not have hit you, *if* you were hit."

"If?" she snapped, looking at him.

"No damage was done after Silas arrived at the hospital."

"That's not completely true," Missy declared. "Dad was on the floor when they found him. He had been unconnected from all the monitors and from the IV drip, left to die there. I suspect that whoever was here maybe got nervous since Dad falling to the floor probably made some noise."

"And I think you're just grasping at straws," he replied as he looked over at Silas. "How're you feeling?"

"As if I've been shipwrecked and lost for weeks," he said cheerfully.

That resulted in a smile on the sheriff's face. "Don't go doing that again, will you? We had search and rescue out there for a hell of a long time, trying to find you."

"Oh, I wasn't planning on doing it again, but, hells bells, I didn't plan on doing it in the first place."

"So, I'm sure your daughter has been asking you about sabotage?"

"Yeah, it was sabotage all right, or have you not checked with Rob?"

The sheriff nodded reluctantly. "Yeah, I've kind of checked with Rob."

"Kind of?" Silas pressed, with a stare.

"Yeah, kind of, but he wasn't willing to say anything else."

"You already know what you need to do," Silas declared, glaring at Woodley. "Good to know where your loyalties lie."

The sheriff hitched his hat back and glared at him. "Whoa, whoa, whoa. What are you talking about here?"

"Nothing," Silas muttered and let it go.

Glaring back at Silas, the angry sheriff snapped, "You better watch where you put your accusations."

"I'm not alone and defenseless now. Trey's got my

back."

"What do you know about this Trey character?"

"If you weren't so busy trying to deny what happened here, you would remember him yourself. He used to live here before he joined the military and was my fishing buddy for years."

"You mean that Boy Scout kid?" the sheriff asked in astonishment.

"Yeah, that kid, the one who I was always bragging about being such a genius fisherman," he said with a laugh. "Then he took off and went into the military. Honest to God, I missed him something awful."

"You did say that. I remember that," Missy shared, smiling, "and you kept trying to convince me to go out more and more on the boat."

"But it wasn't your thing."

"No, it sure wasn't," she admitted, "and I'm not sure you'll get me out in the boat at all now."

He winced at that. "Yeah, both of us might have to reassess our love of boating, at least for a while."

"That boat will never float again," the sheriff snorted. "It's done."

"It better not be," Silas snapped, "because that would really piss me off. The *Forget Me Not* is *not* done, and I'll thank you to not go around saying that it is. Rob will fix her up. You'll see, and you'll eat those words."

Missy huffed. "Oh, so somebody can attack you, and you're okay with that, but, if they touch your boat, it's a whole different story?" Missy exclaimed, frowning at her dad.

"Yeah, that was my father's boat," he stated ruefully. "We worked on that sucker every weekend for a very long time, and it's very special to me," he muttered. "I don't appreciate anybody who would be trying to take her away from us."

"I don't appreciate anybody trying to take *you* away from me," she murmured.

"And yet they didn't," the sheriff noted, staring at her suddenly. "If you think about it, since you were both stranded out there, it wasn't just about you, Silas. This was about the both of you."

And, at that, Missy didn't know what to say.

TREY AND SCHOONER walked up to Mildred's house again. Trey knocked, a determined expression on his face.

This time, Keith, Mildred's son, answered and glared at him. "What the hell are you doing back here?"

"I'm looking for an explanation as to why you were at the hospital on the day Silas was attacked?" Keith frowned at him. "The old man's awake now." At that comment, fear entered Keith's gaze, and that's how Trey knew he'd hit the jackpot.

Keith stepped outside on the front porch and closed the door.

Trey nodded. "Yeah, I know. You don't want to go back to jail, but it seems to me as if you are still pushing the issue, and you could find yourself going back a whole lot sooner than you expected."

"No fucking way," Keith snarled, glaring at him. "No way I'm going back."

"And yet you went into Silas's room."

"I didn't touch him. I didn't do anything."

"So why wear a wig?"

"I didn't want to get recognized."

"Why did you go in there at all?" he asked, staring at him, trying to figure out why and how this mess was happening.

Keith hesitated and then shrugged. "Not like I give a shit, but my ma asked me to. Of course she did."

"What does that mean?"

"I just went into his room, okay? She wanted me to check up on him, but I didn't want him to see me. I didn't want anybody to see me."

"Why not?"

"Because I'm not allowed at the fucking hospital, okay? … I broke into it and stole drugs from there."

"Ah, crap." Trey stared at Keith. "You're not legally allowed in the hospital at all, are you?"

"No, I just told you that."

"Yet knowing that, your mother still asked you to go."

"Yeah, she did, and I was pissed off about it too. Yet she wouldn't give me any cash for gas for the car, and I wanted to get the hell out for a bit. Anyway, she told me that she would pay me as soon as I did that."

"She just wanted you to go in?"

"I was supposed to just go in and check on him, but then he reared up out of the bed. It scared the shit about of me, and, I swear to God, I just took off."

"Where's the wig and the lab coat?"

"In my car," he muttered. "You really think I'll go to jail over it?"

"I don't know what's going on or what this is all about, but we need some more answers," Trey shared. "How close are you to your mother?"

"What do you mean, how close are we? We're close, at

least as close as anybody can be. She wants me out of the house though."

"How much does she want you out of the house?"

"I don't know. Why are you asking?"

"I'm asking if she could have had an ulterior motive for sending you to the hospital."

"I was just supposed to look in on him. She didn't want to be seen going in too often, you know? She's still sweet on him."

"Yet she's been dating the sheriff."

Keith stared at him, surprised.

Trey nodded. "She's been dating Woodley for a while, so I'm not sure what her motive is on keeping up with Silas in the hospital."

"Jesus, I don't know," Keith declared. "I didn't do anything. I wasn't responsible for what happened to him. I had nothing to do with that nightmare out on the ocean. I don't even fucking like boats. Everybody here is just crazy about fishing, and it's just not my thing."

"What is your thing?"

He hesitated and shrugged. "I would tell you, but you'll laugh."

"No, I won't. Tell me. Now you've got me curious," Trey prodded.

"I like pottery," Keith admitted and shrugged. "I've always wanted to just be a potter. I would have my own little studio, but my uncle blew that all to hell. He got me hooked on drugs, and that was that."

"Your uncle?" he asked. "Is this uncle still alive?"

"Yeah, but he's not all there, not anymore. He had a stroke, and now he's got dementia or something funky. He's in a home not far from here, and my ma has to look after him."

"Really. Do you have any idea what she's up to?"

"No. What are you even talking about?"

Just then the front door opened, and Mildred stepped out onto the porch, glaring at Trey. "What are you doing here?" she snapped. "And what's that dog doing here?"

"I'm here because I had questions to ask," Trey explained, studying the woman in front of him. "And Schooner needed some fresh air outside of the hospital."

"You don't need to be here at all. You can just leave. We've done enough talking to you, and you need to leave us alone."

"Maybe so," Trey conceded. "Your son might have a few questions for you though."

Keith turned to face her. "What the hell's going on, Ma?"

"Nothing is going on," she declared, glaring at both of them.

"So, tell me," Trey began. "When did your brother have that stroke?"

She looked at him. "Thomas?"

"When did he have the stroke?"

"Why?" she asked nervously.

"Was it about, oh, I don't know, a few weeks ago?" he asked.

She chewed on her bottom lip.

"It was, wasn't it?"

She shrugged. "I don't know. I don't know anything about it."

Keith shook his head. "That's not true. You told me how you're the one who's looking after him," Keith said, staring at her. "What the hell is going on, Ma?"

Trey suggested, "I think what's going on is that your

uncle Thomas is the one who arranged for Silas's accident and who sabotaged his boat."

"Why the hell would he do that?" Keith asked in confusion. "There's no reason for him to do that."

"It turns out there is," Trey muttered, "and even your mother may not have known about it initially. I'm not really sure how that'll work out, but she did know at the end of the day."

"What are you talking about?" Keith sputtered. "She doesn't know nothing."

"Has she been at your uncle's place any time lately?"

Keith went silent for a moment. "Yeah. A while back she drug me over there one day."

"What for?"

"To clean, said she wanted to surprise him or something."

"And she brought you to help?"

"No, to keep an eye out, so the surprise wouldn't be ruined."

"And did anything unusual happen?" Trey asked Keith.

"No, nothing I know of." Keith frowned from one to the other. "Although we did leave in a hurry, … and there wasn't much cleaning going on."

"Did she take anything with her?" Trey asked.

"Some papers but she told me that we would come back later."

"*Right*," Trey noted, smirking at Mildred. "So, Mildred, was that paperwork the life insurance your brother had on Silas Ragner?"

Her eyes widened, and her bottom lip trembled.

"Wait. … What?" Keith turned to her, waiting for a response. Then asked Trey, "What the hell is going on here?"

"Your uncle was in business with Silas, his partner in the animal clinic way back when. During that time Thomas took out a life insurance policy on Silas. And Silas probably took out one on Thomas. It's a common business practice that covers one business partner when the other one dies. So, when the partnership broke off, Thomas still had the life insurance policy," Trey explained. "Apparently Thomas kept paying the premiums all these years, wondering if it was time to cash it in by killing off Silas. Or maybe that was your mother's idea."

"It was Thomas's idea," Mildred claimed, her arms crossed over her chest, yet visibly trembling.

"*Right*, so the question is, were you part of it?"

"What the hell?" Keith turned and stared at his mother, the reality suddenly dawning on him. "Did Uncle Thomas sabotage Silas's boat to get the life insurance? Was he willing to take out two people over it?"

"It's worth millions of dollars," Mildred declared, staring at her son.

"Jesus, Ma."

"So, let me guess," Trey interjected. "Mildred, you weren't cleaning Thomas's place. You were snooping, and you found out about the insurance and what he'd done. You two had a fight about it, and he ended up having a stroke as a result? Am I close?"

Keith frowned. "Wait. Doesn't it seem odd that suddenly they both nearly died? How would any of that even work? How or who would even collect this life insurance anyway?"

"Nobody, as long as Silas is still alive, but, if Silas died and if your uncle is still alive, Thomas would get the life insurance. Oh, but then he's incapacitated—"

"But if someone had a power of attorney," her son added, turning to stare at his mother, "*you* would have had control over all of it."

"I *would* have," she stated, glaring at Keith, "but you couldn't even do that right."

"What are you talking about?" Keith yelled, and his bewilderment seemed real.

Trey looked at him and shared, "There were signs that Silas was starting to stir, to maybe wake up, but, if he would have woken up to you being there, I wonder if your mother had hoped Silas would have a stroke on his own or something and just die. Unless there was more to the plan which you haven't shared, Keith."

"I wasn't assuming anything," she snapped, "I just wanted to know how he was, based on how he responded. You were just supposed to go and give him a good scare," she exclaimed, looking at Keith.

"You didn't say that," he pointed out. "You told me to go in and check on him."

"I said check on him, move him over to ensure he was breathing, even give him a shake."

"Hell no, I wouldn't touch him. The man was comatose."

"You told me that you would do exactly as I said."

"Yeah, but not all that. Then he woke up, and it freaked me out. I don't know that he really woke up, but he made a strange sound, it scared me and I took off."

"He fell off the side of the bed, by the way," Trey noted, "so I'm pretty sure the authorities would consider that an assault."

Keith stared. "What? I didn't assault him at all."

"You were seen entering the hospital, wearing the wig and the lab coat," Trey murmured. "But you took them off, put them in a plastic bag, and left the hospital."

"So, Keith had everything to do with it," Mildred stated immediately.

Her son straightened and turned ever-so-slowly toward her. "What the hell is going on, Ma?"

Trey snorted. "If she gets rid of Silas, and she gets rid of her brother, then there's really only you stopping her from enjoying all that fortune and freedom."

The son swallowed hard, then stared at his mother. "This is all about money?"

"What do you mean, *all about money?*" she repeated, turning beet red. "This isn't about money. There's so much more to life than money."

"But apparently not for you," Keith replied.

"It's not as if I got any joy from love," she argued bitterly. "I really loved Silas, but nobody seems to give a shit about that."

"But you just tried to kill him," her son said.

"I did not. That was your uncle Thomas."

"You were okay with it though."

She flushed. "It's not that I was okay with it, but, if it would have worked out that way, there would have been millions of dollars. And it's not as if Silas wanted me anyway."

"Yet you're dating the sheriff," Trey pointed out.

"No, I'm not dating the sheriff." She huffed, almost in disgust. When Trey continued to stare at her, she kept talking. "We've been together for a while, but he just broke it off."

"*He* broke it off, or *you* broke it off?"

She shrugged. "I broke it off."

"But just recently, right?"

She stared at him. "What difference does it make?"

"I can imagine the sheriff was handy to have around, wasn't he? You haven't broken it off with him just yet, have you?"

"I will," she declared. "That was one of the next things that I was planning on doing."

"But, in the meantime, it was probably handy to have an authority figure, like the sheriff, in your pocket, while you arrange all these murders."

"No, you don't understand," she snapped. "I didn't do anything. That was Thomas."

"But you sent me in there," Keith said, staring at her in shock, "hoping that Silas would die by my doing what you told me to do."

"What exactly did she tell you to do?" Trey asked Keith.

"She told me to check his lines, and she told me what things to push to check, and I should see if he was breathing. Honest to God, … it sounded funny," he said, with a frown, "but I wasn't suspicious. She's a nurse for fucks' sake, and I don't know fucking anything." He stopped, suddenly looking pale. "You set me up. … You set me up to kill Silas. I was the only one there. You sure weren't," he stated, and his jaw dropped. "You literally set me up."

"That's an interesting thought," Trey pointed out. "You would be going to jail again, prison probably. And she would have the house, right? So, even if you didn't die in prison, she would still have the house and maybe access to a lot of money. So, whenever you came back out again, if you even got back out again, you know a lot can happen while you're in jail. Either way, she would have it all," Trey explained.

Keith looked at his mother, and Trey could see the pain in his expression. "Dear God," Keith muttered, "are you serious?"

She just glared at him.

"What happened to your father?" Trey asked Keith.

He turned and looked at him, confused. "What do you mean?"

"What happened to him? You told me how he left you half the house."

"He died … a long time ago." Then he stiffened and glanced at his mother again, horrified. "Was that you too?"

She turned on him, with such a mean beady look in her eyes, and replied, "That bastard beat the crap out of me. So don't you even begin to blame me for that shit. He died, but it was self-defense. Just like this." With that, she pulled out a handgun.

Her son took a step back in shock, falling against the front door, as he stared at her—as if he'd never seen her before. Schooner, who had been sitting docilely next to Trey the whole time, leaped at her, grabbing her wrist in his jaws, knocking her to the ground, sending the bullet harmlessly into the porch ceiling.

"At least now we're getting to the truth," Trey muttered, as he quickly secured the gun and pinned her to the porch floor, then looked over at Keith. "If you ever want a chance to chase your dreams and to do what you want with your life, I think it's time you phoned the sheriff right now."

He nodded, visibly shaken, but resolute. "I agree." And, with another hard look at his mother, Keith pulled out his cell phone and dialed 9-1-1.

"No way," she wailed. "Absolutely no way."

"It's already a done deal," Trey said. "Silas's awake, and he'll be fine. Your son has had a very hard awakening, which may continue because we'll also take a serious look at your brother and see whether it really was a stroke or something you induced."

From the flush on Mildred's cheeks, Trey realized that it was, indeed, another crime she had committed, just to secure her brother's potential ill-gotten gains for herself.

CHAPTER 17

MISSY LISTENED TO Trey's update, her father shaking his head from time to time, as all the details spilled out in the hospital room. "Oh my God," she kept whispering, too stunned for any of it.

Trey looked over at Silas. "So, I don't know how much of it was Thomas, how much of it was Mildred, and how much of it was the two of them in cahoots, but at least now we know."

Silas closed his eyes briefly. "I'm not sure either, but I'm very grateful that they will no longer try to kill me or the people I love."

"As it turns out, her son was not involved, except for the visit to your room, where he opted not to do her bidding, and we're all in agreement on that."

"That's some comfort," Silas noted. "Another factoid for you to ponder is that Thomas was in the Coast Guard way back when. My guess is he still is—or was, before his stroke or whatever."

Missy gasped.

Trey nodded. "That fits. So Thomas sabotaged your boat and planned to be a member of your search party too, until Mildred stepped in and took over the plan. Believe me that Keith's feeling pretty rough right now, finding out that his mother was really hoping the instructions she gave him to check that you were doing okay were really meant to kill you."

"Yeah, I still don't quite understand the part about adjusting the lines or whatever that was," Missy admitted.

"I'm not sure either," Trey added, shaking his head. "Ultimately I think Mildred hoped that, through this hospital visit, either Silas would wake up scared and have a stroke, or Keith would cut off Silas's oxygen or mess up the IV somehow. I don't really know because Keith can no longer remember exactly what Mildred told him to do. Whether that's on his part or the mother's, I don't know, but I do believe Keith. The shock on his face when he realized that his mother had set him up to go back to jail, plus had killed his father and had given his uncle a stroke, was all definitely genuine. Oh, and Thomas got Keith hooked on drugs to begin with. Also she broke into Dad's house likely looking for legal paperwork on his business and any life insurance or anything else she might be able to use."

"Christ," Silas muttered, staring at Trey in shock, "that poor boy."

"I know, but," Missy said, frowning at her father, "that *poor boy* also has a lot of responsibility in this too, especially in the sense that he now needs to get his life together."

Silas nodded. "It won't be that easy for him."

"Come on, Dad. Let's save yourself before you go back to saving the world, okay?"

He glared at her. "Maybe, but, you know, fishing is good for the soul."

She stared at him for a long moment and then burst into laughter.

Trey agreed. "I may have to fall on your dad's side of this argument. I was heading down a rougher road myself when he brought me into his *fishing boat repair nightmare slash therapy* program," he shared, with a smile.

"Maybe that's something you want to look at, but not just yet, please," she noted. "I'm sure Keith will have a pretty rough time going forward, at least for a while."

"Maybe, but it wasn't his own doing, and that's something we have to remember," her father stated. "Keith wasn't a part of this. He's had a terrible upbringing and paid a high price already."

"I know. I know," Missy agreed, realizing that her father would always see people in the world who needed a mentor in life. And maybe it was a good thing. She didn't know. All she knew at this moment was that a killer would not go free and that she and her father were now safe. She smiled up at Trey. "I am so glad it's over."

He nodded, giving her a gentle smile. "Me too." Schooner woofed from the bedside, and Silas just laughed at the barking. "You too, right? You're just a big hero, aren't you, boy?"

"I can't believe he was there to save the day again," Missy said, reaching down to cuddle him.

"No kidding," Trey added. "I was prepared for Mildred to put up a fuss, but I didn't see the gun play coming."

Schooner just rolled over and lapped up the attention.

"He's enjoying that belly-rubbing part pretty well," Silas noted as he leaned back against the bed. Then he waved his hands at the two of them, shooing them away. "Now, both of you go share an evening, get some dinner and some rest. I'm fine here, and I'll be good as new soon. I'm feeling better all the time, and it'll all be okay. But leave Schooner here with me. I hate to be parted from him if I don't have to be."

Trey looked over at her and raised an eyebrow. "Sounds

like your dad is giving us orders."

"Ya think?" she asked, with an eye roll.

"Go on now," Silas prodded. "I'll have a good solid night's sleep tonight, and I want you two gone. You go on and enjoy your own evening together, do you hear me?"

"What? Now *you're* trying to be a matchmaker too?" she asked, with a laugh.

"If I thought it would do any good, absolutely." She stared at him, and he nodded. "It's all good. Go on, scat, shoo."

"If you say so," she muttered, giving her father a kiss on the cheek.

Trey grabbed her hand. "Come on. Let's go eat. I'm starving."

She looked at his hand and smiled. "Okay. I could be persuaded to eat something. Maybe fish and chips down at the marina."

Her father grumbled, "That's hardly a great date."

"Right about now, that's all I can manage," she stated, with a smile. "That is, if you're up for it?" she asked, turning to Trey.

"I'm always up for fish and chips," he said, "especially if it's with you."

She flushed, and her father laughed. "Now go," he stated. "Go off and do all the good stuff people do to find out if they're right for each other."

"Oh, so you're having doubts now?" she asked, raising one eyebrow.

"I don't have any doubts," he declared, with a wry grin. "It's you who have the doubts."

She looked at him and asked, "Did I say that?"

"No, you sure didn't, which is even better."

She groaned. "We need to leave now, before Dad gets any worse."

"Too late." Silas chuckled. "I'm all about grandbabies now."

She stopped and glared at him, turning quickly back to Trey. "See?"

"At least I'm being honest," Silas muttered, rolling his eyes. "I survived, and now we'll create a whole new generation of fishermen."

"No, no, no," she cried out. "No fishermen babies, not now. Honestly, you'll be lucky if I let you on a boat, much less any future babies. So stop, no more talk about any of that."

"Okay." Silas winked at her. "Just make an old man happy eventually."

"Eventually, yes," she agreed, "but not right now." She glared at him and then turned to find Trey grinning like a crazy man too. "What are you smiling at?"

"The two of you," he said, with a chuckle. "Come on. Let's go see if he's right."

"Wait. What are we seeing if he's right about?" she asked, protesting as Trey led her out of Silas's hospital room.

"Whether we really do have what it takes." She stopped, looked up at him, and he nodded. "I'm serious if you are."

"I'm definitely serious," she replied. "I just didn't expect anything to happen quite so fast."

"I know," he said, giving her a look, "but sometimes when it happens, it's just right, and I think in our case we got lucky."

"I don't know," she muttered. "I feel as if my dad has been waiting for you to come back since forever."

"Maybe so," he murmured. "I'm not sure that's wrong

either. Maybe I just needed the right impetus to come back."

"What? A missing dog?" she asked in astonishment.

He grinned. "Yeah, a missing dog. Whoever would have thought it?"

Laughing, she followed him out of the hospital.

As THEY WALKED along the beach after dinner, Trey said, "You know that your father's right."

"About what?" Missy asked.

"I think we are meant for each other."

"And here I thought we would take our time to figure it out," she replied. "It's so beautiful here, but are you sure you want to come back here?"

"What? You say it's beautiful and then you doubt that I want to come back?"

"No. I think it's the work thing I'm worried about. Are you okay to do whatever you need to do to make a living here? It doesn't make sense to come back if you're not happy here."

"Yeah, I'm not sure what my new career will look like yet, although there has been a suggestion made. I just don't know if I really want to go in that direction yet, but it's something I should at least take a look at."

"What's that?" she asked.

He shrugged. "Maybe working in the sheriff's office in some capacity."

She looked at him and then nodded. "That would be a hell of a good idea. They need someone who's got the brains for it. And maybe isn't a pompous ass."

He snickered at that. "Oh, give the guy a break. The

sheriff was in a bad spot there, and no telling what lies Mildred might have filled his head with. But, back to the job idea, I do have a fair bit of investigative work in my military history," he shared, "so I've got that covered. And the sheriff did approach me about it on the sly, by the way."

"I'm all for it," she said.

"Are you sure? You'll be this fancy vet, working in the clinic with your dad, after all."

"Yeah, and I can't wait to get back to that too," she replied, beaming a smile his way.

"I'll need to fill in my brother and sister in-law, and they've got a baby due to be born in the next six weeks or so."

"Which is all good. So … how serious is *serious?*"

"Oh, we don't have to rush anything."

"No, we sure don't," she agreed, "but I'm invited to the christening of Jackson and Elizabeth's baby."

"Good. I would imagine I am too, although I haven't pushed that."

She laughed. "Just in case you end up pissing them off and losing your invite, you can always be my plus one."

"Oh, *thank you,*" he teased, with a grin. "I don't think it will be an issue. Jackson and I are looking forward to having a chance to get to know each other again."

"Good, it's high time," she said. "I think that's what family is all about."

"According to your dad it is."

She groaned. "He'll really bug me until I get there too."

"But, in the meantime, we'll have fun exploring who and what we are."

"Speaking of which," she began, "do you want to come back to my place?" He stopped and looked at her, and she smiled. "I have been thinking about that a lot."

"I won't lie. … I have been too," he shared, "but I don't want to push you." She rolled her eyes. "We've been getting to this point very, very quickly. Sure, it's fast, and, yes, we could wait another few days, another few weeks," he added, "or we can just go back to your place."

She burst out laughing, and then he grinned, sweeping her up in a hug, then racing her back to her home. She howled with laughter, saying, "As if anybody won't know what's going on now."

"As if I care," he muttered, as he came to a halt, pulling her to him, tilting her head back and kissing her, the first serious kiss they had shared since they met.

When he lifted his head, she murmured, "That was really nice."

"Good. There's definitely more where that came from."

She smiled. "In that case, we better go someplace where the sheriff isn't about to arrest us for indecency."

"Oh, you're thinking about right here, right now?"

"I'm definitely thinking about right here, right now, but I would rather it was right here, right now, at my place, so let's go."

And, with that, it took about fifteen minutes to fast-walk there. As they walked into the house, Trey asked, "Are you okay with this happening in your dad's house?"

"I am for the moment, until we sort out living arrangements and all," she replied. "For the moment, this is where I want to be."

"Good." Trey gave her a beautiful smile.

"Don't be shocked when he asks us to move in here," she noted hesitantly, "though it is a massive house."

"It is, but I don't know how you feel about that."

"I'm okay with it, but that may not be what's on your mind."

He shrugged. "We could always take part of it and remodel it into a private apartment just for us."

"Ooh, I like that idea," she said, staring up at him.

But she hesitated, and he had to ask, "What?"

"Renovations like that … sound pretty expensive."

He smiled. "I don't think you need to worry about that. Turns out that I'm pretty handy with a hammer."

"Really?" she asked, her eyes wide.

"Yep, really, but we have more important things to worry about at the moment."

"What's that?" she asked, frowning.

"This." And he bent down and kissed her again.

<hr>

CHAPTER 18

Missy's toes curled, her breath caught in her chest, and her brain completely ceased to function. When he finally lifted his head, she whispered, "Oh God."

"Is that an *oh God yes* or an *oh God no*?"

"That's an *oh God, why aren't we in bed already?*" He gave a shout of laughter, then scooped her up into his arms again.

"You don't have to, you know? You've got a damaged foot."

He snorted. "I have a prosthetic, yeah," he murmured, "but it won't stop me from doing what I want to do."

"No, but that also doesn't mean you have to hurt yourself."

He shook his head, then entered the bedroom that he had seen when he was here before and presumed was hers, then carefully laid her on the bed. She hopped back up and immediately started tossing off her clothes, left, right, and center. Astonished, he watched, completely enthralled, until she was kneeling on the bed in just a tiny little pair of panties. "Good God," he muttered.

She smiled, then said, "I think you're a little overdressed."

He immediately chucked his clothing just as fast as she had. He smiled, and, when he got down to his leg, she watched in awe as he hit a lever that released the prosthetic and then unrolled a sock. "See? That's it. That's the stump. That's what is left."

"Can you walk on it at all?" she asked.

He nodded. "Yeah, obviously it's shorter, but I can put weight on it if I need to. Just not something I want to have to do." He gave her a quick demonstration. "Other than that, it's just a leg." She kept watching him, and he laughed. "It is just a leg," he repeated with a smile, as he headed back to the bed and fell on top of it. "Now, if your curiosity is satisfied?"

"Oh, I don't know," she teased, her gaze settling on his groin, "because, as far as I can see, my curiosity is really aroused."

"Just like something else," he muttered, feeling his erection rise strong and proud in front of her. As her hand closed around it, he gasped. When she hesitated, he explained, "Just cold hands, but don't stop. Jesus, don't stop."

At that, she giggled and immediately started moving her hand up and down, as the coldness immediately fell away, and the heat took its place. He moaned in joy at her gentle touch. When he couldn't take it anymore, he flipped her over and immediately got to know more about her. His lips and his hands were so busy that she didn't know where one started and one stopped. Her skin melted under the heat of their desire, and her body surged up against his hand when he found her intimate parts.

She shuddered with her release, lying on the bed in shock. "Good God," she whispered, "you're a little too deadly for this."

"No, not at all," he noted, "but I want this to be a two-party activity, not just one."

She opened her arms and whispered, "Then I want to repeat whatever that was."

He smiled, slid into place, and, with a simple surge, seated himself deep inside her. When she cried out in joy, he froze, and she whispered, "I'm fine. Don't stop. Dear God, don't ever stop."

And, with that, he settled into a move that increasingly rose and fell, dragging their passions to the edge of the cliff, before finally tossing them both over.

When he collapsed beside her, she whispered, "That was wonderful."

He pulled her tightly into his arms and held her close, relaxing deep into the mattress. When she finally got her breath back, she lifted herself up on one arm and said, "See? That's why we didn't want to wait." He opened one eye to look at her, a question in his gaze. She added, "Just look at what we would have missed out on."

He grinned and nodded. "I'm glad you feel that way."

"Absolutely," she murmured, and then she poked him in the chest. "Can we do it again?" He laughed, not being able to contain himself, as he pulled her back into his arms.

"Absolutely, time and time again for the rest of our lives."

BADGER STARED AT his wife. "What the hell, Kat? I'm definitely not letting you work with anybody I want to keep local."

She smiled at him. "You already bitch and complain because you want to find more work for these men. You don't want any of them to suffer without enough to keep them going—even if it's not money that they actually need."

"Everybody needs self-esteem. Everybody needs to know that they're useful and that they still have something to offer this world," he declared.

Gently she touched the corner of his mouth and nodded. "I know, and that's only one of the many reasons I love you."

"Only one of the reasons?" he repeated, waggling his eyebrows. "Tell me more."

She burst out laughing and said, "No, I think your ego is doing just fine."

"You're the one who's doing just fine," he replied. "It's freaking unbelievable how on target you always are. It is uncanny."

"I don't know about that," she said. "Yet I'm so happy for Trey and Missy—and Silas and Schooner. And I'm happy that this crazy situation has a happy ending."

"What about Keith, the woman's son? Do you think

he'll get over it?"

"I don't know," Kat admitted. "It depends on how the community handles it. Keith may just sell his home and move away, but, then again, maybe he'll learn to fish," she teased, with a knowing smile.

Badger sighed. "Are we done now?"

At that, she laughed. "Do you really think we're done?"

"No, not likely," he muttered, "but you could consider it."

"No, we have two more files here, and then, chances are, we're done. At least that's all we have for now. I guess we'll cross that bridge when we get there."

"Two more files," Badger muttered, shaking his head. "I can't even imagine. Are you thinking you'll go for the goal?"

"Of course I'll go for the goal," she declared. "Two more. That's not much of a challenge, is it?"

"Sure it is. Where is this one?"

"Cowboy country."

"What do you mean, cowboy country?"

"The War Dog was going with a group who does pack trips, trail riding, and the like."

"And?"

"The War Dog went missing during the night."

He frowned at her. "And we're supposed to track him down? Will you also track down the bear that took him down too?"

She smiled up at him. "We do know one cowboy. He's a bit of a renegade, but I thought maybe somebody who used to do both horseback riding and training dogs might be okay to go to Texas. Plus he's from there."

"Oh, don't tell me," Badger grumbled. "Austin is bound for Austin?"

She burst out laughing. "That's exactly what I was thinking. At least he could fly into Austin, but he wants to drive."

"Long way to go. He's testing the limit of your newest prosthetic, isn't he?"

"Don't we all?" She grinned broadly. "The ranch is in the backwoods, way south of Austin, somewhere closer to the border—or maybe closer to the Gulf of Mexico. I'm not sure, but it's a big cattle ranch, out in the middle of nowhere. The wife of the owner has a side gig with a pack string and trail-riding tours. Her son and her daughter run it with her."

Badger just nodded, as he watched Kat go deep in thought. He finally asked her, "And?"

"There's no *and*," she said, batting her eyelids at him. "No *and*s at all."

"What's the dog's name?"

She laughed. "You won't believe it."

"Probably not. What's the name?"

"Cowboy. They call him Cowboy."

"Oh, for crying out loud," he muttered, with a moan.

She nodded and laughed. "But he's also a beloved member of the team."

"And the war department contacted you?"

"The family contacted the war department, thinking they were in trouble because they lost the War Dog," she explained. "So, in that way, this is already unusual because they fessed up. *Hey, we don't know what happened, but it could be something bad.* So we just don't know much, and now the war department wants us to look into it."

"That is all just too far-fetched."

"It is far-fetched, so let's just say the war department may not really think there's any point looking into it, but I don't feel the same way." When Badger frowned at her, Kat shrugged. "I think he deserves a chance."

"Cowboy or Austin?"

She smiled. "Let's just say, … Austin was named Austin for a reason."

He pinched the bridge of his nose. "So, don't keep me in suspense. Does Austin know this ranching family already or something?"

"Or something," she said.

"You'll have to talk to him and see if he's willing to go."

"Oh, I'm pretty sure he's willing to go."

"And why is that?" Badger asked.

"Because that daughter who runs the side company … is also his estranged wife. It's apparently a marriage that's not working, but they haven't gotten the divorce paperwork done yet."

"Meaning?"

"Meaning that something is still there and needs to be worked out," she stated.

"Have you talked to Austin? What if he doesn't want to go?"

She nodded. "He's already on his way."

This concludes Book 28 of The K9 Files: Trey.

Read about Austin: The K9 Files, Book 29

The K9 Files: Austin (Book #29)

Welcome to the all new K9 Files series reconnecting readers with the unforgettable men from SEALs of Steel in a new series of action packed, page turning romantic suspense that fans have come to expect from USA TODAY Bestselling author Dale Mayer. Pssst… you'll meet other favorite characters from SEALs of Honor and Heroes for Hire too!

Austin hates to think that Kat had tapped into his inner psyche and had pulled out the one job he both wants yet is terrified to do. He'd walked away—or maybe had been chased away from Rox. He is no longer sure; he only knows that he needs closure on a marriage that had been heaven, until it turned to hell. And now the same family he'd married into had gotten, then lost, a War Dog. And, sure enough, Kat had found out about his entanglement, asking him point-blank if it was time to get his life together.

Rox had sent Austin away in the red heat of temper, and he'd gone, as in gone and never to return. Now here he is, sitting in her kitchen as if they'd never had such a tumultuous past. Finding out he'd returned for the missing War Dog and not for her bit hard. Still, she'd called in about Cowboy, the missing dog, but hadn't expected them to send Austin. It's as if the gods weren't done ruining her life.

Finding the missing War Dog and sorting out the other unsettling issues on the ranch Austin had fallen in love with years ago isn't going to be easy—particularly with Rox at his side—but he knows he is fighting for more than just peace and justice. He is fighting for his—their—future. One that, deep down, he never truly let go of.

Find Book 29 here!
To find out more visit Dale Mayer's website.
https://geni.us/DMSAustin

Author's Note

Thank you for reading Trey: The K9 Files, Book 28! If you enjoyed the book, please take a moment and leave a short review.

Dear reader,

I love to hear from readers, and you can contact me at my website: www.dalemayer.com or at my Facebook author page. To be informed of new releases and special offers, sign up for my newsletter or follow me on BookBub. And if you are interested in joining Dale Mayer's Reader Group, here is the Facebook sign up page.
http://geni.us/DaleMayerFBGroup

Cheers,
Dale Mayer

About the Author

Dale Mayer is a *USA Today* best-selling author, best known for her SEALs military romances, her Psychic Visions series, and her Lovely Lethal Garden cozy series. Her contemporary romances are raw and full of passion and emotion (Broken But … Mending, Hathaway House series). Her thrillers will keep you guessing (Kate Morgan, By Death series), and her romantic comedies will keep you giggling (*It's a Dog's Life*, a stand-alone novella; and the Broken Protocols series, starring Charming Marvin, the cat).

Dale honors the stories that come to her—and some of them are crazy, break all the rules and cross multiple genres!

To go with her fiction, she also writes nonfiction in many different fields, with books available on résumé writing, companion gardening, and the US mortgage system. All her books are available in print and ebook format.

Connect with Dale Mayer Online

Dale's Website – www.dalemayer.com
Twitter – @DaleMayer
Facebook Page – geni.us/DaleMayerFBFanPage
Facebook Group – geni.us/DaleMayerFBGroup
BookBub – geni.us/DaleMayerBookbub
Instagram – geni.us/DaleMayerInstagram
Goodreads – geni.us/DaleMayerGoodreads
Newsletter – geni.us/DaleNews